MASQUERADE & MURDER

AT THE
BOURBON BALL

MURDERS IN BOURBON COUNTRY

SCARLETT DUNN

SCARLETT DUNN BOOKS

<u>Historical Novels</u>

Promises Kept
Finding Promise
Last Promise
Christmas at Dove Creek
Whispering Pines
Return to Whispering Pines
Christmas in Whispering Pines
The Cowboy Who Saved Christmas (Christmas Road)
Chase the Wind (coming 2022)

<u>Mystery Novels</u>

Murder on the Bluegrass Bourbon Train
Masquerade and Murder at the Bourbon Ball

Dedicated to Terry Meiners

My sincere appreciation to Terry for allowing me to include him as a character in my book. Not only is he the absolute best in his profession, he always gives selflessly to others—a real blessing to our community.

PROLOGUE

WITH PERSPIRATION SNAKING DOWN HIS spine, Trey Sullivan watched in his rearview mirror as the black convertible Mercedes pulled in behind his car. The Mercedes rocked back and forth when it came to an abrupt halt. *Can you get any closer to my bumper, you jerk?* He wasn't happy about the isolated location for their meeting, but he'd agreed, thinking nothing could happen in the middle of the day. The only thing that interested him was being paid what he was owed, then he would be done with this entire sordid affair. *The jerk better hope he brought the cash with him.* When Trey became involved with politics, he'd quickly learned you could never trust a politician. Not even the one paying you. At one time, he'd been a naïve, starry-eyed young man who wanted to make a difference, but it didn't take him long to see most politicians lied about everything. They lied to their constituents, telling them what they wanted to hear to get elected. After they were in office, they continued to lie and pander to keep their position. It was all about power. Power and money. Power was their primary goal. Once they had enough power, they accumulated the wealth. A vicious cycle for unscrupulous people.

Trey looked in the driver's side mirror, and kept his eyes on the man as he got out of the car and walked toward the trunk. After he retrieved a briefcase, he headed toward Trey's car. Trey smiled to himself, thinking that briefcase was filled with his money. All he had to do for a hundred thousand was install a little camera. *Easy peasy.* In his mind, he was already counting the cash. Expecting the man to walk to his window,

Trey pushed the button to lower the glass. Instead, the man opened the door behind the driver's side and slid in behind him. The hairs on the back of Trey's neck tingled, the telltale warning that he should have taken more precautions. But he chose to ignore that little voice in his head. Greed overrode any cautionary thought. Without turning around, he adjusted his rearview mirror down so he could see the man's face. "Did you bring the money?"

"Yes, it's in my briefcase. Do you have the flash drive?"

Pulling the flash drive from the console, Trey held it up for him to see. "You have all of the money?"

"Yes, I have all of it. How do I know you didn't make copies?"

Trey stared at him in the rearview mirror and shrugged. "Why would I? You paid me to do the job, and you are paying me enough to keep it quiet."

"Just want to make certain I won't have any surprises down the road. Did you erase your computer?"

Trey glanced down at the laptop in the passenger seat. He realized he should have left it somewhere safe before their meeting. "It's wiped."

"Good. And no one saw the camera?"

"No, I was careful." Trey heard him open his briefcase. *Finally.*

CHAPTER ONE

SOMETHING COLD AND SLIGHTLY WET pressed against Honey Howell's nose, rousing her from a rather pleasant early morning dream. It wasn't necessary for her to open her eyes to identify the offending culprit trying to awaken her. This was Elvis's preferred way of saying he was ready to start his day. She didn't mind her bloodhound's cold snout; in her estimation, it beat a blaring alarm clock any day. Finally, she opened one eye and stared at the black nose resting against her own. Two huge dark eyes were staring back at her.

"I was having a wonderful dream, buddy."

On hearing her voice, Elvis jumped up, placed his front paws on the mattress and gave her a gentle nudge with his big head. Honey grinned at his antics and tossed back the covers. "Okay, I'm getting up." She moved to a sitting position, glanced at the clock and groaned. "Seven o'clock." She leaned over, took a floppy ear in each hand and narrowed her eyes at her beloved canine. "Elvis, it's Saturday and I wanted to sleep until eight. I told Gramps we'd be at his house at nine o'clock." Honey was meeting a representative from the company that was handling the decorations for their upcoming Bluegrass Bourbon masquerade ball at her grandfather's home. Since his home was only a ten-minute walk up the pathway from her cottage, she had planned to enjoy a rare morning where she could sleep a few more hours.

Elvis snagged her robe from the chair next to the bed and dropped it in her lap.

Honey ruffled his fur. "You win. Best laid plan." She stood and shoved her arms in her robe. "Do you need to go outside?"

At his favorite word, Elvis bolted from the bedroom, down the hallway toward the kitchen, with Honey lagging far behind. When she finally caught up with him, she slid open the door. "There you go. I'll get your breakfast ready while you're doing your thing, so don't go too far." Instead of going through the door, Elvis sat down as if he was waiting for her to join him.

Honey looked at him, trying to understand what he wanted. "What? Do you want to go to Woodrow's now?"

At her question, he jumped up and barked.

"Gramps has probably already left for his golf game, so you won't even get to see him."

But when Elvis didn't move Honey became concerned. Elvis obviously wasn't in a hurry to go outside for his morning ritual, and that indicated something else was on his mind. She'd learned not to ignore him when he didn't stick to his usual routine. Her first thought was something might be wrong at her grandfather's house. She ran to her bedroom and hurriedly dressed in shorts and a tee shirt. She quickly brushed her teeth, ran a brush though her hair, and slipped on her running shoes as she hurried back to the patio door where Elvis was impatiently waiting.

With Elvis beside her, they jogged the quarter of a mile to her grandfather's home. Woodrow's home was a massive century-old Southern Colonial, and before the turn of the century one of their ancestors added a large ballroom to the rear of the home. Honey thought it must have been a huge extravagance, but at the time formal balls were more commonplace. Instead of renting a venue for the upcoming masquerade ball, she decided there was not a more charming setting than Woodrow's home. The home seemed to lend itself to the evening since all of the guests would be wearing historical costumes.

Instead of stopping at the sprawling columned front porch, Elvis raced to the back of the house. When Honey reached the back patio she saw Elvis had plopped down at the other end of the pool, with his big front paws dangling in the water.

Honey's gaze zeroed in on the man swimming laps. Seeing his dark hair and muscled arms breaking the surface of the water, she thought it was Sam. She'd been dating Sam Gentry for several months—that is, when he had time to date. As the town's newest detective, his free time seemed about as rare as a red diamond. She watched him effortlessly glide the length of the pool to where Elvis was waiting for him to surface. She figured that was the reason Elvis was in a hurry this morning; somehow he knew Sam was here. *Must have heard his car.* Due to their busy work schedules, she hadn't seen Sam for a couple of weeks, and Elvis missed him. *But what was he doing at her grandfather's house so early swimming laps?*

Reaching the end of the pool, Sam emerged from the water directly in front of Elvis. Bracing one arm on the deck, he reached up and scratched Elvis behind his ears. Honey could hear his deep voice, but she couldn't hear what he was saying. Whatever it was, Elvis's tail was wagging uncontrollably.

Honey made her way around the pool, but before she reached the end she realized it wasn't Sam in the pool. Like Sam, the man had dark curly hair and a muscled physique, but he was speaking with an accent. She recalled her grandfather had told her that he would be having a houseguest for the next several months, but it had slipped her mind. Theo Parker was the grandson of Richard Parker, who had been a good friend of Woodrow's for many years before his death. Richard owned a whiskey distillery in England that Woodrow visited often throughout the years. Theo had inherited the business from his grandfather. Her grandfather had stayed in touch with Theo, and was aware he we was interested in purchasing a distillery in Kentucky. Recently, Bunny Spencer, the owner of Pickett's Distillery, asked Woodrow to discreetly find a buyer for her business. She preferred to keep her search private, hoping to avoid the local media attention if they became aware of the sale. Bunny's husband, Troy Spencer, had been involved in two murders, and the theft of Woodrow's bourbon. He'd been killed by the wife of a wealthy local businessman, and his death had been the fodder for the press for weeks. Trying to help Bunny, Woodrow called Theo to see if he had an interest in the distillery and Theo jumped at the chance.

Honey thought Theo Parker didn't look like anything like she expected. With his dark golden skin, she thought he looked more like a

Greek god. He was a bit taller than Sam, but he wasn't as broad in the shoulders. Elvis jumped on him as though they were long-lost friends. She knew Elvis didn't mistake him for Sam, he was much too smart for that.

"Hello," Honey said.

Theo Parker turned abruptly, obviously caught by surprise. "Ah, you must be Honey, since I assume this handsome guy is Elvis." He stroked Elvis's back. "Other than bourbon, all Woodrow talks about is you and Elvis."

Honey walked closer. "Mr. Parker?"

"Theo, please." He glanced down at Elvis and rubbed his ears. "Hello, Elvis."

Honey smiled at him. "I think you've already made a friend."

"I would think he makes friends easily."

"Not necessarily, but he usually knows when people like dogs." Honey thought Elvis was reacting to Theo the same way he did when he first met Sam.

Theo returned her smile. "Then he's correct in his judgment. I love dogs."

Honey couldn't help but notice he was a very handsome man. Movie star handsome; strong jaw, expressive eyes the color of an exquisitely aged bourbon. Honey almost felt like she was cheating on Sam, at least in her thoughts.

"If you are looking for Woodrow, he already left to play golf."

"Actually, I wasn't looking for him. I expected you both to be playing golf today. I have a meeting with decorators here later, but Elvis was eager to get here."

"My flight was delayed arriving last night, so I told Woodrow I would enjoy the pool instead of golf today. I was so tired I didn't think I could do the game justice."

Honey chuckled. "It's probably a blessing you didn't play golf today. Gramps plays with two politicians who happen to represent opposing political parties. He told me the conversations of late were getting rather testy."

Theo picked up his towel. "The less time spent with politicians, the better."

Honey grinned. "I agree."

"I have some proper English tea with me. Would you fancy a cup?"

"I know Woodrow's housekeeper doesn't arrive until noon today, have you had breakfast?"

"No, not yet."

"If you will give me a few minutes, I'll bring some coffee cake back with me to go with your tea. I baked it last night."

He arched his brow at her. "What kind of coffee cake?"

"Lemon."

Theo's eyes lit up. "My favorite. Would you consider leaving your partner with me so we can become better acquainted?"

Honey had a feeling Elvis wanted to get to know him as well. "He can stay with you, but be forewarned, he will be expecting some bones from the pantry." Honey jogged back to the cottage and hurried to take a quick shower. Once she applied a little makeup, she dressed in a different pair of shorts and a nicer tee shirt.

Theo was sitting at the kitchen counter talking to Elvis when Honey returned carrying the coffee cake.

Theo eyed the coffee cake. "That looks delicious. Woodrow told me you are a great cook."

Honey wondered what else her grandfather told him. Funny, he didn't mention how handsome Theo was. Instead of standing there gawking at him, Honey busied herself retrieving plates from the cabinet and slicing the coffee cake.

Theo poured the tea, and then pulled the chair out for Honey when she joined him at the counter.

"I can make you a real breakfast if you like."

Theo eyed the lemon coffee cake appreciatively. "This will do nicely."

After spending a few moments chitchatting about Kentucky weather, Theo asked, "Why haven't you ever visited our distillery with your grandfather?"

"My vacation time never coincided with my grandfather's trips." Honey told him about her career in marketing in California before she came home to work at her grandfather's distillery, Bluegrass Bourbon.

"Woodrow mentioned you will be running the distillery."

Honey nodded. "That's the plan. Although, I hope he never retires." Honey remembered that Theo had lost his own grandfather two years prior. "I was sorry to hear about your grandfather. Gramps considered him a good friend."

Theo looked away as though the memory was too painful to discuss. "I miss him every day. He didn't get the chance to retire and enjoy life. Though, like Woodrow, the distillery was his life. That's what he enjoyed."

"You're right, I think staying in the business keeps my grandfather young."

Theo clinked his cup to hers. "Here's hoping we'll feel the same way after twenty-five years."

Honey smiled up at him. "Let's hope."

"You said you were meeting decorators here. Is Woodrow redecorating his home?"

"No, I'm meeting the decorators who are handling the masquerade ball."

"Oh, I see. I've been looking forward to your ball. Thank you for inviting me. It sounds like a fascinating evening."

"Did you need a costume?"

"I brought one with me."

"Don't tell me who you are going to be. I would rather be surprised."

"Okay, I'll surprise you. Now, tell me about your home state. I plan on living here part of the year, and this is the first time I've been to Kentucky."

"Does that mean you've already decided to buy the distillery?" Honey asked.

"Yes, assuming Mrs. Spencer accepts my offer. Woodrow sent me all of the information I needed, including videos of the distillery. Without Woodrow's expertise, I couldn't have moved so quickly. He's been more than generous helping me. I can hardly wait to see the place."

"We have the keys to the distillery. I can take you there today," Honey offered.

"That's very kind of you. You must allow me to take you to lunch. Of course, that's assuming I don't eat all of this delicious cake."

Honey laughed. "We can make it a light lunch."

"I'd love to see the distillery. Can Elvis accompany us?"

"Of course, and we can have a picnic lunch if that would suit you. Elvis is not at his best when left in the car alone."

CHAPTER TWO

AFTER HER MEETING WITH THE decorators, Honey left Elvis with Theo while she walked to the cottage to get her Jeep. She couldn't stop thinking about how quickly Elvis warmed to Theo. She smiled to herself, thinking she was also quite taken with him. Theo was not only physically appealing, he was undeniably charming and seemed to be a genuinely nice guy.

Once inside the cottage, she glanced in the mirror and thought she needed to freshen her makeup. Since lunch would probably be carryout, she saw no reason to change clothes. After grabbing her handbag, she stuffed some goodies for Elvis inside and walked out the door. Before she reached the Jeep, her cell phone rang.

"Hi, Sam."

"Hi, Honey. How are you?"

"Great. How are you?"

"I have about two hours before I need to be in Louisville, and I thought I would see if you would like to go to lunch."

"Oh, Sam, I can't. I just promised Woodrow's guest from England that I would show him the distillery he's purchasing and have lunch after. Gramps is playing golf and I hated to leave him alone." Honey was disappointed she couldn't see Sam, considering it had been so long since they'd had an actual date.

"I forgot he was in town. What's his name? What kind of guy is he?"

"His name is Theo Parker and he's very nice. Elvis seems to like him."

"Really?"

"Elvis couldn't wait to get to Woodrow's this morning, and when he saw Theo in the pool, he greeted him like an old friend. At first, I thought it was you in the pool."

"Why?"

"All I could see was his dark curly hair." Honey prudently ended her description of Theo with the color of his hair.

Sam didn't comment. "Should I be worried?"

"Worried about what?"

"This guy replacing me in Elvis's heart."

Honey chuckled. "I doubt it."

"Let me talk to Elvis so I can tell him I miss him."

"He's not here. I left him with Theo. I came back to the cottage to get the Jeep."

Sam didn't say anything for a few seconds, then said, "I see."

Honey didn't think it was her imagination that their conversation seemed a little awkward. She hoped it was due to the fact they hadn't seen each other for a while. Even though they talked on the phone almost every night, it wasn't the same as spending time with each other.

"I'll call you tonight, maybe I can talk to Elvis then."

"Okay. Be safe." Honey stared at the phone when she ended the call. She hated that their busy careers were keeping them apart. It wasn't necessarily her career, but Sam's occupation was much more demanding. There was no way she would ever ask him to change professions. Sam loved being a detective, and any woman who dated him would need to be accepting of that fact.

After touring Pickett's Distillery, Honey, Theo, and Elvis were sitting at a picnic table at one of Honey's favorite burger joints. Theo picked up his second triple burger, removed one of the burger patties and handed it to Elvis. "I'm going to need to run ten miles later today to work off this lunch.

"You're a runner?"

"Yes, I try to run several times a week."

"You can run on our path at home."

Theo removed the bun from another burger and held more meat out to Elvis.

"How did you know he doesn't like the bun?"

Theo shrugged. "He's a real guy. It's all about the beef."

Honey couldn't help but laugh at his response. She enjoyed the easiness they shared, almost as if they'd been friends for years. The discussion turned to horses, and Honey asked him if he rode.

"I do, and Woodrow said we would ride while I'm here. I also ride motorcycles, and he mentioned your brother has a couple of bikes."

"Yes, and I'm certain he would be up for a ride anytime if you're interested."

Theo's eyes lit up. "I'd love to ride with him."

Honey had debated on how she could entertain him until her grandfather returned from his golf game, but hearing of his interest in motorcycles, she made a quick plan. "Would you like to see my family's horse farm? I'm sure my brother would love to talk horses and motorcycles until your ears hurt."

He smiled wide. "I thought you would never ask. If you're sure we won't be intruding, I'd enjoy it very much."

On the way back to Woodrow's later that day, Honey drove to the back road behind the estate to show Theo how the running trail circled the property. She was on the access road behind the farm when she noticed a car parked on one of the gravel utility roads. It was unusual to see a car parked there, so she turned onto the road to see if someone was having car problems. She glanced at Theo and explained, "No one is ever on this road and they may need help."

Honey pulled her Jeep behind the dark blue Lexus, but she couldn't see anyone sitting in the car. "Maybe they've already walked to get help. Cell service isn't always the greatest back here."

Elvis barked when Honey opened her door, and she turned to him. "I'll be right back."

Theo reached over and placed his hand on her forearm. "You can never be too careful. Let me see if I can help." He opened his door and hopped out.

"I'll go with you. It might be someone I know." Before Honey could close her door, Elvis jumped over the seat and leaped to the ground. He ran to the car ahead of Theo, stood by the driver's side and barked.

Theo noticed the back passenger door on the driver's side was slightly ajar. Thinking that was odd, he called to Elvis. "Come here, Elvis."

Elvis ran back to him, and Theo glanced at Honey and pointed to the door. "You and Elvis stay right here. I'll see if anyone is in the car." Theo made a wide arc around the driver's side of the car and saw a man slumped over the steering wheel. He approached the car slowly, keeping his eyes on the man, as well as trying to see if there was someone in the back seat. Seeing the back seat was empty, he opened the driver's door. "Sir, did you need help?" Getting no response, Theo moved closer and saw the reason the man didn't respond.

Honey walked up behind Theo and peeked around his shoulder. She saw the trail of blood streaming from the back of the man's head. "Oh, no! Not again."

Theo pressed his fingers to the man's neck, but he felt no pulse. "He's deceased. You should call the authorities."

Remembering Sam was in Louisville, Honey called the chief of police, Hap Nelson. Hap told her to sit tight and stay in the Jeep to keep any evidence from being disturbed. He was at least twenty minutes away.

Once they were back in the Jeep, Theo asked, "Honey, what did you mean when you said *not again*?"

"Just a few months ago, I found two bodies."

Theo turned in the seat to face her. "Really?"

Honey nodded. She told him about her lifelong friend she'd found dead in the park. "He was murdered, and then I found our master distiller on the dinner train. He was also murdered. The same man murdered both of them." Honey proceeded to tell him the story behind the murders.

When she finished the story, Theo whistled softly. "Woodrow told me the husband of the woman who is selling me the distillery had committed murder, and that a woman had shot him. I had no idea one of the murdered men was a friend of yours."

"Yes, he killed both men, and it was all about greed."

"I'm sorry about your friend," Theo told her.

Woodrow pulled into his driveway when his phone rang. "Hi, Honey,

I just got home." Listening to what Honey had to say, he turned around and drove to the utility road. Parking his car behind Honey's, Woodrow joined them in the Jeep to wait for Hap. "Theo, I'm sorry you had to see this on your first day in Kentucky."

"Before we found this gentleman, I had a wonderful day with Honey and Elvis."

Hap Nelson pulled beside Honey's Jeep and inclined his head in greeting. He didn't stop to talk when he jumped from his vehicle, he walked directly to the Lexus. Without touching the door to the Lexus, Hap leaned in and, seeing the wound in the back of the man's head, he felt for a pulse. He didn't want to disturb the body to get a look at his face, which was resting on the steering wheel. Pulling his handkerchief from his pocket, he used it to slip his fingers inside the man's jacket pocket, searching for his wallet. After he pulled his wallet free, he found his identification. Recognizing the name on the driver's license, he glanced at the side of the man's face. He closed his eyes and shook his head. *This is all I need.* He scanned the interior of the car to see if there was a murder weapon visible before he made the call to the crime scene technicians.

Hap walked back to Honey's Jeep. Bracing his hand on the top of the vehicle, he leaned down and said, "Hi, Honey." He saw Woodrow and nodded. "Woodrow." Before he could ask the identity of the man in the passenger seat, Woodrow introduced him.

"Nice to meet you, Mr. Parker." His eyes drifted back to Honey. "Why were you two out here on the utility road?"

Honey explained the reason they were on the back road. "I saw the car and thought the driver might need help." She told him Theo opened the car door and saw the man first.

Hap looked at Theo. "You checked for a pulse, Mr. Parker?"

"Theo, please. Yes, I did. He was dead, but I did notice his skin was still warm."

Hap nodded, thinking he'd noticed the same thing, but then, it was a warm day. He looked at Woodrow. "How about you, Woodrow?"

"I arrived a minute or two before you. I've been playing golf all day, and when Honey called me I was pulling into my driveway. I drove back here and waited with Honey and Theo."

"Great day for golf. When I retire, I hope we can play more often. Who did you play with today?" Hap asked congenially.

"Actually, the first nine holes were miserable. I played with Will McNeal and Jeffrey Younger. They wouldn't stop their bickering, so I left them at the clubhouse after the ninth hole. I told them last week that the next time they ruined our game with their political arguments, I wouldn't play another hole. Lucky for me, I ran into Terry Meiners in the clubhouse, and one of his foursome didn't show, so I finished the day with his group. It's been a long time since I've had such a good nine holes on the golf course. I'd forgotten how much fun it can be playing with people who actually enjoy the game."

"No one is more fun than Terry."

Woodrow nodded toward the Lexus. "Do you know who he is?"

Hap held up the driver's license still in his handkerchief. "Looks like Trey Sullivan."

Woodrow thought the name sounded familiar, and then it finally clicked. "Trey Sullivan? Will McNeal's campaign manager?"

"Yeah."

"What in the world was he doing on this road?" Woodrow asked.

"Getting killed," Hap replied. "The boys will be here in a few minutes to go over the scene. Y'all can go on home now. But don't mention this to anyone until we are positive of his identity."

CHAPTER THREE

FINDING A DEAD BODY HAD a way of placing a pall over the evening Woodrow had planned. Instead of going out for dinner, Honey, Theo, and Woodrow decided to have dinner at home. Honey stopped at her cottage, took a quick shower, and prepared a large salad before she returned to Woodrow's.

While the men were on the patio readying the grill for steaks, Theo told Woodrow about his day with Honey and Elvis. "After the tour of the distillery, I'm even more excited about the purchase. Do you think Mrs. Spencer will accept my offer?"

Woodrow placed the steaks over the hot coals. "Yes, I'm confident she will. Your offer is more than fair, and she wants to rid herself of all of the bad memories."

Their conversation turned to the dead man. Theo asked if he was one of Woodrow's acquaintances.

"No, I didn't know Trey well, though he did work for one of my golfing friends, Will McNeal. Will is running for governor, and he'd mentioned several times that Trey was an excellent campaign manager. I guess I should say Will and Jeff Younger are my ex-golfing friends. I won't be playing with either one of them again."

"It must have been a miserable nine holes."

Woodrow walked to the table, poured bourbon in two glasses and handed one to Theo. "I don't know what's happened to people today, but they can't seem to have a civil conversation when they differ politically. I've played golf with these guys for a few years now, but the last year has been unbearable. They constantly accuse each other of spying on their respective campaigns." Woodrow shook his head. "It's taken the joy out of the game for me. I didn't realize what I'd missed until I played with Terry and his friends. Terry Meiners is a radio personality in Louisville. We've known him for years, he's a great guy and a joy to be around."

"Since I will be living here for most of the year we can start a new foursome, if you're interested," Theo suggested.

Woodrow clinked his glass to Theo's. "I'm very interested. It's time for a fresh start." Woodrow held up one finger and added, "There's only one condition."

Theo arched his brow. "No politicians allowed in the group?"

Woodrow grinned. "You read my mind."

Theo nodded his agreement. "No problem. I have no fondness for politicians. As you know, politics can get fairly nasty in my homeland."

After dinner, they sat in Woodrow's living room discussing the merits of having a cooperage on site of the distillery that Theo was purchasing. Elvis was lying on the floor beside Theo, and everyone thought he was sleeping until he suddenly lurched to his feet and ran down the hallway.

"Someone must be here," Honey said.

"How do you know?" Theo asked as Woodrow stood and motioned for Honey to stay seated just as the doorbell chimed.

"Elvis hears everything before we do. One of his many talents," Honey explained.

Woodrow returned to the living room with Sam Gentry. Elvis was excitedly jumping on Sam, telling him in his own way how much he'd missed him.

After introducing the men, Woodrow said, "Sam, I'm sure you've heard Theo is going to buy Pickett's Distillery."

Sam and Theo shook hands and exchanged greetings before Sam walked to Honey and kissed her cheek. "I thought you might be here after Hap told me what happened today."

"Have they confirmed that it was Trey Sullivan?" Honey asked.

"Yes, Hap's meeting with the family right now." Sam glanced at Woodrow. "Hap said you played golf earlier today with Will McNeal."

"Nine holes. He will be devastated over the news. Will was quite taken with Trey, always complimenting his work ethic." Woodrow extended his hand toward the sofa. "Sam, can I get you a bourbon?"

"No, thanks, I still have to go back to the station tonight." He placed his black Stetson on the table as he sat on the sofa next to Honey.

"Have you had dinner?" Honey asked. She thought that he looked tired. She also noticed he was wearing a dark shirt; Sam normally wore white or blue. He also looked more muscular than ever.

"I grabbed something quick on the ride back from Louisville." Sam leaned over and rubbed Elvis behind the ears. "How's my buddy doing?"

"He's had a full day. I'm surprised he isn't worn out," Honey replied.

Sam turned his attention on Theo, silently taking his measure. "Sounds like you had an interesting first day in our fair town."

"Honey and Elvis were kind enough to show me around. It was a rather macabre ending to an otherwise perfect day," Theo replied.

At the mention of his name, Elvis walked over to Theo and waited for an ear rub from him. Theo didn't disappoint.

Sam noticed Elvis's reaction to Theo, though he told himself he shouldn't take it personally since he'd neglected both Honey and Elvis over the last few weeks. Still, it was difficult to ignore that, like Elvis, Honey seemed equally taken with Theo. "Are you planning to move to Bardstown, Theo?"

"That's my plan. Of course, I'm assuming that I will strike a deal with Mrs. Spencer. If we come to an agreement, I will be spending most of my time in Kentucky, at least for the next few years. After that, I'll see what happens."

Sam noticed that when Theo added that last sentence his eyes drifted to Honey. He figured it didn't take a rocket scientist to know Theo was already intrigued by her. It frustrated Sam that he couldn't stay longer; he wanted to make sure Theo knew the lay of the land. After twenty minutes, he stood to leave. Theo stood and shook his hand. Sam noted the Englishman was an inch or so taller than himself. He also looked to be in excellent condition. He wanted to find a reason to dislike him, but he had to admit Theo seemed to be a likeable guy.

Honey and Elvis walked Sam to the door. "It's nice to see you, even if it was for only for a few minutes," she told him.

Sam put his arm around her waist and pulled her closer. "It's good to see you. I'm sorry I haven't had a lot of time lately. I've missed you and Elvis."

Honey was determined not to interfere with his work. "I know you've been busy."

"It won't be like this forever. I'm working a lot of cases right now. I hope you'll be patient with me."

Honey didn't think that sounded optimistic for them getting together anytime soon. She placed her hand on his chest, and she felt the reason he looked larger. "Why are you wearing a bulletproof vest?"

Sam had intended to remove the vest before he saw her, but he was so tired, he forgot. "I was backup on a call earlier, strictly protocol. Nothing to worry about. I just forgot to take it off."

Honey had no reason not to accept his explanation. "Are you still planning on coming to the masquerade ball?"

"Of course. Even Hap is excited about wearing a costume, and you know nothing excites Hap," Sam teased. "But I did want to talk to you about the party."

"Oh?"

"I told you about my best friend, Rick Cameron."

"That's Cam, right? Your friend in Texas?"

Sam nodded. "He's asked to visit for a couple of days, but he wants to come on the day before the party and leave the day after. He's bringing someone with him. I hated to put him off because he said he had something important to discuss with me. I tried to get him to tell me what was on his mind on the phone, but he said he needed to talk to me in person. I have a strange feeling he's going to tell me he's getting married."

"Is he engaged?"

"Not that he's told me. On the other hand, I have been so busy that I haven't talked to him in weeks. He's left me several messages, and I intended to call him back, but I've been too busy. I had no idea he was serious with anyone. He was always the one who said he would never get married. The confirmed bachelor."

"Maybe he wants to see you about something else," Honey suggested.

Sam gave her a thoughtful look. "Maybe, but I know Cam pretty well. He sounded like this was something very serious." He grinned at her. "And what could be more serious than getting married?"

Honey laughed, thinking he'd paled at the thought of marriage. "Invite them to the ball if you want."

"Thanks, I was hoping it wouldn't be a problem. I'll tell them to bring a costume."

"If they can't find costumes that quickly, I'll make an exception for them."

"Does that mean I don't have to wear a costume?"

"Absolutely not. You've had more than enough time to get your cowboy costume together." She tapped the Stetson in his hand. "You didn't even have to buy a Stetson, you probably have twenty."

Sam arched his dark brow at her. "How did you know I was planning on being a cowboy?"

Honey grinned up at him and shrugged. "What else?"

"I only have ten hats. Maybe I'm too predictable," Sam muttered as he lowered his head and found her lips with his. It wasn't his usual kind of lingering kiss, but a rather quick one, which told her his mind was preoccupied, and he was probably as exhausted as he looked. When he released her, he looked down to say goodbye to Elvis, but Elvis wasn't beside him.

Honey saw the question in Sam's eyes. "He must have gone back to the living room."

As soon as Honey walked back to the living room, she saw Elvis lying at Theo's feet, enjoying his attention.

"Theo, what time did you say your solicitor and master distiller will be here Monday morning?" Woodrow asked.

"Their flight arrives a little after nine," Theo replied.

"Good, we'll meet Bunny Spencer and her attorney in my office at eleven a.m."

"I appreciate your opening your home to the three of us. We can certainly stay in a hotel."

"Nonsense, it's no problem. It's my pleasure to have you stay here. I'm tired of rattling around in this big old home by myself. It will be nice to have company for a change."

Honey felt a pang of guilt thinking she wasn't spending enough time with Woodrow. Even though he'd been dating Sam's grandmother,

Virginia, and taking her to dinner a couple times each week, Honey thought he sounded lonely.

"Gramps, I can drive Theo to the airport Monday morning, and we can meet you at the distillery."

"Perfect. If the flight is delayed, I can entertain Bunny until you arrive."

Honey walked over and gave Woodrow a kiss on the cheek. "Elvis and I should head home. It's been a long day."

Theo stood and said, "I'll walk you home."

"That really isn't necessary." Honey pointed to Elvis. "I have my protector."

"I insist. There was a murder today not far from here, so I would feel better if you weren't walking alone tonight."

When they reached Honey's cottage, Theo remarked that he'd envisioned her cottage to be a small little two-room bungalow. "This is much larger than I expected."

"Gramps had it renovated before I moved back from California. The contractor did a fabulous job." Honey opened her door. "Would you like to see inside?"

"Very much. Your grandfather's home is lovely, but I prefer something smaller, like this."

Honey remembered her grandfather told her that Theo's family lived in an old castle with huge rooms, and massive fireplaces in every room. She gave him a tour of the cottage and when they reached the kitchen, she said, "I'm particularly pleased with the work the contractor did in this room. I love cooking in here, it has everything I need."

"I'm afraid my skills stop at grilling, but this looks very well-appointed."

Honey turned on the outside lights, and opened the patio door. "The patio area was also renovated, but the pool isn't heated. Gramps likes to swim all winter, so his is heated."

Theo walked around the patio area. "Do you think I could find a place like this to buy?"

"You might have to do some renovations on a place if you want some land."

"I would prefer some acreage, something ideally situated like your cottage."

"It's nice to have some space for Elvis to roam. He likes to have a lot of territory."

Theo rubbed Elvis's head. "This is a great place for him."

When they walked back to the front door, Theo said, "I want to thank you and Elvis for a wonderful day. I'm afraid I've monopolized your time today."

"It was very enjoyable."

Theo leaned over and brushed a kiss over her cheek. "For me as well. I will say good night."

CHAPTER FOUR

Honey, Theo, and his friends barely made it back to the distillery by eleven. Bunny Spencer and her attorney were in Woodrow's office when they arrived.

Honey introduced everyone before going to her office where she found Georgia and Elvis waiting for her. Georgia was bursting with curiosity. "Oh my goodness, I can't believe you have spent the last two days with that man."

"I think I should ask Gramps for hazard pay," Honey joked.

"I'll pay you if you'd like me to chauffeur him around."

Honey waggled her finger at Georgia. "Tsk, tsk. I'm going to tell Preston." Georgia had been dating Honey's brother for several months, and their relationship seemed to be getting very serious.

"Just because I'm dating Preston doesn't mean I'm dead. I mean, Theo is beautiful."

"Fickle, fickle," Honey teased. "What happened to your infatuation with Detective Gorgeous?"

"Sam would be a great model for a cowboy magazine, but Theo Parker should be on the cover of one of those bodice-ripping romance novels. He's more handsome than all of those British movies stars put together. His two friends aren't bad either. Which one is the attorney?"

Honey had to agree that all three men were handsome. "Oliver Dalton is the attorney. Jacob Newbury is his master distiller."

"I was so busy gawking at Theo I can't even remember if I said anything to his friends," Georgia quipped. "Please say I didn't look stupid."

Honey laughed. "You didn't look stupid, but you *were* gawking at Theo. It reminded me of the way you drool over bourbon balls."

Georgia grinned at her. "He does look as yummy as your bourbon balls. And I did notice they aren't wearing wedding rings."

Honey lifted her shoulders and shook her head. "I didn't notice."

Georgia rolled her eyes. "Have I not taught you anything? Speaking of Detective Gorgeous, has he met Theo Parker yet?"

"Yes, they've met."

Georgia's eyes widened. "And?"

"Sam stopped by after he heard about the murdered man we found." Honey knew that comment would get her mind off handsome men. Georgia obviously hadn't heard about the murder, or Honey knew she would have been on the phone first thing.

Georgia gasped. "Murdered man! What murdered man? Don't tell me that you found another dead body."

Honey filled Georgia in on her day with Theo, and how they had found Trey Sullivan in his car.

"I can't believe we are going to go through this again. Did you know him?"

"No, I had never met him. I feel so sorry for his family. He was a young man." Honey told Georgia that Trey Sullivan worked for one of the men running for governor.

Georgia exhausted all of her questions, and circled back to their original subject. "Back to Detective Gorgeous. What did he say about Theo?"

"Nothing, but I think Elvis hurt his feelings."

"Elvis?" Georgia's eyes darted to Elvis. "How did Elvis hurt his feelings?"

Honey grinned. "Elvis really likes Theo too."

"Really? As much as he likes Sam?"

Honey nodded. "Elvis greeted Theo like he was a long lost friend. The same way he acted when he first met Sam."

Ruffling Elvis's ears, Georgia whispered to Elvis, "Elvis, maybe you're the one who is fickle."

Elvis groaned.

Georgia turned her eyes back on Honey. "So, what's up with you and Detective Gorgeous?"

Honey walked around her desk and sat down. "Nothing. Unfortunately. He's very busy at work, and we haven't been on a date in weeks. It was the first time I've even seen him in almost three weeks."

"I understand being busy, but his schedule is kind of difficult on a relationship."

"We seem to be drifting apart. He tries to call every night, though he sounds so tired I doubt he remembers our conversations. Maybe that's why Elvis was so taken with Theo—he misses Sam's attention."

Georgia sighed. "I'm taken with Theo too. Think he'll rub my ears?"

Honey laughed at the dreamy expression on Georgia's face. "You wait until I tell Preston you have a major crush on Theo."

"Preston told me he met Theo Saturday. Funny, he failed to mention how good-looking he is. So, are you going out with him?"

"Of course not. Our relationship is strictly professional," Honey responded.

"Mm-hmm." Georgia was quiet for a few moments, then asked, "Why do you think that guy was murdered on your property?"

"I've been asking myself that question over and over. It's so out of the way that it makes no sense."

"And you're sure you didn't know him?"

Honey shook her head. "I'm sure."

"When is the funeral?" Georgia asked.

"They're having a graveside service on Wednesday."

"We should go and see who shows up," Georgia suggested.

Honey stared at her a moment, then replied, "I was planning on it."

"Don't think you are going to go without me."

Theo and Bunny Spencer agreed to the terms of the sale, and once the meeting ended, Honey gave Theo and his friends a tour of their new restaurant and gift shop on the grounds of the distillery. "Theo, the contractor who did the work on the cottage, also did the renovations on this building."

Theo was impressed by the renovations of the older buildings. "He does great work. I'm anxious to meet him."

They reached the gift shop, and Honey grabbed a box of bourbon balls. "Have you gentlemen tried bourbon balls before?"

"Not me," Theo said, and Oliver and Jacob shook their heads.

Honey opened the box and extended it to the men. "This is our old family recipe."

Theo's eyes widened when he tasted the bourbon ball. "These are delicious."

Oliver and Jacob agreed, and Honey handed them the box. "Have some more."

Theo reached in and removed several pieces from the box. "These could be addictive."

Honey led them through the gift shop, and gave Theo some suggestions for his distillery. "We sold some things in our welcome center, but we decided to add a larger gift shop and offer more items, many from our local artisans. We enjoy showcasing the products made in Kentucky. Next summer we are planning a festival and inviting our local artists to set up booths on the grounds for three days."

"You have great ideas. Do you think I could hire you away from Woodrow?" Theo teased.

Honey smiled at him. "You will find our industry is a tightly knit group, and we want to make sure everyone succeeds."

"That's evident by Woodrow's generosity helping me with this purchase. I admire the sense of community here," Theo replied.

On their way back to Honey's office, Georgia met them in the hallway. "Do you have your costumes for the ball?"

"Yes, we came prepared," Oliver replied. "I'm going to be..."

Georgia held up her hand, silencing Oliver. "Don't tell. Honey wants to be surprised."

Elvis ran to Honey when they walked in her office, and once he had received some attention from her, he ran to Theo. When Theo took a seat, Elvis plopped down and rested his head on his lap.

Honey tried to move Elvis away. "Elvis, Theo may not want your hair or your slobber on his suit."

Theo waved her hand away. "He's fine, a little hair is no bother."

They discussed business for several minutes before the master distiller, Jacob, asked Honey about the murders. "Woodrow mentioned two master distillers have been murdered in the last several months." He glanced at Theo, and added, "Theo failed to mention that fact when he talked me into coming to Kentucky. Sounds like master distillers might not have a lengthy lifespan here."

Honey told Jacob and Oliver about the murders, and the theft of their bourbon. "My best friend was murdered. He was part owner, as well as the master distiller of Cleary's Distillery. And the second victim was our own master distiller. But you can rest easy, Jacob, it had nothing to do with being a master distiller. The owner of Pickett's was stealing product with the help of our master distiller. My friend K. C. Cleary uncovered their scheme, and we think that was the reason he was killed."

Woodrow walked into the office. "Are you gentlemen ready to go to Pickett's? I know you have a lot to do to get the place in order, and I'm sure you are ready to meet your employees."

Theo stood. "Yes, we are anxious to get started." Everyone left Honey's office, but Theo lagged behind. "Honey, Woodrow has agreed to have dinner with us tonight, but I wanted to ask if you could join us. I've made reservations for five, hoping you were free."

Honey's initial thought was to wait to see if Sam had any free time tonight, but then she thought she'd been doing that very thing for the last few weeks. "I'd love to join you."

Even if it was a business dinner, Honey was looking forward to spending an evening out. She'd secured her last earring when Elvis ran from her bedroom. A few seconds later she heard the doorbell. She hurried to the door to see Elvis standing there with his tail swishing back and forth, watching Theo through the window. As soon as she opened the door, Elvis jumped on Theo before she could stop him. "Elvis, down."

"He's fine." Theo petted Elvis as he pulled a huge bone from his pocket. "Can I give him this treat? I figured since he must stay home tonight alone, I should bring him something."

"Yes, he's had his dinner. That can be his dessert."

Honey glanced at the car in the driveway—a limo. "Let me grab my handbag."

Theo stepped inside and gave Elvis his treat, then watched Honey walk to the table for her handbag. "You look beautiful."

Turning to him, Honey smiled. "Thank you." She noticed he'd changed his suit, and he looked just as handsome as he did earlier.

"I hired a limo for tonight."

"I could have driven," Honey responded.

"I don't want to tire you out being our chauffeur." Theo grinned. "And since I've never driven in the States, I may need your help learning to drive at some point."

Honey laughed. "I'd be happy to help. You're a brave man, there is no way I would drive in England. I know I would forget what I was doing and end up on the wrong side."

"When you come to England again, I promise I will return the favor. As a matter of fact, why don't you come for a visit when I go back in a few months? I'd love to show you England."

"I don't know if I'll be able to get away in a few months. We're still busy with the new bourbon," Honey replied.

"Please think about it and see if there is a way you can work it out."

After they returned from dinner, Theo walked Honey to her cottage door. "Thank you for accompanying us tonight. Not only did you add beauty to our group, the conversation was much more enjoyable."

Honey thoroughly enjoyed the evening. Theo, Oliver, and Jacob had been friends since childhood, and they entertained her and Woodrow with exploits of their youth. They were an entertaining trio, and Honey couldn't remember the last time she'd laughed so much. She could tell her grandfather really enjoyed the evening as well. "It was a wonderful evening. I haven't been out to dinner in a few weeks, and I'm afraid I was becoming a bit of a hermit. It was a fun evening."

Surprised by her response, Theo said, "I would think you would have a different date every night of the week."

Honey laughed. "Hardly. I've been very busy at the distillery and I'm afraid that doesn't leave much time for socializing."

Reaching the door, Theo hesitated a moment, then said, "Well, I want to remedy that, unless you are otherwise attached to someone in particular?"

Honey thought about Sam. She didn't want to lie to Theo, but she couldn't say she wanted to discourage him either. "Sam Gentry and I had been dating regularly, but lately our schedules do not seem to coincide."

"I see." He leaned over and kissed her cheek. "I can't imagine any man allowing a schedule that would keep him from you." He opened her door and said goodbye to Elvis with an ear rub. "You two have a nice night."

Sam called just as Honey crawled into bed. Their conversation was brief, and once they said good night Honey realized Sam didn't even ask how she'd spent her evening. She couldn't help but question if he was really so busy that he couldn't find time for their relationship, or if it was a matter of waning interest. Deciding it served no purpose to worry about the situation, she thought about her schedule for the next two weeks. Along with Woodrow, she would be spending most of her time with Theo at his new distillery. Thankfully, Georgia was capable of handling the final details for the masquerade ball. She smiled, thinking of Georgia's reaction to Theo. Honey knew Georgia was crazy about Preston, but even she wasn't immune to the charms of the handsome Englishman.

CHAPTER FIVE

HONEY DROVE BY THE ROW of cars with flags on their fenders, identifying them as the funeral procession for Trey Sullivan.

"A lot of people are attending his graveside service," Georgia said.

"He was in politics. Everyone will show up." Honey kept driving until she found a secluded place to park her Jeep, where it would not be easily seen. They left the Jeep just as all of the funeral-goers were walking to the gravesite. Instead of joining them, Honey pointed to a massive statuary some twenty yards away. "That looks like a good place to watch who comes and goes."

Once they were situated behind the ten-foot marble angel, Georgia whispered, "Do you see anyone you know?"

Honey peeked around the angel's wing and pointed to a man at the end of the first row of people. "That's Mr. McNeal, you know, the gubernatorial candidate. Trey Sullivan worked for him."

"The man in the navy suit?"

Honey nodded.

"He's attractive, very elegant looking. Is that his wife holding on to his arm?"

"I think so. I've never met her, but I've seen her on the local news."

Georgia arched her brow. "They make a rather odd couple."

"What do you mean?"

"I don't know. They don't look like they go together. You know, he looks like Ken, but she doesn't look like Barbie."

Not far from where Honey and Georgia were watching people gathered around the gravesite, Sam stood somberly by a grave holding a bouquet. Though his head was lowered as if in prayer, his sunglasses concealed his observant eyes surveying the people surrounding Trey Sullivan's casket. He slowly made his way to another grave, trying to get a better view of the faces. He noticed some movement at another gravesite. He lowered his glasses to get a better look at the unusual marble angel with an eight-foot wingspan. The angel had three heads. *Three heads. And two were not marble.* On the heels of that thought, one of the heads bobbed up and down. He turned to look at the row of cars lining the road closest to Sullivan's gravesite. He didn't see a red Jeep, but when he glanced farther down the road, there it was.

"First time I've seen an angel with three heads."

Honey and Georgia whipped their heads around to see Sam standing behind them, dark and imposing, a stark contrast to the archangel in front of them.

Honey noticed the handful of colorful flowers in his grip. "What are you doing here?"

"I think I should be the one asking you two that question." Sam's eyes flicked to the mourners to see if anyone had noticed them.

"We wanted to see who attended Mr. Sullivan's funeral," Honey whispered.

"Why?"

"He was murdered on our property and I want to know why. We were curious to see who might show up for his funeral."

Sam expelled a loud breath. "Honey, once again, you need to leave investigations to the police."

Honey rolled her eyes at him. "We're just curious."

"Why are you incognito?" Georgia asked Sam.

Sam frowned at her. "What do you mean? I'm not incognito."

"Where's your cowboy hat?"

"In the car."

"I've never seen you without it. Looks to me like you didn't want to be recognized," Georgia responded.

"I'm the detective, and I'm investigating a murder. Now, you two need to leave." Out of the corner of his eye, Sam saw a dark sedan driving slowly on the road behind them. He turned to see who was driving. The windows were darkly tinted, but Sam thought he could make out four people inside. He turned to walk away and said over his shoulder, "Go home." He dropped the flowers he was clutching onto a grave as he jogged toward his car.

Honey looked at Georgia and shrugged. "I wonder what that was all about. I mean, he didn't even say goodbye."

"Do you think he's mad at us?"

"I don't know why he would be."

"He's going to the gym too much, he's getting too muscular," Georgia commented.

"I noticed that the other night, but it was because he was wearing a bulletproof vest."

"Why was he wearing that?"

"He said he was on a backup call." Honey watched Sam get in his car and drive away at a speed that wasn't allowed in a cemetery.

"He seemed very interested in that car that drove by," Georgia said.

"I know."

"Terry! It's so good to see you." Honey hugged Terry as soon as he walked inside Woodrow's home.

"I can't believe how long it's been since I last saw you." Terry leaned and rubbed Elvis's head. "How's the big guy doing?"

Elvis leaped on Terry and licked his cheek. "Does Elvis have a costume for the ball?"

"Yes, but he's the only one who will be a fictional character. I'm so happy you are going to be our master of ceremonies. That will ensure a fun-filled evening." She motioned for him to follow her down the hallway. "Come on, Gramps is in the living room." As they walked toward the living room, Honey told him about their guests from England.

"Woodrow told me about his visitors when we played golf."

Woodrow greeted Terry and made the introductions. "As I told you,

Theo is purchasing Pickett's Distillery. Oliver is his attorney, and Jacob is the master distiller."

Theo shook Terry's hand. "Honey and I listened to your program earlier. She said you have the best voice in radio, and I must say I certainly enjoyed your show."

"Honey is generous in her praise." Terry turned to shake hands with Oliver and Jacob, then took a seat across from Theo. "Woodrow said you own a distillery in England. How did you become interested in bourbon?"

"I must credit my interest to my grandfather. He was friends with Woodrow for many years, and he'd been talking about buying a bourbon distillery for a long time. Sadly, he died before he could see that dream come true. When Woodrow told me there was a distillery for sale, I knew it was an opportunity that may not come along again."

"Woodrow also mentioned that you play golf. I hope you can join us while you're here," Terry said.

"Indeed, I do, and I would love to join you."

"Terry, can I get you something to drink? Bourbon?" Woodrow asked.

Terry nodded. "I haven't tried Devil's Due yet."

Theo held the glass he was holding in the air. "I give it the highest recommendation."

Woodrow walked to the bar, poured a shot of bourbon and handed it to Terry. "I know Honey wants to show you the ballroom. Let's walk back there so you can have a look around."

"Honey, Woodrow tells me that you plan to have a string quartet and there will be ballroom dancing," Terry said.

"Do you think many of the guests know how to waltz?" Theo asked.

"I doubt it, but we will have instructors here to teach the dances to the guests who want to participate," Honey replied.

"You can count on three of your guests who already know how to waltz," Oliver said.

Honey stopped and turned to Oliver. "Seriously?"

Oliver made a cross over his heart with his forefinger. "Honest."

Her eyes darted from Oliver to Jacob to Theo. She thought they were teasing her. "All three of you know how to waltz?"

The three friends exchanged a look and grinned at her. "Yeah. Like we told you, we've been friends since childhood. Our mothers thought it was a good idea for us to learn to dance when we were about twelve years of age. I think she thought it would save our teeth if we gave up rugby," Jacob explained.

"We all grumbled about it, but once we saw all the good-looking girls in dance class that first day, we didn't mind it so much," Oliver added.

"You don't look like dancers," Terry told them.

"We didn't forsake rugby, but in this instance, I'm glad I learned to waltz. I'm claiming the first waltz with Honey," Theo said.

"I get the second," Oliver added.

Jacob elbowed Oliver. "I was going to say that."

Oliver slapped him on the back. "You were always too slow. Guess you get the third dance."

Honey laughed. "There will be many ladies attending who will be more than willing to dance. I'm certain none of you will have a problem finding partners."

"I hope they're all as pretty as you," Oliver said.

"Hearing you argue over dancing with Honey has given me an idea. Honey, since the ball benefits charity, why don't we have a dance where the men bid on their partners?" Terry suggested.

"That sounds fun," Theo said.

"I love the idea. Perhaps the women could also bid on the men for a dance," Honey suggested.

Terry nodded his head. "Why not?" He slapped Woodrow on the shoulder. "Just have plenty of bourbon so the money will fly freely from their wallets."

They reached the arched entryway leading to the ballroom. Woodrow turned on the five crystal chandeliers suspended from the gold tin ceiling tiles. The room was painted a pale creamy color, and with the gleaming hardwood floors, the area radiated a warm golden glow.

Honey said, "I've always loved this room."

"It reminds me of grand ballrooms in England," Theo commented.

"It must have been an extravagance to build this room at that time. Sadly, we haven't used it enough through the years. I should have made more of an effort to have parties here," Woodrow told them.

"Whatever the cost, it was worth every penny. It feels like we've stepped back in time." Terry pointed to the balcony area overlooking the ballroom. "Will the musicians be located up there?"

"Yes. But as master of ceremonies, you can decide what will be most convenient for you." Honey turned and pointed to a raised platform on one side of the room. "You could use that as a stage if you prefer, whatever works best for you."

"I'll welcome everyone from the balcony, and afterward I'll be mingling with the guests most of the time. I can use the stage to announce the dances, and encourage participation with the professional dancers."

"The guests might need a few cocktails to muster the courage to try some of the dances," Oliver told him.

"I may need a drink or two to learn to waltz," Terry joked.

"I know you can dance, Terry. Haven't you ever waltzed?" Honey asked.

"Nope, that's one I've never learned."

"I'm sure you will pick it up quickly. You'd better, because someone might bid on you," Honey teased. She looked at the other men and added, "Terry has as many women listeners as men."

"My women friends tell me women are partial to men with a good sense of humor," Theo said.

Honey nodded her agreement. "True, and there's no one better than Terry at making people laugh and feel comfortable."

"You're making me blush. I hope I live up to your expectations," Terry replied.

"I have no doubt as long as you're here, the party will be a great success." Honey pointed to the double doors on one side of the room, which led to a large outdoor patio area. "We will have a huge heated tent if the evening is a little cool. That's where we plan to have tables for bartenders. Buffet tables will be in the center of the room, surrounded by tables and chairs. We will also have seating areas on the outside patio if the weather is cooperative."

"Will you have some of your bourbon balls for dessert?" Theo asked.

Honey smiled at him. "As many as you want."

"Be careful what you promise, Honey. You saw how much the man can eat," Jacob said.

Terry talked with Theo as they walked back through the house.

"When you get settled I hope you'll come on my show to discuss your new business."

"Thank you for the offer, but I'm not sure anyone would want to hear me," Theo replied.

"Our listeners like to hear about local businesses." Terry turned to Honey. "Don't you think the women listeners would like to hear his accent?"

"Absolutely."

"I'm not so sure about that. I tried to talk to Honey while she was listening to you on the radio and she didn't hear a word I said," Theo responded.

Honey laughed. "I seem to remember you were also laughing at Terry's stories, but your accent will definitely attract the ladies. Seriously, it will be a great way to get the word out about your business."

Theo considered Honey's comment. "Well, if you think I won't be too boring, I'll gladly accept your invitation."

Everyone followed Honey to the kitchen, where she pulled out a platter of burger patties ready to be grilled and handed it to Woodrow. "Terry, you are staying for dinner, aren't you?"

"I can't pass up a good grilled burger."

Woodrow slid the patio door open and Elvis ran outside. "I hope everyone is okay with grilled burgers tonight."

"My favorite," Theo added, with Oliver and Jacob adding their approval.

Honey shooed the men outside. "Go outside with Woodrow and Terry. I'm sure you want to talk golf, and I'm going to prepare a salad and some fries."

"I heard Honey found Trey Sullivan," Terry commented to Woodrow once he joined him at the grill.

"Yeah, Honey and Theo saw a car on the back access road. They thought someone had car trouble."

Terry turned to look at Theo. "That's one interesting welcome to our state."

"One I will certainly remember."

Woodrow pointed them to the bar area. "Help yourself to whatever you want. Glasses and ice are on the cabinet."

The men filled their glasses, and Terry handed a fresh bourbon to Woodrow. "It's hard to believe that it was McNeal's campaign manager who was murdered. Have you talked to McNeal since it happened?"

"No, I haven't spoken to him yet."

"Did you know McNeal and Younger didn't finish their golf game after you left them at the ninth hole?" Terry asked.

Woodrow turned from the grill. "I can't say I'm surprised. They didn't have me to separate them. I think they've gotten to the point that they can't tolerate each other without another person acting as referee."

Terry nodded his agreement. "I was told they both stormed out of the clubhouse without speaking to anyone. There's a lot of bitterness between them. What surprises me the most is Younger and his wife used to play golf with McNeal and his wife every weekend. They were all good friends at one time."

"I know, but I don't think the wives even play with their husbands now," Woodrow replied.

"The women don't play together either," Terry replied.

Theo excused himself and joined Honey in the kitchen. "What can I do to help?"

"I'm just waiting on the fries. The salad is ready."

"I'll keep you company then." Theo sat down at the counter and noticed her glass of iced tea.

"I see you aren't drinking bourbon."

"No, I must admit I am addicted to iced tea."

Theo tapped the glass. "With lots of ice, I see."

Honey smiled. "I know when I visited England I would rarely get more than one cube of ice in a glass."

Theo chuckled. "True enough." He took a sip of his bourbon. "I wanted to ask your opinion about changing the name of the distillery."

"I think it might makes sense to have a fresh start, considering the circumstances."

"You mean considering the deceased owner was a thief and a murderer?"

Honey nodded. "As long as the name is the same, the press will always tell that story when the distillery is mentioned."

"That was my thinking. Speaking of murder, how are you doing?"

Honey shrugged. "Some people might think I'm getting accustomed to finding dead bodies, but you can't put something like that out of your mind quickly, if ever."

Theo nodded. "Yes, you're right. One never forgets these things. When I got out of the military it took me a while to get back to normal, whatever normal might mean."

Woodrow stuck his head inside the patio door. "Burgers are almost ready."

"Perfect timing. The fries will be ready in a few seconds." Honey removed the fries from the fryer and placed them on a large platter. After she pulled the salad from the refrigerator, she handed the bowl to Theo. "Now you can help."

Theo reached over and nabbed one of the fries and stuffed it in his mouth. "With pleasure."

CHAPTER SIX

As Honey was about to step outside with Elvis beside her, he abruptly whirled around and ran through the kitchen. Honey could hear him racing down the hallway toward the front door. Knowing the doorbell would ring in a matter of seconds, she set the fries on the counter and ran after him. Just as she expected, the doorbell chimed before she was halfway to the front door. Elvis was sitting at the door waiting for her with a look on his face as if asking what took her so long. Since his tail wasn't wagging, she had a feeling he didn't know who was on the other side, or he wasn't thrilled with the visitor. She held onto his collar as she opened the door. To her surprise, Jeff Younger, one of Woodrow's golfing partners, was standing there.

Jeff gave her a wide smile. "Hello, Honey. What a pleasant surprise. I hadn't expected you to answer Woodrow's door. I must say, you are certainly a beautiful substitute."

Elvis growled low, and though Honey felt like growling along with him, only good manners forced her to refrain. She'd never been particularly fond of Jeff Younger, and she was certain Elvis sensed her uneasiness. *Creepy* was the only word that suited Younger. Every time she was in his presence, he always seemed to find a way to put his hands on her. Even though he was a married man, it didn't seem to deter him from being flirty with other women. To the unaware observer, it might look innocent enough, but Honey thought it wasn't as harmless as he wanted it to appear. Fortunately, Elvis would keep him away from her, and it wouldn't be necessary for her to tell him to keep his hands to himself. "Gramps is on the patio. We were sitting down to dinner." She hoped her latter statement would shorten his unannounced visit.

"Sorry to interrupt, but I did need to speak to Woodrow on an urgent matter."

Honey thought he wasn't the least bit sorry. He was too self-important to worry about inconveniencing others.

As soon as Younger stepped over the threshold, Elvis immediately maneuvered his big body in front of Honey.

"I see he's still as protective as ever." Younger made a wide arch around Elvis, keeping his distance.

Honey chose not to disabuse him of his fear of Elvis. "He's even more so now. He doesn't like anyone getting too close to me."

When they reached the kitchen, Honey was relieved to see Theo standing there. She introduced Theo to Younger, and then said, "You can go on out to the patio, Mr. Younger."

"Honey, I told you before to call me Jeff." When Younger walked outside, Honey looked at Theo and rolled her eyes. "He's one of the politicians who golfs with Gramps."

Theo leaned over and whispered in her ear, "You mean his ex-golfing partner. I take it you don't like him very much."

Honey shook her head. "Neither does Elvis."

Theo looked down at Elvis and rubbed his ears. "That tells me everything I need to know."

"My thoughts exactly," Honey agreed.

Theo snagged another fry. "I am curious why you don't like him."

"He's handsy."

Theo furrowed his brow. "Handsy?"

"You know the type of man who always finds a way to touch a woman without her consent."

"Ah, I see. Quite right, keep your distance."

"I try to stay as far away from him as possible."

Theo slid the patio door open and motioned for her to precede him. "I can promise you he won't get handsy with me around."

Woodrow had introduced Younger to Oliver and Jacob before Honey and Theo walked outside. Terry had walked back to his car to retrieve his new putter that Woodrow wanted to see.

"I apologize for interrupting your dinner, Woodrow, but I needed to speak to you," Younger said.

Woodrow stood and asked, "Do you need to speak in private?"

"No. I heard Trey Sullivan was found on your property."

Woodrow didn't tell him Honey was the one who found him. "Yes."

"I'm sure he got what he deserved. I mean, he did work for that crook, McNeal," Younger stated.

Woodrow was stunned by his comment. "I can't believe you think the man deserved to be murdered, no matter what you think of your opponent."

At that moment, Terry returned to the group carrying his putter. When Younger saw Terry, he snapped, "What are you doing here?"

Before Terry responded, Woodrow interjected, "Terry is having dinner with us. Now, what did you need to speak to me about?"

Younger ignored Woodrow's question and turned to confront Terry. "Don't you think it's time to tell your audience the truth and admit that you are supporting McNeal? You claim to be fair to all politicians, but we all know that's a lie. You have McNeal on your show much more often than me."

"I make every attempt to be fair, and I can assure you that you have been on the show an equal number of times," Terry replied politely.

Younger moved closer to Terry and looked up at him. He poked him in the chest with his forefinger. "We all know you want McNeal to win. My campaign manager has called you several times trying to book a time on your show and you're ignoring him."

Terry smelled alcohol on Younger's breath. "I spoke to Aaron, and the dates he requested were already booked. We offered him some alternative dates."

Honey couldn't believe what she was seeing. She glanced at Theo and by the expression on his face, he couldn't believe it either. Younger, who might be five feet tall at best, looked out of place next to all of the men standing there; each one was well over six feet. Terry was six two, in great shape, and he was holding a putter in his hand. Honey thought Younger was either drunk or crazy to provoke him.

Younger continued his rant. "It's obvious who you favor, and you're trying to help him win. We all know you have a large audience, and you're using your influence to get him votes."

"Are you on the crack pipe again?" Terry joked, attempting to calm the situation.

Younger's face contorted with rage. His gaze flicked over everyone standing there before he turned back Terry. "Don't you dare insinuate that I'm an addict! I will sue you and take everything you own!"

Woodrow stepped forward, gripped Younger's arm and pulled him aside. "Jeff, in case you didn't notice, Terry is my guest. I suggest you save this conversation for another time and place. Although I can't imagine why you would want to insult Terry. Everyone knows he is a fair interviewer and doesn't play favorites. At least, those who think logically recognize that fact."

Younger yanked his arm from Woodrow's grip. "You're just like Meiners! You want McNeal to win too. I came here to see where your loyalties lie, Woodrow. I know you've donated to both campaigns, but enough is enough. I demand to know who you are going to support."

Woodrow gave him a hard look. "My loyalties are none of your business. We have played golf together for a few years, but that doesn't give you a right to demand anything."

Jabbing his finger in Terry's direction, Younger snarled, "You wait, I'm going to take care of you. You'll be lucky if you have one listener left when I get through with you."

"That's quite enough," Woodrow said. "I think it's time you left."

Theo moved to Woodrow's side. "Woodrow, would you like me to show Mr. Younger to the front door?"

"Thank you, Theo. That would be most kind of you. Our dinner is getting cold."

"I'd like Honey to walk me to the door," Younger slurred.

Theo pointed to the patio door. "I'm afraid that's not an option."

Younger looked up at Theo, and seeing the steely look in his eyes, he wisely didn't mount an argument. But he had one last parting shot to Terry. "Meiners, I'm going to make sure no one wants to be a guest on your show."

Forcefully gripping Younger's elbow, Theo nearly lifted him off his feet assisting him through the patio door. Elvis was on their heels as

Theo efficiently escorted Younger to the front door. Younger didn't utter another word. Once Theo closed the door behind the uninvited guest, he reached down and petted Elvis's head. "Thanks for the backup, partner."

When they returned to the patio, Woodrow handed Theo a fresh bourbon. "Thank you for seeing Jeff to the door. I do apologize for the interruption."

"His behavior was rather boorish. I can see why you've ended your golfing partnership. Plus, I think he had one too many," Theo replied.

Terry handed his putter to Theo. "I think you're right. I've smelled alcohol on him the last few times he's been on my show. He's always confrontational even though I try to keep the conversation off of his opponent, but he always tries to engage me in their arguments."

Woodrow shook his head. "Then you understand what I go through on the golf course with the two of them together."

"I've often wondered how you tolerated them on the course. Talking politics is the perfect recipe to ruin a great day," Terry replied.

"It won't be an issue in the future."

"Do you know his campaign manager, Aaron Branson?"

Woodrow nodded. "I've met him a few times. Seems fairly capable."

Terry nodded. "He's more reasonable than Younger."

"This is a fine putter," Theo said, taking a few practice swings.

"That must be your secret weapon, Terry. If I putted as well, I might be able to give you a game," Woodrow said.

Terry smiled. "I've been having some success with it."

"Dinner is getting cold," Honey reminded them. "If you don't sit down, Elvis will eat all of the burgers."

"After dinner, we can take the putter to the practice green," Woodrow told them.

Everyone sat at the table and Terry asked, "Did you hear Elvis's low growl when Younger was here?"

Honey nodded. "He doesn't like Mr. Younger."

"I've never heard him growl like that before," Woodrow commented.

Honey sat back in her chair. "You know, Gramps, now that you mention it, the only time I really remember hearing him make that menacing growl was with Troy Spencer."

"That's the man who owned the distillery and committed murder," Theo reminded Oliver and Jacob.

"One night, Sam, Elvis, and I ran into Troy and Bunny, and Elvis wouldn't let them near me," Honey told them.

"He's a smart dog. He obviously smelled a murderer," Oliver commented.

Woodrow told the men stories about Elvis finding lost children and senior citizens. "He's been a godsend to the community."

"I wish my designer dog could do something spectacular. It would justify what I paid for him. He cost more than my first car," Terry joked.

Honey smacked him on his arm. "You love your dog."

"Yeah, but he could earn his keep. He could at least growl at my detractors. He doesn't have to actually take a plug out of them. Maybe I should borrow Elvis and take him to the station the next time Younger is booked. He might be less argumentative."

Everyone laughed, and Honey said, "Anytime you want to borrow him, let me know."

Dinner ended, and while Honey was pouring coffee the conversation turned to murder. When Honey handed Terry a cup of coffee, she said, "We can't figure out why Trey was on that road."

"That's a good question. It's not likely he was lost," Terry replied.

"Hap did tell me there was nothing wrong with his car," Woodrow told them.

"Woodrow, do you think he could have been coming to see you?" Theo asked.

"I don't know why he would want to see me; I didn't know him well. And if he was visiting, why didn't he just come through the front gate?"

"Maybe he didn't want to be seen." Terry glanced at Honey. "What about you, Honey? Did you know him?"

"No, I've never met him."

"Maybe he wanted to get to know you," Terry teased.

Honey rolled her eyes at him. "Very funny."

"It seems everyone agrees there was a reason he was on that road, since it is not a usual route," Theo stated.

"Perhaps he was being followed and was trying to get away from someone," Jacob suggested.

Theo grinned at his friend. "You're just glad to know he wasn't a master distiller."

"You can say that again. I still think it odd you didn't tell me about two murdered master distillers before I agreed to come here," Jacob replied.

"I'm not worried about you. You can handle yourself," Theo responded.

Woodrow nodded his agreement. "One look at any of you and a murderer would run for cover. Hopefully, that sad chapter is well behind us."

Honey redirected the conversation back to the murdered man, Trey Sullivan. "Other than being followed, what other possible reason would Mr. Sullivan have to be on that access road?"

"How was he dressed? Could he have been going for a run?" Oliver asked.

"He was in a suit," Theo answered.

"No Trespassing signs are posted everywhere to inform hunters," Woodrow added.

"Perhaps he was meeting someone and thought it would be a nice private spot," Theo mused.

Woodrow sat back in his chair and considered Theo's suggestion. "It's certainly an isolated road, but why meet someone on my property?"

"Maybe because he knew people were rarely back there, or perhaps the person he was meeting suggested the location," Terry added.

Woodrow stood and said, "I guess that's one mystery we can't solve. Honey, let's carry everything to the kitchen while our guests go to the putting green and try out Terry's new putter before it gets dark."

Theo stood and grabbed several plates. "We'll all help and it will be done that much faster."

Jeff Younger walked to the back of the restaurant to the private room he'd reserved. Sliding into the booth, he leaned over and tried to give his assistant and girlfriend, Lela Knight, a kiss.

Lela pulled away from him. "You're late."

"Sorry." He brushed his lips over her cheek. "Don't be angry with me. I stopped to see Woodrow Howell."

"Did you and Woodrow kiss and make up?" Lela snapped.

"I'm afraid I dug a deeper hole. Meiners was there and we had words." Younger had sobered up enough to know he'd made a huge mistake by going to Woodrow's. He told Lela about his conversation with Meiners—at least, as much as he could remember.

Before Lela responded, the waiter appeared to take their drink order. After the waiter left the room, Lela glared at him. "I hope it's nothing Aaron can't smooth over. But why on earth would you argue with Meiners again? That certainly isn't in your best interest, considering his fan base."

"He gets under my skin. I know he's going to vote for McNeal, and he gives him more airtime. Everyone tells me McNeal is more entertaining when he's on his show."

"I've heard the interviews with McNeal, and he does have a good sense of humor. He has a good rapport with Terry." Lela frowned at him. "You could try to be a little more personable. I'd suggest you don't drink first. You know you are belligerent when you drink too much."

"McNeal is an idiot. I make more sense drunk than he does sober," Younger snapped.

Lela sighed loudly. "Have you forgotten Terry is going to be the master of ceremonies at the ball? You're going to be seeing him again very soon. It's stupid to antagonize the man."

Younger dropped his head in his hand. "I had too much to drink."

Lela shook her head. "You're always drinking too much. Aaron told you to watch it before the election."

"I'm getting tired of listening to Aaron." Younger took a sip of his water. "Now tell me if you like your costume."

"I will certainly surprise everyone."

"I know you'll look beautiful. Aaron will pick you up in a limo."

Lela started to pout. "This had better be the last party I have to go to with Aaron. I like him, but people are always asking me if we're a couple. Maybe I should be dating him."

"Is that what you want to do?"

"I should. I'm getting tired of sneaking around. Aaron is very handsome and smart too."

Younger pulled her closer to his side. "But he's not going to be governor. After I win the election, I can make some changes."

"You can, but will you?"

"Of course, I will." He put his hand on her thigh. "Let's eat and go to your condo. I can't be too late tonight, I have an early morning appointment."

CHAPTER SEVEN

PAIGE YOUNGER WAS WAITING FOR her husband when he walked through the door. "Where have you been?"

"Not now, Paige," Younger muttered as he headed to his library. He wanted a drink, not the third degree from his wife.

Paige had been waiting for him for two hours. He'd told her he would be home for dinner, and when he didn't show she'd left countless messages on his cell phone. Not to be put off, she followed him down the hallway. "In case you forgot, you said you would be here for dinner."

"Yeah, I forgot." Younger picked up a bottle of bourbon and filled a glass. He took a long drink before he turned to face her.

Paige put her hands on her hips and gave him a withering look. "I'd say you don't need more to drink. Where have you been?"

"Stop sniffing me, Paige."

"I can smell her perfume!"

Younger laughed. "What do you have to complain about? You married me under false pretenses. You have no interest in me now that you have what you've always wanted, and you don't even have to pretend. I'm going to be governor and you'll be first lady." He held his glass in the air in a mock toast and sneered at her. "Isn't that why you married me? You wanted my money and my name."

"You're not governor yet. If you don't fire that woman, the press is going to find out."

"Stay off my back. You have nothing to complain about. I'm going to win. You need to worry about your own affairs."

Paige stared at the man she no longer knew. "I know you plan on running for president in four years. Aaron told you to get yourself together. This kind of scandal will ruin you."

Taking another swallow of bourbon, Younger couldn't deny her words. It was his plan to become president. It had been in the works for years. Everyone had always underestimated him. No one thought he could become governor. Even Aaron told him Americans voted for tall presidents. It didn't matter if they were dumber than dumb, being tall, good-looking, and charismatic went a long way toward getting elected. His height had been a disadvantage during his entire political career, but his family money went a long way toward making friends in high places. A lot of people owed him, and he wasn't going to let them forget their debts.

When he married Paige, he thought everyone would finally see his success as a man. She was a beauty queen, a decade younger, poised in front of the press, and with her on his arm he received all of the attention he needed and craved. One look at Paige said he was a man to be envied. Problem was, his nemesis, McNeal, was everything the voters wanted in a politician. He was tall, dark, handsome, had charisma out the wazoo, a quick wit, and as much as he hated to admit it, McNeal was bright. McNeal's one disadvantage was his wife; she wasn't in Paige's league, and she hated to be in the public eye. Susan McNeal's family had money, but they hadn't collected favors as he'd done over the years.

Paige waggled her forefinger in her husband's face. "Don't bring her to the ball. You're right, I don't care what you do, but you should be discreet if you don't plan on dropping out of the race. You and your political ambitions aren't worth the embarrassment any longer."

Tossing back the remainder of his drink, Younger wasn't in the mood to stand there and listen to her haranguing. "Yeah, you know all about being discreet. I'm going to bed."

Honey had just crawled into bed when her phone rang. "Hi, Sam."

"I didn't wake you, did I?"

"No. Elvis and I were at Woodrow's late, so I'm just getting into bed."

"How's Woodrow?"

"He's very upset over Trey Sullivan being killed on the property. Woodrow didn't know him well, and we are all questioning why he was on the property." Honey hesitated, then added, "I would have told you this earlier today, but you left."

"Yes, I apologize for that. I have a lot on my mind," Sam explained.

Honey thought his excuse was rather lame. "So it seems. Anyway, Hap told Woodrow there was nothing wrong with Trey's car."

"That's right. Not only that, but I can't find one person who has a negative word to say about him."

Honey snorted. "He was in politics. I would seriously doubt if someone didn't like him."

"Yeah, there is that."

After Honey told him about Younger's visit to Woodrow's earlier, Sam asked, "Aren't they golfing buddies?"

"Yes, he played with Younger and McNeal, but he told both men he wouldn't be playing with them again. Younger actually insisted Gramps tell him who he was going to vote for."

"Younger asked Woodrow that question in front of his guests?"

"Yes, he was very rude. That's not all, he was very offensive to Terry Meiners. He accused Terry of showing favoritism to his competitor." Honey told him about Younger poking Terry in the chest.

"That was a dumb move. Terry's at least a foot taller than Younger, and he's in great shape. What did Terry say?"

"He didn't have a chance to say much. Woodrow intervened, and then Theo escorted Younger to the door."

"Did Younger go willingly?"

"Theo didn't give him a choice. I've never cared for Younger, and after today I hope he won't attend the party," Honey added.

"What do you have against Younger?"

"Like I told Theo, he's is too handsy for me."

"He tries to put his hands on you?"

"Correct."

"Can't say I blame him there. I've thought of the same thing once or twice. But I'll break his neck if he's inappropriate with you."

Honey smiled at the vehemence in his tone. Before she responded, Sam asked, "Did he try to get too friendly with you tonight?"

"No. Before I opened the door, Elvis wedged his body in front of me. Elvis doesn't like him either."

"Elvis is a good boy. Tell him I'll bring extra treats with me the next time I come."

"He is a good boy." Honey hesitated a moment, then asked, "Have you spoken to your friend?"

"Cam?"

"Mm-hmm."

"Yes, he called me earlier. I told him that you invited him and his guest to the ball. He still won't tell me who he's bringing with him, or why he wants to see me now."

"You'll know what's on his mind soon." There was another brief silence, then Honey asked, "How was your day?"

"Long."

Honey heard him yawn. "You sound exhausted. Get some sleep."

"Honey, leave this investigation to me."

"'Night, Sam."

Honey couldn't fall asleep for thinking about her relationship with Sam. Every time he called, the same thoughts seemed to roll around in her mind. She cared for him, but at this point, their relationship seemed to be stagnant. She wanted marriage one day, perhaps children at some point. At this rate, both seemed to be beyond her reach with Sam. Today at the cemetery was the first time he hadn't given her a kiss goodbye.

She wasn't going to push him; either things flowed naturally, or they would simply drift apart. She set aside thoughts of Sam and moved on to murder. Why was Trey Sullivan on that road and who killed him? She picked up her phone and called Georgia.

"Hi, Honey, is something wrong?" Georgia asked.

"No, I'm sorry I'm calling so late, but I have an idea."

It was another beautiful, warm September day, and Honey, Georgia, and Elvis decided to have lunch outside. They grabbed some salads from a drive-through and a burger for Elvis before heading to Honey's cottage.

As they carried their food and drinks to the patio, Honey filled Georgia in on the events at Woodrow's the prior night.

Georgia pulled all of the food from the bags. "I haven't met Mr. Younger."

"I don't know if he will show up to the ball, but if he does, stay as far away from him as possible." Honey went on to tell Georgia about Younger's penchant for inappropriate touching.

"That's disgusting."

"Yeah. Elvis doesn't like him either."

Georgia rubbed Elvis's head. "Elvis, you're so smart."

They finished lunch, and when they jumped into the Jeep to leave, Honey had an idea. "Before we go back to the office, let's go over to the access road and look at the spot where Trey Sullivan was parked."

"Won't the cops still have that area blocked off?" Georgia asked.

"I don't know, let's go see."

Seeing nothing blocking the road, Honey said, "I guess it's okay if we look around." As soon as Elvis's paws hit the ground, he started sniffing around.

"What are we looking for exactly?" Georgia asked.

"I really don't know. I'm trying to figure out why he was out here."

"I wonder where he was before he came here," Georgia said.

"I'd like to know that too. Last night, Theo suggested maybe he was meeting someone out here because it's so isolated and they wouldn't be seen."

"But why would he meet someone on private property?" Georgia asked.

Honey showed Georgia where Trey Sullivan was parked. "Theo saw that the back door was ajar, so he was careful approaching the vehicle."

"Maybe someone surprised him and jumped in the back seat of his car," Georgia theorized.

"If Trey was caught unaware, someone had to park elsewhere and walk in."

"There's too much we don't know to even guess why he was here." Georgia glanced at Elvis. "He seems to have found a scent."

"Elvis can always find a scent." Honey walked over to Elvis to see what held his interest. Seeing nothing, she turned and looked at Georgia. "It seems like a weird coincidence to me."

"What do you mean?"

"Sullivan worked for one of the politicians who was golfing with Gramps that day."

Georgia nodded. "I see what you mean. Weird coincidence—or something more nefarious."

"Exactly."

"You're not thinking someone was trying to implicate Woodrow, are you?" Georgia asked.

"No one would believe Gramps would have something to do with Sullivan's murder."

"Yeah, I remember a lot of people said that when you were a suspect in a couple of murders a few months ago, when you simply found the bodies, but Sam still questioned you," Georgia reminded her.

Honey heard a car pulling off the road and turned to see who it was. "Speak of the devil."

Sam stopped behind Honey's Jeep, and as he jumped out Elvis skidded to a halt in front of him. Kneeling down to Elvis's level, Sam scratched him behind the ears. "How's my buddy doing?"

Elvis excitedly jumped around, his tail flopping back and forth as though he had a motor attached to him.

Honey walked to Sam and said, "I think that means he's glad to see you."

Sam grinned. "Why aren't you jumping around like that?"

"You'd have to at least buy me dinner before I did that," Honey quipped.

"Hey, Detective Gorgeous." Georgia pointed to his hat. "I see you are not incognito today."

Sam glanced at Georgia, noting the streaks in her hair were no longer blue, they were pink. "Like the pink hair."

Georgia shrugged. "I like to change it up for Preston. He can pretend he's dating more than one woman."

Sam's eyes shifted back to Honey. "I'd like to have some time with one woman."

Honey looked at him. "You've been busy."

Sam nodded. "Need I ask what you two are doing here?"

"Just looking around, trying to figure out why Sullivan was on this road. The police tape is gone, so we aren't breaking any rules. What are you doing here?"

Sam sighed loudly as he pushed his hat back on his head. "I knew I should have saved my breath last night. Hap asked me to take a look around to see if the guys missed anything. As you said, Sullivan didn't have car trouble, so it's anyone's guess what he was doing here." He looked down at Elvis, who was sniffing the ground. "Did Elvis seem interested in any area in particular?"

"He's sniffed around, but he hasn't found anything," Honey replied.

"Will you show me exactly where Sullivan's car was parked?"

Honey pointed to her Jeep. "I'm in almost the exact spot where I was that day. Sullivan's car was in front of mine, about five feet separating our bumpers."

Sam walked in front of Honey's Jeep and looked around.

Another car pulled up and parked behind Sam's sedan. Honey turned to see her grandfather and Theo get out of the car. Elvis ran past Honey and headed straight to Theo.

Like Sam, Theo leaned over and gave Elvis an ear rub.

"Looks like a convention," Georgia joked.

Honey walked over to greet Woodrow and Theo. "What are you two doing here?"

"It looks like we had the same idea," Woodrow responded. "Theo and I just had lunch, so I decided to stop and have a look around."

"We haven't found anything," Honey replied.

Sam joined their group. "Woodrow, Theo."

Theo extended his hand. "Nice to see you again."

"Woodrow, Hap said you didn't know Sullivan well," Sam commented.

"No, I think we met on a couple of occasions, but I can't remember ever having a conversation with him. I'm at a loss as to why he was on my property."

"We didn't find a cell phone on Sullivan, or in his car," Sam told them.

"Who doesn't carry their cell phone with them at all times?" Georgia asked.

Sam nodded. "Yeah."

They talked a few more minutes before Sam had to leave. Once he drove away, Woodrow asked Honey to come by the house for dinner because he had something he wanted to discuss with her. "I'm having dinner delivered, so don't worry about cooking. And Chance McComb is going to come by tonight to talk to Theo about building him a home."

"I'll be there. Georgia and I are headed back to the office. See you tonight."

CHAPTER EIGHT

"Where's the handsome trio?" Honey asked Woodrow when he answered the door.

"They are outside on the patio. I wanted to talk to you alone for a few minutes. Let's go into the living room."

A frown furrowed Honey's brow. "This sounds serious. Are you okay, Gramps?"

Woodrow placed his arm over her shoulders. "Of course. I want your opinion on something." He looked down at Elvis. "Go on out to the patio and see Theo." Elvis trotted off toward the kitchen.

When they reached the living room, Woodrow had iced tea waiting for Honey on a table between two chairs. "Let's sit."

"You're making me nervous. What is it, Gramps?"

"You know Theo is planning to buy a home here. He'll most likely have to build to get one that will please him. That's the reason I invited Chance to dinner tonight. Theo liked his work, and I'm sure Chance will help him out."

"That's a wonderful idea," Honey agreed.

"I wanted to know if you had any objection if I sold some acreage to Theo. Since your brother has a home at Morning Glory Farm, there's really no reason we couldn't part with some acres here. It might be nice to have another person on the property. Virginia and I have discussed traveling, since I have you to take care of business now. I think it would be comforting to know there was another person nearby for you when I'm not here."

Honey was surprised by his question; she didn't think he would ever part with some acres on his estate to someone other than a family member. That told her how much he cared for Theo. "The property is yours, Gramps. If you want to sell some acreage to Theo, that's fine with me."

"This will all be yours one day, and I wanted to make sure you had no objections."

"I know you are very fond of Theo. Elvis and I like him, and I agree that it might be wise to have someone close. I can't think of a better neighbor."

"I am fond of Theo. He's a fine man—the kind of man I'd want you to marry one day."

Before Honey could respond, Woodrow held his hand in the air. "No, I'm not matchmaking. I'm just saying that's how much I like and admire him."

Honey grinned at him. "I like Theo, but really, Gramps, I haven't known him long enough to ask him to marry me."

Woodrow laughed. "What about Sam?"

Honey shook her head. "We haven't seen much of each other lately."

"Virginia said she hasn't seen him much either."

"Sam promises he will be at the ball, so I'm holding him to that."

"I hope he keeps that promise. I know he's working long hours, but I also know it's important to make time for the ones you love."

Honey had thought the same thing many times. "It sounds like you and Virginia are getting serious if you're planning on traveling together?"

"We enjoy our time together, and she wants to see the world before we slow down. At our age, we don't have time to waste."

Honey smiled at him. "I think that's wonderful."

"Now, back to the topic at hand. I'm thinking that I could give Theo a choice of acres in the east section, and then he could use the main entryway and build a driveway to his house."

"Sounds perfect."

Honey and Woodrow joined the others and talked to Theo about their plan.

"Woodrow, I'm beyond grateful, but are you certain you want to sell some of your land?"

"I'm sure. Honey and I agree on this. I won't part with more than fifty acres, but you said you didn't want a lot of land. It might be the perfect solution for you. It's close to your business and it's private."

"This is typically generous of you, and no, I don't want much acreage. I have more than I need in England."

"Tomorrow, if we have time, we'll walk the area I have in mind. There is a knoll that offers a picturesque view of the land. It might be the ideal spot to build."

"Perfect." Theo shook Woodrow's hand. "Thank you, Woodrow. I know I will love it here."

Elvis ran to the door, and Woodrow said, "Chance must be here."

Everyone was enjoying their bourbon after dinner when Elvis streaked from the room, headed to the front door. Woodrow followed Elvis to the door, and when he pulled it open, he saw Will McNeal standing there. "Hi, Will. This is a surprise."

"Sorry to barge in on you like this, Woodrow. Would you have a moment to speak with me?"

"I have guests, but we can go in the library for a few minutes." Woodrow turned to lead McNeal down the hallway.

Elvis sniffed McNeal, and sensing he was not going to receive an ear rub, trotted back to the living room.

Woodrow pointed to a chair. "Have a seat. What can I do for you?"

"Hap Nelson told me that your granddaughter was the one who found Trey."

Woodrow nodded. "Correct."

"I was wondering if she found anything in, or around his car."

Woodrow gave him a puzzled look. "No, she saw Trey and walked back to her car immediately to call Hap. She didn't look around. But if there was anything in his car, I assume Hap found it."

"Hap said nothing was in Trey's car, but I'm missing a laptop. I gave it to Trey to use, but it's not at our office. I wouldn't be so concerned, but it contained rather private information on my campaign. I'm sure you understand the sensitivity of that kind of information."

"I'm sorry, but I'm certain Honey didn't find anything." Woodrow stood, hoping to put an end to the visit.

McNeal didn't move. "Have you seen Younger?"

Woodrow walked around his desk and stood in front of Will. "Why do you ask?"

"He called me ranting about something. I couldn't understand what he was saying, so I hung up on him." McNeal took a deep breath and continued. "I also wanted to tell you how sorry I am about my behavior on the golf course. I'm afraid Younger and I can no longer be around each other without having an argument. I wanted to ask if we could continue our game without him."

"I'm afraid not. I've already made other arrangements. I think we all need a fresh start," Woodrow replied politely.

McNeal stood and offered his hand to Woodrow. "Perhaps you're right. Since Younger started seeing that girlfriend of his, he's impossible to be around. I don't know if he feels guilty or what. Maybe he's afraid his wife is going to find out. Did you know about his affairs?"

"I have no idea what you're talking about, and I try not to listen to gossip."

McNeal shrugged and turned toward the door. "I thought everyone knew about his girlfriend." He turned around and gave Woodrow his trademark politician's smile. "I'll see you at the ball. I'm looking forward to it."

"It should be a wonderful evening."

After McNeal left, Woodrow returned to the living room and sat next to Honey. "Honey, Will McNeal was at the door. He asked me if you found a laptop when you found Sullivan."

"We didn't look inside the car."

"That's what I told him. He's coming to the ball, so I imagine you will see him there."

"Thanks for the warning," Honey teased. "Although, he is somewhat more likeable than Mr. Younger."

Woodrow laughed. "Faint praise, indeed."

Honey gave him a mischievous grin. "Do you think Mr. Younger will be at the ball?"

"I don't think he would miss it. He'd be afraid it might give McNeal an advantage if any undecided voters happen to attend."

Honey groaned. "I want the guests to enjoy themselves and not be hounded by politicians."

"I'll put a stop to it if I hear either one of them talking politics," Woodrow promised.

Elvis ran to the door again, and Honey groaned. "I'll get it this time."

Honey came back with Elvis. "Gramps, speak of the devil. Mr. Younger is here again. He's waiting in the library."

Woodrow shook his head. "I'm beginning to think Younger and McNeal are watching each other."

CHAPTER NINE

HONEY WAS A FLURRY OF motion the morning of the ball. By midmorning, she walked with Elvis to Woodrow's house to check on the ballroom decorations. When Elvis ran around the side of the house, Honey figured Theo was swimming again.

Seeing them, Theo hopped out of the pool and grabbed his towel. "Seems like I keep meeting you two here."

"I came to make sure all of the decorations are in order."

"I have to admit I already took a peek and the room looks grand. I was going to make some tea. Could I tempt you to a cup after your inspection?"

Honey smiled up at him, trying to keep her eyes on his face and off of his muscled physique. "Sounds wonderful, but I'm afraid I don't have coffee cake to tempt you this morning."

Theo opened the patio door and pointed to a bakery box on the counter. "I bought some scones at your local bakery yesterday, and I've only had two earlier."

"Tea and scones. I almost feel like I'm in England. I'll be right back." Honey made a quick tour of the ballroom before she returned to the kitchen. As she neared the doorway, she heard Theo talking to Elvis. She stopped outside the door to listen.

"Your master didn't tell me I couldn't give you a bone. Just in case I'm not supposed to indulge you, I must have your word that you will not tell her."

Honey stifled a laugh. She entered the room to see Elvis crunching on a massive bone. "Did he give you his word?"

Theo grinned at her. "He most certainly did." He pulled a chair out for her before he poured her a cup of tea. "What did you think of the decorations?"

"You were right, the room is dazzling." Honey realized she hadn't seen Oliver or Jacob. "Where is everyone this morning?"

"They all left to go hit some golf balls this morning."

"Why didn't you join them?"

Theo opened the box of scones on the counter and offered the sweets to her. "Don't you like my company?"

Honey reached inside the box and plucked out a scone. "Yes, I do, particularly when you offer me tea and scones."

"I think you prefer my English tea," he teased.

"There is that. I think I like your hot tea more than you like my sweet iced tea."

Theo pulled out a chair and sat next to her. "I think you could get me to like almost anything."

Honey felt a blush rising from her neck. "Didn't I tell you that it's a rule that if you want to be accepted as a true southern-fried Kentuckian, you must love sweet iced tea?"

"I thought all I had to do was learn to say *y'all*."

Honey laughed. "You said that like a native. We're already rubbing off on you. Are you looking forward to tonight?"

"Very much. Will you save the first dance for me?"

Honey thought about Sam. He hadn't called last night, and she doubted he'd even be there for the first dance. "I will."

"Please tell me you won't be wearing a costume that totally disguises you."

"You'll know me," Honey promised.

Theo released an exaggerated breath. "Good. You're too beautiful to mask your identity, not to mention, I'd hate to have the wrong woman in my arms. It might prove embarrassing."

"Are you excited?" Georgia asked Honey as soon as she answered her phone.

"Yes, I know it's going to be a fun evening. I'll get to see some people I haven't seen in a long time, and I hope to see Sam for more than five minutes."

"I'm so excited, I've never been to a masked ball. Preston wouldn't tell me his costume."

"Did you tell him yours?"

"No! I wanted to surprise him. He's been guessing, but he's been wrong every time."

"I'm sure Sam will come as a cowboy."

"Yeah, that's what I thought," Georgia agreed. "What about Woodrow?"

"He's been letting his hair grow longer, so I'm thinking a president." Honey thought he wouldn't want to wear a white wig. "My bet would be George Washington."

"I bet you're right. I thought he might be going through some male thing, letting his hair grow so long," Georgia joked.

Honey laughed at the thought. "Gramps is well past the age of a male midlife crisis."

"True, and I bet he didn't buy a Corvette in his fifties. He's much too secure for that stuff."

"You're right about that."

"What about Terry's costume? Did he tell you who he was going to be?" Georgia asked.

"He didn't tell me. All he said was he was going to make a memorable entrance. Knowing Terry, I wouldn't be surprised at anything he comes up with."

"Even wearing a mask, we'll recognize him by his distinctive voice," Georgia added.

"Not to mention his blue eyes are a dead giveaway."

"I better let you go so you and Elvis can get ready. See you soon."

Honey and Elvis walked to Woodrow's home an hour before the guests were to arrive. It took her longer than normal to walk the short distance, due to her Southern belle dress. The wide crinoline beneath the voluminous skirt forced her to move at a slower pace. She thought about Sam as they walked, wondering why he hadn't called. She'd tried to call him to make sure he was going to be able to make it tonight, but her call went straight to his voicemail. Since he didn't return her call, she had no idea if, or even when he would arrive. "Elvis, I hope Sam gets to see how handsome you look tonight." At the mention of Sam's name, Elvis lifted his head, looked at her, and made a sound between a moan and a loud sigh, as if he understood what she was saying.

Approaching the porch, they saw a man wearing Western clothing, a large black Stetson, and two Colt revolvers worn butt forward. Honey was so impressed by the authentic costume, it took her a minute to realize it was Theo behind the black mask and not Sam. He jumped from the porch and walked to meet her.

Theo stared at her for several seconds, admiring her lavender gown. "You look beautiful, just as I imagine Southern belles looked in the eighteen hundreds."

"Thank you, and your costume is wonderful." Honey thought he made a handsome cowboy. "Wild Bill Hickok, isn't it?"

Theo's eyes widened. "Exactly. How did you know I was Wild Bill and not another Western figure?"

"How you're wearing your revolvers. Very historically accurate. Your costume designer did a wonderful job."

"I gave him a photograph of Wild Bill, but I have Woodrow to thank for finding me the revolvers."

Honey thought he sounded as excited as a little boy.

Elvis was nudging Theo's hand with his nose, so he forced his eyes from Honey to give him some attention. "I take it by Elvis's Inverness cape and deerstalker hat that he is Sherlock Holmes. He looks very dashing."

"Elvis is the only one who is allowed to be a fictional character tonight. It seemed to be a fitting costume for him."

Elvis turned and looked down the driveway, and within seconds Woodrow's car came into view. Parking in front of the colonnade, Woodrow jumped from the car and walked to open the passenger door for his date, Sam's grandmother, Virginia Gentry.

Honey gave Virginia a hug. "You make a lovely Martha Washington."

Virginia smiled wide. "Thank you, dear. I'm glad you know who I am."

Honey introduced Virginia to Theo. "This is Theo Parker, but tonight, he is Wild Bill Hickok."

Honey kissed Woodrow on the cheek. "I told Georgia you were going to be George Washington. The hair is perfect."

"You look lovely, Honey." Woodrow smiled at Theo's costume. "Theo, you look like the original Wild Bill."

Theo pulled one of the Colts from his holster and handed it to Woodrow. "I have you to thank for making my costume more realistic with these wonderful revolvers. Beautiful weapons."

"You can thank one of our guests tonight, Rudy Lewis. He's a collector and he loaned them to me." Woodrow noticed Elvis's costume and laughed. "Perfect costume for you, Elvis."

Woodrow pulled his pocket watch from his vest to check the time. "I'm sure our valet will be here momentarily. We'll wait for him, and greet any early guests."

"Good, I need to check the tent to see if the caterer has everything in hand," Honey said.

Theo extended his arm to Honey. "Elvis and I will accompany you."

Honey was pleased to see all the tables in the tent were beautifully decorated and the buffet tables were filled with mouth-watering delights. "Feel free to taste anything that appeals to you, Theo. You can be my guinea pig."

"How did you know I'm starving?" Theo picked up a tidbit off one tray and popped it in his mouth. "I don't know what it is, but I like it. Bacon makes everything tasty. I like your bacon here."

Honey laughed. "It's rumaki." She pointed to a row of appetizers covering one table. "Keep going."

Theo picked up another piece of rumaki and gave Elvis the bacon. Elvis made quick work of the tasty morsel.

"Elvis likes the bacon, too."

"Elvis likes most food," Honey teased.

Theo sampled everything on one table while Honey spoke to the woman overseeing the room. She joined Theo a few minutes later. "What do you think?"

"It's all great. But I'm going to need a bourbon now."

"I think we can handle that. Would you like Devil's Due?"

"Perfect, thank you."

Honey turned to one of the bartenders and ordered two drinks. "I hear the musicians warming up in the ballroom. I guess we should return to the front door to see if guests are arriving."

From the large tent they entered the ballroom and the musicians were playing a waltz. Theo took Honey's glass from her and set both drinks on a nearby table along with his hat. He held his hand out to her. "Give me a few moments, I might need a little practice."

"Don't expect me to be as good as you."

Theo pulled her into his arms. "I doubt dancing is easy in that dress." Theo expertly led her around the room as the musicians played a Johann Strauss waltz. He leaned down and whispered in her ear, "This doesn't count as our first dance. This is just practice."

Honey thought it was the perfect beginning to what she expected to be a lovely evening. Waltzing with a handsome man who was holding her tightly in his arms and looking down at her as if to say there was no place on earth he would rather be. It was a magical moment. Theo definitely knew his way around a dance floor, not to mention the heart of a woman.

When the music ended, Theo continued to hold her in his arms. They were gazing into each other's eyes, both acutely aware of the growing attraction between them. When they heard applause, they turned to see who was intruding on their private moment. The musicians and the waiters were applauding their efforts.

Theo released Honey and politely bowed. "Thank you for the dance, Honey."

"My pleasure." Honey thought about Sam as they walked back to the table to retrieve their drinks. She cared deeply for Sam, but she couldn't deny she was definitely enjoying Theo's company and his attention. Elvis wedged his way between Honey and Theo as they walked back to the front door. Several guests were already on the porch talking with Woodrow and Virginia.

"I feel like we have stepped back in time," Theo commented, seeing all of the period costumes.

"I hadn't even thought that we might not be able to identify some of the guests with their masks on. If I don't introduce you right away, just know I don't recognized them," Honey whispered. She looked over the crowd and saw her brother and Georgia approaching. "At least I know Preston, even in the cavalry uniform."

"Preston, I know you are Custer, but Georgia, who are you?" Honey asked.

"Clara Barton."

"Who's Clara Barton?" Theo asked.

"She was a nurse in the Civil War and founded the Red Cross," Honey replied.

Theo furrowed his brow and whispered in Honey's ear, "She had pink hair?"

Honey laughed. "Probably not."

"You were right about Woodrow. He looks great as George Washington," Georgia told Honey. "Wait until you see your mom and dad. Their costumes are awesome."

Preston looked his sister up and down. "You look beautiful, but who are you?"

"I'm a Southern belle," she answered.

Georgia and Preston petted Elvis and complimented his costume.

"Very appropriate, but you do know Sherlock Holmes was a fictional character, don't you, Sis?" Preston teased.

Honey rolled her eyes at her brother. "Yes, but he's the only one who can be a fictional character tonight."

Seeing her father's car stop in the circular drive, she watched as the valet opened the passenger door, and her father hurried around the car to assist her mother. Honey motioned for them. "You two are Brits and Theo is an American."

"Theo, you make a great cowboy. Which one are you?" Lorraine asked.

"Wild Bill Hickok. And I assume you two are Queen Victoria and Prince Albert."

Thomas Howell extended his hand. "You're exactly right. I'm the only one in the family who hasn't met you. I'm Honey's father, Thomas Howell."

Theo gave him a firm shake. "A pleasure. Preston and Honey gave me a tour of your lovely farm."

"Preston tells me you're a motorcycle enthusiast as well."

"One of my guilty pleasures, I'll admit."

Woodrow interrupted the conversation on the porch with an announcement. "It looks like Paul Revere has arrived."

Everyone turned to see a man riding a black horse approaching, shouting, "The guests are coming!" He reined in at the porch and dismounted. Handing the reins to the valet, he asked, "Would you park my horse in Woodrow's stable?"

"I should have known," Honey laughed as she walked to greet Paul Revere. "That's some entrance and one great costume, Terry."

Paul Revere removed his tricorn hat, bowed, and reached for her hand. After he brushed his lips over the back of her hand, he said, "Ma'am, a multitude of guests are arriving momentarily."

Preston walked over to shake Terry's hand. "Terry, I wouldn't have recognized you until I heard you voice."

"Seeing all of you in costume standing on this columned porch as I rode in made me feel like I was riding into a different era."

"I thought the same thing. The costumes are amazing," Theo added.

"Are we ready to get this party started?" Terry asked.

Woodrow opened the doors and turned to Terry. "Mrs. Harris is taking over the duties at the door so she can see all of the costumes, so lead the way to the ballroom, Mr. Revere."

CHAPTER TEN

NOT LONG AFTER THE MUSIC started playing, the guests began flowing into the ballroom. Terry took the stage to welcome everyone and introduce the musicians. He shared with the guests the plans for the evening. "We will have a waltz where the men must bid on the lady they would like to partner, and another waltz where the ladies must bid on the gentleman of their choice. Remember, everything goes to charity, so be generous tonight. Now, for all of you with two left feet out there, you will see professional dance instructors are among the guests to help if you need some pointers. I know I'm going to need help with the waltz, so feel free to join me as I make a fool of myself."

Woodrow, Honey, and Elvis mingled among the guests, welcoming everyone. Woodrow spotted two of his good friends, Sharon and Rudy Lewis. "Rudy, I thought I recognized your long white hair. What a great Buffalo Bill costume."

"I was thinking about being a pirate, but Sharon said my hair looked more like Buffalo Bill Cody," Rudy responded.

"And who could make a better Annie Oakley?" Honey said to Sharon.

Theo approached Honey to ask her to dance as Preston and Georgia joined them. Before Theo could say a word, Woodrow introduced him to Rudy and Sharon.

"I understand you are the gentleman I should thank for these wonderful revolvers," Theo said as he shook Rudy's hand.

"I'm glad I could help," Rudy replied.

As they were chatting, Sharon said, "Here comes another Paul Revere. I've already seen a few of them."

Woodrow glanced at the man, but didn't recognize him until he spoke. It was Woodrow's master distiller, Cullen Webb. "Cullen, I didn't recognize you. Your costume is very similar to our master of ceremonies." Woodrow introduced everyone, but said, "Cullen, I'm sorry, but I don't think I know your date."

"This is Gloria Barnes. She works for Cleary's Distillery."

Honey and Georgia exchanged a look. They both recognized the woman who had dated Honey's best friend, K. C. Cleary, before his death. Georgia leaned over and whispered in Honey's ear. "Isn't that the same *store-bought boobs* Gloria Barnes?"

Honey tried not to laugh at the moniker one of Gloria's acquaintances had given her. She noticed Gloria's saloon girl costume had a very low-cut bodice. "That's her."

"She spills over no matter what she is wearing," Georgia mumbled, her eyes fixed on Gloria's costume.

Cullen introduced Gloria to everyone.

"We've met before," Honey said.

"Yes, I met Honey and Georgia right after K. C. Cleary's death," Gloria reminded them.

"That woman is so uncouth that it defies the imagination," Georgia murmured when Cullen turned to introduce Gloria to another guest.

Preston lowered his head to Georgia's ear. "What did you mean about *store bought*… Did you say *boobs*?"

Georgia elbowed him and whispered her response, "Yes, I did, and isn't it obvious what I meant?"

Preston chuckled.

Honey rolled her eyes at Preston and hissed, "Keep your eyeballs in your head, or Georgia might pluck them out."

"I swear, Sis, you have better ears than Elvis. Do you think anyone else heard me?"

"I can't believe Cullen is dating *her*," Georgia commented.

Overhearing the entire exchange, Theo asked, "Who is she?"

Honey turned to him and said quietly, "I'll explain later, it's a long story. Not one for a party."

Theo nodded and held his hand out to her. "I came over to ask you for my first dance."

Placing her hand in his, Honey replied, "It would be my pleasure." Not only was she thrilled to dance with him again, she was equally thrilled to put some distance between herself and Gloria Barnes. She glanced at Elvis before she walked away, saying, "If you would like to find a nice comfy spot for the night, that's okay."

Woodrow offered to take Elvis to his library and remove his coat so he would be more comfortable.

"Thanks, Gramps." Honey kissed Elvis on the head. "You have the best costume."

Honey and Theo were the first couple to take the floor, and Theo had already asked the musicians to play a long waltz when he gave them a signal. Within seconds, the buzz of conversation stopped as people turned to watch the handsome couple glide around the dance floor. They were, by far, the most handsome couple in the room.

Theo couldn't take his eyes off of Honey. He didn't think he'd ever seen a more beautiful woman. "Everyone is watching you."

"I bet the women are watching you," Honey countered, thinking that few men were as handsome or charming as Theo.

Across the room, Sam Gentry walked into the ballroom with his two guests in tow. He noticed the entire roomful of people were turned toward the dance floor, so he maneuvered his way through the crowd to see what was going on. He spotted Hap in his Teddy Roosevelt costume standing by Preston and Georgia. After he said hello, and introduced his guests, he said, "What's going on?"

Hap inclined his head toward the dance floor. "See for yourself."

Though the dancing couple were wearing masks, Sam immediately recognized Honey's long blond hair. Sam knew it was Theo Parker in the Wild Bill Hickok costume.

Sam's best friend, Cam, stood beside him watching the attractive couple. "Wow, they're good. Who are they?"

Sam didn't respond. His eyes were glued on the couple, waiting for the dance to end.

The waltz ended and the crowd gave them resounding applause. Once again, Theo bowed politely, befitting the custom of a time long past. "I've never enjoyed a dance more, and I think our audience approves."

"I'm happy I didn't stumble. That's all due to you." Honey looked over the throng of people and immediately spotted Sam standing next to her brother. "There's Sam with his friends."

Theo politely placed his hand in the small of Honey's back as they made their way to Sam.

Honey smiled at Sam. "I was beginning to worry that you wouldn't be able to make it." She pointed to his costume. "I had a feeling you would be Wyatt Earp."

Sam leaned over and kissed her cheek. "You look beautiful." He didn't know if Theo was acting as her date, or if he was her date, but he politely extended his hand to him. "Guess you are Wild Bill."

Theo shook his hand. "Yes, I thought I'd honor the American West I loved to read about as a boy."

"Honey, you and Theo looked like professional dancers out there," Georgia gushed.

"Everyone was watching you two," Preston added.

Honey glanced at Sam to see what his reaction was, but his expression gave no hint as to what he was thinking. "It was all due to Theo, he's a marvelous dancer."

"Nonsense, I've never had such a graceful partner," Theo replied.

Sam was waiting for Theo to drop his hand from Honey's back, and the moment he did, he replaced it with his own and urged her closer. "Honey, I want you to meet my best friend, Rick Cameron."

"Thank you for allowing us to crash your party," Cam said.

"Not at all. We're happy you could join us."

Sam glanced at the woman standing close to his other side. "This is Cam's fiancée, Liz Simmons." Sam then introduced the couple to everyone in the group.

Honey couldn't help but stare at Liz's costume. She was wearing a long black sheer robe covering over a barely-there nude body suit that left little to the imagination. The costume was obviously created from an early photograph purported to be of the infamous Josephine Earp.

While Sam was making his introductions to Theo, Georgia leaned close to Honey and whispered, "If she has a mole on her rear, I bet we could see it."

Honey shook her head, thinking the woman's costume was far more risqué than anything Gloria Barnes would wear.

"Odd that her fiancé is dressed as Doc Holliday, yet she chose to be the wife of Wyatt Earp instead of Big Nose Kate," Georgia added softly.

Honey looked at Cam's costume. Georgia was right, Cam was Doc Holliday. Sam was Wyatt Earp. Interesting.

Sam, Theo, and Cam were discussing revolvers when Liz maneuvered her way in front of Honey. "I imagine it was a big surprise when Sam told you I would be here."

"Actually, Sam didn't mention you. I don't think he was aware who would be traveling with Cam."

"Oh, I assumed he called you after we went to dinner last night." She reached over and placed her arm through Sam's, forcing him into their conversation. "Darling, I can't believe you didn't tell her about me. I mean, it's not like we're strangers just because our engagement didn't work out. We're still close friends."

Sam gave Honey an apologetic look. "I didn't have a chance to call Honey after dinner."

Honey noticed Sam didn't pull away from Liz's grasp. Fiancé? He'd never mentioned he'd been engaged. Not that he had an obligation to tell her, but she remembered how he'd pressed her about her relationship with K. C. Cleary when he was found murdered. When the silence stretched to an uncomfortable level, Honey touched Theo on the arm and pointed across the room. "I think those three tall men across the room must be Oliver and Jacob with Chance McComb. We need to see their costumes and I did promise them a dance." She briefly glanced at Liz and Cam and said, "Lovely to meet you." Her gaze barely passed over Sam. "Please excuse us."

Liz held on to Sam's arm as Honey and Theo walked away. "Looks like she found herself a handsome Englishman for the evening."

"Honey's a beautiful woman. She could have any man she wants." Sam was angry with himself for not calling Honey last night and telling her about Cam's guest. But he didn't want to spoil the evening for her by dropping the bombshell about a previous engagement. He wished he'd told her long ago. Now, he knew it was going to be even more difficult to explain. He stopped a passing waiter and grabbed a bourbon from his tray. "Cam, would you like one?"

"That woman was wearing an interesting costume. I imagine that will draw a lot of attention tonight," Theo remarked.

"Yes, I think that was the point," Honey replied.

When they reached the men, Theo slapped Oliver on the back. "Well, if it isn't Sir Winston Churchill."

"Wonderful costume, Oliver," Honey told him.

"Jacob, I think you are the third Paul Revere I've seen so far," Theo said.

"Do you know who Chance is supposed to be tonight?" Oliver asked.

Theo studied Chance's fringed suede shirt and huge knife in a leather sheath at his waist. "He's Jim Bowie."

Oliver was surprised at Theo's knowledge of American history. "How did you know that?"

"I've read a lot of American history," Theo replied.

"Chance, you look great." Honey thought he actually resembled images she had seen of Jim Bowie, with his cleft chin and thick hair.

Chance stared at Honey and grinned. "You look even more beautiful than normal, if that's possible."

Jacob nodded his agreement. "She'd make any costume look great."

A woman approached the group and smiled. "Honey, I thought that was you surrounded by all of these men."

"RuthAnne! I'm so happy you could come." Honey introduced her friend to the men.

Theo pointed to RuthAnne's costume. "I like your costume, but I'm sorry, I must admit I don't know who you are."

"Sybil Ludington," RuthAnne replied.

"What a perfect costume for you." Honey told the men that RuthAnne was an excellent horsewoman and writer.

"But who was Sybil Ludington?" Oliver asked.

"Sybil rode more miles than Paul Revere over dangerous roads to raise patriot troops to fight in the Battle of Danbury," RuthAnne responded.

"Are you saying Sybil outrode me?" Jacob asked.

RuthAnne smiled at the attorney. "Sorry, Paul, but my ride was twice as long as yours."

Honey saw Woodrow approaching with a man wearing an ornate light blue brocade waistcoat, vest, and tight white pants. Even though he wore a feathery light blue mask, Honey immediately knew the man was Jeffrey Younger. "Oh, great."

Everyone turned to see Younger strutting toward them dressed as Napoleon.

RuthAnne leaned close to Honey. "He makes the perfect peacock."

"My thoughts exactly." Honey noticed Mrs. Younger and Sam's grandmother walking behind Woodrow and Younger.

Everyone had met Jeff Younger, so Woodrow introduced Mrs. Younger to Theo and his friends.

"Tonight I am Josephine Bonaparte," Mrs. Younger told them.

"Have you seen my campaign manager, Aaron?" Younger asked Woodrow.

"I'm afraid not," Woodrow replied.

Honey remembered adding his name to the guest list when Woodrow told her Younger asked if he could have an additional invitation.

Abraham Lincoln and Mary Todd joined their group. Mr. Lincoln acknowledged everyone in the group.

Woodrow recognized them immediately. "Great costumes, Will." He turned to Susan, Will's wife. "Nice to see you, Mrs. Lincoln." He then introduced everyone in the group to the McNeals.

"I didn't think you would come to the ball, considering your assistant was recently murdered," Younger quipped to Will.

Will ignored him and turned his back. "Woodrow, this is an absolutely fascinating party. The costumes are wonderful."

"We can thank Honey for the lovely evening. It was all her idea," Woodrow responded.

Younger moved closer to Honey. "Honey, did I tell you that you look absolutely ravishing tonight?"

Theo reached for Honey's hand. "If you will excuse us, this ravishing lady promised me this dance."

Honey whispered her thanks to Theo as they walked away. A few feet from the dance floor they were stopped by Honey's mother, Lorraine, and another woman.

Honey recognized Bunny Spencer as soon as she said hello.

"Honey, I wanted you to see Bunny's costume," Lorraine said.

"It's a beautiful costume, but…"

"I know, no one knows who I'm supposed to be. I'm Belle Brezing. Apparently, I was related to her on my grandmother's side of the family."

Theo told Bunny it was nice to see her, then asked, "Who was Belle Brezing?"

"She was a nationally known madam who lived Lexington. Supposedly, the madam portrayed in the movie *Gone with the Wind* was inspired by Belle," Bunny replied.

"I saw that film. Tonight has been as interesting as an American history lesson." Hearing the first notes of one of his favorite waltzes, Theo nodded to the ladies. "Please excuse us, Honey has promised me this dance."

Not too far away, Sam stood with another bourbon on ice in his hand, eyes fixated on the waltzing couple, trying to figure out how in the world he was going to explain things to Honey. He saw a man approach Theo, making an attempt to tap him on the shoulder, trying to cut in on his dance. Even dressed as Napoleon and wearing a mask, Sam knew his identity. Jeffrey Younger. Sam had to hand it to Theo, he must have seen Younger approaching and managed to make a deft maneuver to avoid the interruption. A woman in a red dress grabbed Younger's arm, and even at a distance, he could see the woman was giving him a piece of her mind. Sam smiled, thinking Younger was about to meet his Waterloo.

He glanced back at Honey and Theo. He didn't know what he had to smile about—another man was dancing with his woman, and presently whispering something in her ear. But was Honey his, or had he blown it? After Liz mentioned their engagement, he saw Honey's shocked expression. He imagined he was about to face his own Waterloo.

CHAPTER ELEVEN

Aᴼᴛᴇʀ Honey's waltz with Theo ended, Oliver claimed her hand for the next dance, followed by a dance with Jacob. Theo stepped in for one more waltz, before they walked to the tent to get something to eat.

Theo walked the length of one table and filled his plate to overflowing. Honey raised her brow at his heaping plate. Theo grinned, saying, "What? I need to keep my strength up if I keep dancing like this."

"I hope you can move after you eat all of that," Honey teased.

"Ah, this is simply an appetizer."

Before they made it to a table, Jeff Younger approached them along with another man dressed as Paul Revere and a woman in a red gown.

"Honey, I want to introduce you to Aaron Branson, my campaign manager, or should I say John Wilkes Booth." He reached for the woman and slid his arm around her waist. "And this lovely woman is Maria Walewska."

Honey wondered where Mrs. Bonaparte was while he was cuddling another woman. "Nice to meet you both." Honey politely introduced Theo.

A few pleasantries were exchanged, and Honey and Theo turned to find a table when Terry Meiners approached.

"Ah, the great Terry Meiners," Younger commented snidely.

Terry didn't respond, and Aaron intervened before Younger said another word. "I think some fresh air might be in order." He smiled at

Honey and Theo. "Pleasure to meet you." He then escorted Napoleon and Maria Walewska to the doorway leading to the patio area.

"Terry, do you know that woman with Younger?" Honey asked.

Terry turned to look at the back of the woman. "I don't recognize her with that mask."

She looked up at Theo, and asked, "Who did he say the woman was?"

"Maria Walewska. I don't know if that was her costume or her name?"

Terry pulled out his phone and googled Maria Walewska. He chuckled. "That's pretty funny."

"What's funny?" Honey asked.

"Maria Walewska was one of Napoleon's mistresses."

Theo arched his brow at her. "That explains why he was *handsy* with her."

Honey elbowed him in the side. "Funny."

"Handsy?" Terry asked.

"That's what Honey calls it. I call it boorish behavior."

Honey looked up at Theo and smiled. "You're so proper, Theo."

Theo winked at her. "Not all of the time."

Honey's cheeks started to color and she turned to Terry. "Terry, did you need me?"

"I think we should start the bidding dances in an hour or so. Give everyone time to have some food and a few bourbons to loosen their wallets. Many of the guests have been practicing with the instructors, so they'll be ready for the dances."

"Sounds great."

"Terry, please give me time to eat first," Theo joked.

"Yeah, you better keep your strength up because I'm sure some women will be bidding on you. I expect you to bring top dollar," Terry joked.

"How does this work? Do all of the women participate?" Theo asked.

Terry reached for a plate and followed Theo down another table filled with delicious-looking morsels, and filled his own plate. "I think most everyone here will join in the fun since it's for a good cause. Honey, what do you think about starting the bidding at one thousand per lady?"

"I'll leave that up to you, Terry. I don't want anyone left on stage if no one bids, so I'll tell Gramps to be prepared to bid."

"I'll make certain Oliver and Jacob will bid on the ladies," Theo added.

Georgia and Preston walked into the tent, and once they filled their plates, they joined Honey and Theo at their table. While Preston and Theo were discussing motorcycles, Georgia whispered to Honey, "Did you know Sam had been engaged?"

"No, he never mentioned it." Honey was upset with Sam. He hadn't denied he'd been engaged to Liz, but she refused to allow her disappointment to ruin her evening. She had been so excited to see Sam tonight, and even dance with him, but it appeared she was the only one who felt that way.

"He was watching you the entire time you danced with Theo."

Honey shrugged. "He hasn't sought me out to dance." It was some consolation knowing there were several other handsome, eligible men who wanted to dance with her.

"I wonder what he saw in that woman. That just proves there is no accounting for taste," Georgia mumbled. "Do you think his friend Cam thinks there is anything odd about the way *his* fiancée hangs on to Sam?"

"You would think he might find it strange."

Preston nudged Georgia. "Theo said the bidding on the ladies will start soon. Did you want me to bid on you?"

"Only if you want to be the one driving your date home this evening."

Preston leaned over and kissed her cheek. "I don't know, I was thinking about bidding on that woman with Sam. You know, the one that is practically nude."

Georgia responded by elbowing him in the ribs. "I didn't think you noticed."

Clutching his ribs, Preston laughed. "Heck, a blind man would have noticed her."

"You might be blind before the end of the night if you look at her one more time," Georgia threatened.

Honey and Georgia excused themselves for a few moments to go to the ladies' room. The two lavatories located by the ballroom were both occupied, so Honey directed Georgia to the hallway. "Let's go to the library, no one will think to go there."

As they approached the library, Honey noticed the door was ajar and the light on Woodrow's desk was turned on. She assumed Woodrow turned on the light for Elvis earlier.

"I haven't been in Woodrow's library before," Georgia commented as Honey pushed the door wider.

Once Honey stepped into the room, she came to an abrupt halt. Sam was standing there with his body pressed from lips to toe with a woman. Honey immediately recognized the woman's costume. Josephine Earp's arms were wrapped around Sam's neck. There wasn't a centimeter of space between them.

Georgia moved beside Honey and saw the reason Honey came to a stop. "Uh-oh."

Sam pulled Liz's arms from his neck and turned to face Honey. "This isn't what it looks like."

Honey was so shocked that all she could do was stand there and stare at them. Her eyes bounced from Sam to Liz.

Sam took a step toward her. "Honey, I wasn't…"

Honey cut him off and took a step to the side. "I don't care what you were doing. It's none of my business." She managed to regain her composure, and hurried past them without sparing a glance at either one. When she reached the bathroom, she slammed the door shut and clicked the lock.

"Honey!" Sam shouted after her. He glanced at Georgia and started to say something, but Georgia held her hand in the air, indicating he had nothing to say she wanted to hear. "What? Were you giving her mouth-to-mouth?"

Sam sighed. He turned back to Liz and snapped, "You've caused enough trouble, go back to Cam."

"Sam, we need to talk about this," Liz said in a sultry voice.

Sam put his hands on his hips, looked her in the eyes and shook his head. "We have nothing to talk about. I won't say anything about this to Cam—not for your sake, but for his. For whatever reason, he cares about you." His eyes were cold when he added, "Never give me a reason to change my mind."

Liz reached out and ran her hand over his chest. "You know you still care for me, Sam."

Sam backed away from her and pointed toward the door. "Liz, go."

Georgia waited until Liz walked out of the room before she looked at Sam and frowned. "I didn't know you were such an idiot."

Sam raked his fingers through his hair in frustration. "I didn't know I was either." He walked over to the bathroom door and tapped lightly. "Can I talk to you, Honey?"

"Go away. We have nothing to say to each other."

"Honey, we need to talk." He turned the doorknob only to find it locked.

"Leave me alone."

He turned from the door and faced Georgia, who looked as though she might take his head off. "I wouldn't talk to you, either."

He slowly walked out of the library.

Georgia tapped on the bathroom door. "He's gone."

On the way back to the ballroom, Honey didn't say a word. They spotted Preston and Theo in the doorway leading to the ballroom. Honey stopped to tell Woodrow that Terry was about to start the bidding. "Please bid on any woman if no one is bidding."

Honey was so upset by what she saw in the library that she forgot to notice if Elvis was in the room. "Georgia, did you see Elvis in the library?"

"No, I didn't. If he was in there, I would have asked him to bite Sam in the rear."

"He must be in another room." When they were a few feet from Theo and Preston, Honey saw Liz join the men and she stopped. "Georgia, look who is talking to Theo and Preston."

"That witch. If she gets any closer to Theo, she'll be in his drink."

Honey watched Theo's reaction to Liz. To the man's credit, he kept his eyes on her face. "I guess Cam and Sam aren't enough for her."

Theo looked up, saw Honey and smiled. He walked to her and held out a drink he was holding. "I thought you might want some iced tea."

"Thank you." Honey wished Liz would walk away, but no such luck.

"Honey, I've been trying to convince your partner he should dance with me," Liz purred.

Theo looked down at Honey and smiled warmly. "I told her I'm saving myself for you."

Liz started to respond, but Terry Meiners stepped to the microphone, drawing everyone's attention. "Gentlemen, if you want to dance the next waltz, you will have to bid on your partner. Ladies, please join me on stage so the men can see who they are bidding on." As the ladies climbed the stairs to the stage, Terry added, "Now, men, be generous, remember it's for charity and you don't want to appear cheap to your partner. And for all of you married men out there, I must warn you, we have some single men here tonight who are wanting to dance. Some of them came all of the way from England just to see our beautiful Kentucky ladies, and they are eager to bid."

Liz touched Theo's arm as she headed to the stage. "I hope you bid on me."

Honey stared at her in disbelief.

Georgia grabbed Honey's arm, directing her to the stage. "Do you think it would be polite for the hostess to kick a guest?"

"The thought has some appeal," Honey retorted.

"Theo deserves a big kiss for ignoring her," Georgia whispered.

"Unlike Sam, Theo doesn't have a problem resisting her charms."

As the women lined up on the stage, the men gathered in front, waiting for Terry to start the bidding.

Terry reached for Lorraine's hand, urging her to the front of the ladies. "Let's begin the bidding with Queen Victoria. Who will start the bid at one thousand dollars?"

After several men bid on Lorraine, Terry prompted, "How often do you men get to dance with a queen?" Honey's father finally won the bid at four thousand dollars.

Terry congratulated the successful bidder. "That's the way to start the bidding. Remember gentlemen, this is for charity. Let's keep it going. Next we have..." He glanced at Honey and grinned. "Maria Walewska, Napoleon's paramour." Terry looked at the men in the audience and asked, "Who is the first bidder?"

Jeffrey Younger was in the midst of men in front of the stage, and despite the amount of alcohol he'd consumed, he was still standing. "I'll bid one thousand."

Paige Younger was on the opposite end of the stage from Maria Walewska, glaring at her husband. Aaron, Jeffrey's campaign manager, pushed his way through the throng of men to reach him. He whispered in his ear, "Sir, you need to remember that your wife is on that stage. Don't make a fool of yourself."

"Then you bid on her for me," Younger ordered without lowering his voice.

Someone outbid Younger, and Younger started to raise his hand, but Aaron yanked his arm down, and made the bid.

"Mr. John Wilkes Booth wins the bid with two thousand." When Maria Walewska walked off the stage, Terry leaned toward Honey and whispered, "I think I've seen Maria Walewska playing golf with Younger and his campaign manager, but I don't know her real name."

Terry motioned for Sybil Ludington to join him by the microphone. "Do I hear a thousand dollars for the best woman on horseback?"

Several men started bidding, and Terry urged them on. "Wonderful, Mr. Paul Revere has won that bid at five thousand. In case you folks didn't notice, we have a few Paul Reveres here tonight. Maybe Paul had several siblings."The audience laughed and Terry added, "I want to let the other men know that I'm the only Paul who rode a horse to this party, so you can't steal my ride." He pointed to the Paul Revere who won the bid and said, "Remember, Sybil already outrode you once, my friend."

Honey didn't recognize the man wearing the Paul Revere costume. "Terry, who is that Paul Revere?"

Terry looked at the man and shook his head. "I don't know, I didn't recognize his voice either." He motioned for the next lady to join him. "Gentlemen, have another bourbon and open those wallets wide. I want to see the bidding go higher." Terry put his arm around Annie Oakley, and told the crowd, "You better dance well if you bid on this one. I hear Annie Oakley is a great shot, and I wouldn't want her shooting off your toes if you can't perform, or you can't outbid the previous bidders." When the laughter died down, he opened the bid at two thousand.

After several men bid, Buffalo Bill Cody, Annie's husband, raised his hand and shouted, "Six thousand. If I don't win, she might find someone she likes better."

"Since starting at two thousand has been so successful, we'll do it again with Mrs. Napoleon Bonaparte." Aaron remained beside Younger to make certain he placed a bid on his wife. As it turned out, Aaron took up the bidding when Younger walked away, and found himself in a bidding war with Teddy Roosevelt and Ben Franklin.

Next in line was the woman no one could ignore. "Who is brave enough to bid on Josephine Earp?" Terry asked.

To Honey's surprise, Cullen raised his hand for the first bid of two thousand dollars. She wondered what his date, Gloria Barnes, would make of that bid. A different Paul Revere bid, and Honey realized she didn't recognize that Paul Revere either. Honey tried not to look Sam's way, but she did notice he didn't bid on Liz. Cam bid three thousand and won the dance with his fiancée.

"I'm happy to see everyone is being so generous, now let's keep it up," Terry encouraged.

Theo's solicitor, Oliver, won the next bid for Belle Brezing at three thousand.

"Next up, we have Mary Todd Lincoln," Terry announced.

John Wilkes Booth bid on Mrs. Lincoln, causing the crowd to give a collective groan. Woodrow looked for Will McNeal in the crowd, but he didn't see him, so he bid on Mrs. Lincoln. Another Paul Revere made a bid, but in the end, John Wilkes Booth won the bid at four thousand.

It didn't escape Terry's notice that Mr. Booth had won two dances. "Mr. Booth is a busy man. I think I should advise Mrs. Lincoln to avoid theaters tonight."

The bidding went on and on until Honey was the last woman standing beside Terry.

"I thought we'd save our hostess until last. Who is going to open the bid for this Southern belle?"

Sam raised his hand and bid two thousand dollars. Honey didn't even spare him a glance. Theo quickly bid three thousand. Jacob bid three thousand five hundred, and then, not to be outdone, Oliver bid four thousand. Theo laughed at his friends. Sam surprised Honey when he bid five thousand dollars. She didn't know his salary as a detective, but she doubted it justified such a generous bid. Chance McComb upped the bid to six thousand dollars.

Honey could hardly believe the bidding. She looked at the crowd, trying to see who bid seven thousand, and she saw Hap making his way through the people heading in Sam's direction. Just then, Theo countered with an eight-thousand-dollar bid. The crowd grew quiet as the bidding went higher, all eyes bouncing from one bidder to the next. Chance bid nine thousand.

Terry leaned over and said softly in Honey's ear, "I thought Sam might continue, but I don't see him now."

"I would rather dance with Theo," Honey responded.

Another man Honey didn't recognize bid ten thousand dollars.

"Fifteen thousand dollars," Theo called out. He glanced Chance's way, determined to let him know he wasn't going to stop bidding, no matter what it cost him.

After he waited a few seconds for a challenging bid, Terry said, "Wild Bill, I think you have a dancing partner." He turned away from the microphone and whispered to Honey, "You got your wish. I think Theo likes you." He turned his attention back on the audience. "Folks, thank you for your generosity. Later, the ladies can bid on the gentleman of their choice. Ladies, I expect you to be as generous as the men have been." He turned to the musicians and instructed them to play a waltz. "Make it a long one, these men deserve their money's worth."

Conversation died down as the music filled the room and the men claimed their partners. Theo extended his hand to Honey, saying, "I'm the luckiest man here."

"Theo, you were much too generous with your bid."

"For a waltz with you? Never. Though I must admit, I expected your detective to stay in the bidding."

"He's not *my* detective." After tonight, Honey didn't know what she was feeling for Sam.

Theo smiled at her warmly as he pulled her into his arms. "His misfortune is my good fortune."

The waltz ended and Honey asked Theo if he would like to meet some of the guests who had arrived later. Theo was eager to meet some of his new neighbors.

It was a surprise to Honey that she didn't recognize many people behind their masks. Many of the guests didn't reveal their identity, and Honey suspected they relished their anonymity for one night.Of course,

Theo was a hit with all of the ladies in his Wild Bill Hickok costume. "I'm sorry I couldn't introduce you to everyone, I simply didn't recognize some people."

"They did seem rather pleased that no one recognized them. Did you ever figure out the identity of Maria Walewska?" Theo asked.

"No, I have no idea who she is. I'll ask Woodrow."

"You could ask Younger," Theo teased.

Honey rolled her eyes at him. "Very funny."

"Did you notice he quit bidding on his wife?" Theo asked.

"I did. But I can't say it surprises me. I saw him with his wife at dinner one night not too long ago, but they didn't see me. When they left the restaurant, he walked through the door and didn't even hold it for her. It almost hit her in the face. I couldn't believe how rude he was in public."

"Ah, not only a philanderer, he is no gentleman."

"Theo, a philanderer is never a gentleman," Honey countered.

CHAPTER TWELVE

MAKING THEIR WAY THROUGH THE crowd, Honey and Theo were headed across the room to ask Woodrow where he had taken Elvis. They passed Younger's wife and campaign manager, who appeared to be in the middle of a heated discussion. Suddenly, Mrs. Younger abruptly turned around and stomped away.

"Did you hear what they were arguing about?" Honey whispered.

"Before she walked off I heard her say, *I told you not to bring that woman here. You know how he is when he's drinking.*"

"I guess she was referring to Maria Walewska."

When they reached Woodrow, Honey asked him about Elvis.

"He's in the library. I removed his jacket and filled his water bowl. When I left the room, he was curled up on his sofa. The poor fellow was exhausted, too much excitement today."

"I was in the library earlier and didn't see him, but then..." She wasn't going to mention her encounter with Sam and Liz. "I'm sure he was probably sleeping soundly."

Before she walked away, Woodrow asked, "Have you seen Will McNeal? His wife asked me a few minutes ago if I had seen him."

"No, we haven't seen him. He didn't bid on his wife."

"I noticed that, as did many others," Woodrow replied.

"Perhaps we should go check on Elvis before Terry starts the bidding on the men?" Theo suggested.

"I don't think we have time. I wouldn't want the women to miss the chance to bid on you. I'm sure Elvis is sleeping peacefully."

When they walked toward the stage, Theo asked, "Do you plan to bid on me?"

Honey gave him a sideways glance. "Maybe."

Georgia joined Honey in front of the stage, and said, "I don't see Sam up there."

At that moment, Liz walked up beside Honey. "I wonder where Sam went, I wanted to bid on him."

"What about your fiancé?" Georgia asked.

Liz arched her brow at Georgia. "I guess I'll have to bid on both men."

"Can you dance with them both?" Georgia quipped.

"I think I can work out that little problem. I might even bid on that handsome Brit."

Honey couldn't believe the gall of the woman. "If you're going to bid on Theo, I hope you have your checkbook with you." There was no way she was going to let her have a dance with Theo.

Georgia laughed out loud.

The bidding on the men started off with a bang. Sam wasn't on stage, so Liz bid on her fiancé. Women in the audience were very generous bidding on Oliver and Jacob. Theo was the last man on the stage, and when Terry started the bidding at one thousand, Liz was the first woman to lift her hand even though her fiancé was standing beside her.

"Look at poor Theo, he looks like a deer caught in the headlights," Georgia murmured in Honey's ear.

Honey bid two thousand. "I wonder what Cam is thinking right now?"

When Liz bid two thousand five hundred, she looked at Honey and gave her a little smirk.

"What are you doing, Liz?" Cam questioned.

"Just getting more money for charity, darling."

When Honey bid four thousand, Liz didn't counter, but another woman bid five thousand. Honey thought the voice sounded like Bunny Spencer. Another woman made a generous bid, but Honey didn't even turn to see who was bidding. The higher bid didn't dissuade her; she continued bidding until she won the dance with Theo at eight thousand dollars.

Georgia gave Honey a hug. "Good for you, Honey. I'm glad you didn't let that woman intimidate you."

"There was no way she was going to win, even if I had to empty my entire savings account." Honey walked on stage and told Terry she had an announcement. When he relinquished the microphone to her she said, "To thank our wonderful master of ceremonies, I think you ladies should start the bid on him at three thousand dollars. I've seen him practicing with the instructors tonight, and I think he will make a wonderful partner." The bidding kept going and going until one woman dressed as Marie Antoinette was the victor with a sixteen-thousand-dollar bid.

"That's the highest bid of the night, but I know Terry is well worth every penny." Honey walked off the stage and Theo was waiting for her.

The musicians started playing, and Theo held out his hand. "I'll try to make our dance worth your bid."

Honey gave him a smile as she placed her hand in his. "Dancing with you is worth every penny, and it's for a good cause."

"I owe you a dinner for not letting that woman win."

"Which one? You have garnered quite a fan club in a short amount of time."

Theo wrapped his arm around her waist. "It was rather flattering to have several women bidding, but I was referring to Sam's friend."

Honey raised her brows in response. "Many men might have enjoyed dancing with her. Especially in that daring costume."

"Any man could see she's trouble. I'm amazed we've almost made it to the end of the night without her fiancé getting into a fistfight."

"What do you mean?"

"She's the kind of woman who enjoys having men fight over her. I'd say she thrives on making them jealous. Some men are so in love they can't see what's right before their eyes until it's too late."

"You think Cam doesn't know she wants to make him jealous?"

"I doubt it. He's probably so in love that I imagine he's blind to her less virtuous traits."

Honey wondered if Sam had been afflicted with the same problem. "You sound like a man with some experience."

"Not me, but I have a few friends who have fallen victim to women like her."

The evening came to an end, and judging by the comments from the guests as they left, it was a great success.

Cam thanked Honey and Woodrow again for inviting them with such late notice.

"I haven't seen Sam. Do you know what happened to him?" Woodrow asked.

"He and Hap had to leave earlier. He gave me the keys to his house and car. He said if he wasn't back by the end of the party, he'd see me tomorrow," Cam replied.

Woodrow left to drive his date home, and Oliver and Jacob retired to their bedrooms. Honey, Theo, Terry, Preston, and Georgia decided to have some snacks in the kitchen before calling it a night.

Honey pulled some platters from the refrigerator before she said, "I'm going to the library to see if Elvis is still there. It's not like him to stay away from me so long." Finding the library empty, she checked a few rooms on her way back to the kitchen.

Theo stuck his head out of the kitchen doorway and shouted, "Honey, Elvis is in the kitchen!"

Hearing her footsteps, Elvis ran down the hallway toward her. "Where have you been?"

"He was locked in the pantry," Theo told her.

Honey watched Elvis quickly empty his water bowl. "I wonder how long he was in there."

Theo refilled his bowl. "I bet he's hungry."

Elvis stopped drinking long enough to lick Theo's hand.

"I'll get him some bones." Honey walked inside the pantry to pull out some treats, and she noticed the container wasn't in its usual spot on the shelf. She grabbed several bones and held them out to Elvis. "The container was on a different shelf."

"Someone must have intentionally locked Elvis in the pantry. He's so large, I don't see how they could miss him." Georgia said.

"I'll ask Mrs. Harris tomorrow. She may have gotten distracted and accidentally closed him in there." Honey rubbed Elvis's head as he chomped on a bone. "Do you want to go outside?"

Elvis ran to the patio door, and Theo slid it open for him. "I'll go with you."

Theo and Honey walked at a leisurely pace through the garden, allowing Elvis time to sniff as much as he wanted.

"Theo, I feel as though I've monopolized all of your time tonight." Not only had Theo been a wonderful dancing partner, he'd been considerate and attentive all evening. Unlike Sam. Theo placed his hand on the small of her back. "I didn't want to be with anyone else."

They stopped walking while they waited for Elvis to take care of business, and Theo turned to face Honey. "In case I didn't tell you, you look beautiful tonight."

Honey looked up at him and smiled. "Thank you, but you did tell me."

"Honey…"

"Yes…"

Theo leaned over and kissed her. When she didn't pull away, he wrapped his arms around her waist and pulled her closer.

Honey thought Theo was almost too good to be true: handsome, intelligent, charming, and as an added bonus, the man could kiss. There wasn't one thing about him she didn't like.

When their kiss ended, Theo said, "Honey, I guess you've already have figured out I'm very attracted to you and I'd like to spend more time with you."

Honey was attracted to him as well, yet she had to work out her feelings about Sam. "I guess you can tell I'm equally attracted to you. But…I want to be honest with you. Sam and I, well, we have, or perhaps I should say we had, an understanding."

"By understanding, I guess you mean you were dating exclusively."

"Yes. We…or, I thought things were getting more serious than they were. We haven't had a chance to really talk things through."

Theo smiled at her. "Fair enough." He took her hand in his. "Just understand that I intend to give Sam some competition unless you have an objection to that."

Honey was flattered that he wasn't a man who would give up easily. She didn't want to discourage him, particularly since Sam hadn't been honest with her. She no longer knew the direction of her relationship with Sam, or even if there was a relationship. "I don't object."

They continued following Elvis, until he suddenly ran off the path into the brush. Honey yelled for him, and they waited for a few seconds, but Elvis didn't return.

"Elvis, you know I can't go through that brush in this dress," Honey called after him.

Theo laughed. "I can go after him." He pushed aside the dense foliage as Elvis peeked his nose through the thicket and barked.

"Come on, Elvis, let's go to the kitchen. We need a snack," Honey urged.

Elvis reluctantly joined them on the walkway, but he didn't turn back toward the kitchen. He loped ahead, leading Honey to believe he was going to the tent. Honey and Theo had no choice but to follow him. "He probably wants some more of that bacon you were feeding him earlier."

Theo grinned. "Or, he may need to burn some energy if he was locked up for a few hours."

Honey noticed the pathway was growing darker, and she wondered why the lights weren't on in this area. She lost sight of Elvis. "There should be a lamppost in this area. The light must be burned out."

Theo pulled his phone from his pocket and turned on the flashlight. "I see the lamp." He walked ahead of Honey to inspect the light. "It's broken. I walked this way yesterday and I didn't notice glass on the walkway."

Theo spotted Elvis down the pathway near a bench. "There's Elvis, and I think someone is sitting on that bench."

"Just one person?" Honey asked.

Theo turned to wait for her to reach him. "Can't you see in the dark?"

"Not very well."

Theo walked back to her and took her hand in his. "All I see is one person. Looks like a man."

"Maybe he had too much to drink and wanted some air."

"Probably passed out," Theo suggested.

"Let's see if he needs coffee." When they were closer to the man, Honey couldn't actually see his face, but she recognized the light-colored costume. She stopped a few feet from him. "Mr. Younger, could I get you some coffee?"

When Younger didn't respond, Theo walked closer and leaned over to him. "Mr. Younger?" He held his phone's flashlight to his face. "He won't be needing coffee."

Honey saw that Mr. Younger's head was slumped over, his chin touching his chest. "I can't believe he passed out here."

Theo felt for a pulse. "Honey, he's not passed out, he's dead."

"Oh, no! Please tell me you are joking!"

Theo walked the few feet back to her and pulled her into his arms. "I'm afraid not."

Elvis started sniffing around Mr. Younger's feet.

Fortunately, Honey maintained the presence of mind to say, "Elvis, come here. We don't want to disturb anything." Elvis ran to her side. "Let's go back to the kitchen and call Hap."

Hurrying to the house, all Honey could think about was Mr. Younger's wife. The poor woman was going to be devastated. Suddenly, it occurred to her she hadn't seen Mrs. Younger leave tonight.

Woodrow had returned from taking Virginia home when Honey, Theo, and Elvis walked through the patio door. "Gramps, we need to call Hap."

Hearing the urgency in her voice, Woodrow asked, "What's wrong?"

"We found Mr. Younger. He's dead," Theo answered.

"Dead?" Terry repeated as if he thought he'd heard incorrectly.

Theo nodded.

"I can't believe this keeps happening," Georgia lamented.

"Do you think he had a heart attack?" Preston asked.

"No, he was murdered," Theo replied.

Woodrow pulled his phone from his pocket. "Hap, Woodrow here. Are you close to the house?" Woodrow listened for a few seconds, then said, "Jeffrey Younger is dead."

When the call ended, Woodrow said, "Hap and Sam are on the way."

Woodrow waited for them on the front porch. When they arrived, he led them to the kitchen. "Honey and Theo found him."

Sam's eyes immediately went to Honey, who was sitting next to Theo at the table. "Are you sure it's Younger?"

Honey nodded her head. "I recognized the costume, but Theo checked for a pulse. He saw him up close."

Theo nodded his confirmation to Sam. "The lamp in that area was broken, and I'm positive it was working last night when I went out for a walk. But I held my flashlight to his face."

Hap and Sam walked to the patio door. "We'll take a look."

Theo stood and placed his hand over Honey's. "I'll show them. I know you are worn out."

Honey smiled up at him. "Thank you."

Sam watched the interaction between Honey and Theo before he followed Hap out the door.

Sam inspected Younger's body closely, holding his flashlight up to the back of his head. "Someone bashed in the back of his head."

"Not a gunshot wound?" Theo asked.

"No," Sam answered.

Sam and Hap looked around the immediate area for the weapon, but found nothing.

"I imagine it's here somewhere, but we may not find it until morning," Sam said.

"If they used the butt of a gun, they probably carried it off with them," Hap suggested.

Hap called for the crime scene team before they all walked back to the house.

While Hap was on the phone, Sam spoke to Theo. "What were you two doing out here?"

"We were walking Elvis. He'd been locked in the pantry, and we didn't find him until after the guests left. We didn't know how long he'd been in there."

"I don't remember seeing him at the party before we left," Sam commented.

"Woodrow took him to the library not long after the first guests arrived. Elvis was tired, and we thought he was sleeping," Theo replied.

"I didn't see him when I was…" Sam was about to say he didn't see Elvis when he was in the library with Liz, but he caught himself before he said too much. He didn't know if Honey told Theo about the incident in the library.

Preston and Georgia were leaving when the men came back in the kitchen. Hap asked them if they saw anything out of the ordinary during the party.

Georgia glared at Sam. "I saw several people being jerks."

"What do you mean?" Hap asked.

Georgia wasn't going to mention seeing Sam in the library with his ex-fiancée. "I did see Mr. Younger arguing with someone in the ballroom."

"Who was he arguing with?" Sam asked.

"I don't know. I saw him and I heard him raise his voice, but I couldn't see who he was with. Several people were blocking my view."

"Did you hear anything specific that he said?"

"Not really. I knew he looked and sounded angry."

"I noticed he walked outside with his wife, and I could tell they were not having a pleasant conversation. I also saw him with one of the Paul Reveres in what looked to be a heated discussion," Preston added.

Hap looked at Terry. "Was it you?"

Terry shrugged. "He tried to corner me a few times, but I walked away."

Hap told them to go home. "If you think of anything, you know how to reach me."

Sam turned his attention on Theo. "Where's Oliver and Jacob?"

"They're upstairs in their rooms. Do you want me to wake them?"

"We can talk to them tomorrow. Does anyone know if Mrs. Younger drove herself home?"

They all looked at each other.

Terry answered first. "I didn't see her leave. And I don't remember seeing Aaron and Maria Walewska leave either."

Sam and Hap exchanged a look. "Who is Maria Walewska?"

"Napoleon's girlfriend," Terry responded.

"Are you saying this woman…Maria…is, or was, Younger's girlfriend?" Sam asked.

"I didn't say that. All I know is Younger, who was dressed as Napoleon, bid on the woman dressed as Maria Walewska while his wife was standing on the stage. Aaron took over the bidding and won, but Younger danced with Walewska instead of his wife," Terry answered.

"Who is she?" Sam asked.

"No one knows," Woodrow replied. "No one recognized her."

"I bet Mrs. Younger knows who she is." Honey told them about the comments they overheard between Mrs. Younger and the campaign manager.

"What about McNeal? Did anyone see him leave?" Hap asked.

Everyone shook their head.

Terry stood to leave. "If you have no more questions for me, I'm going to head home."

"Call us if you remember anything," Sam told him.

"You're not going on horseback?" Theo questioned.

"No, the horse belongs to Woodrow. I parked my car behind the stable and rode the horse to Woodrow's house."

Theo laughed. "It was very entertaining."

"Terry, I forgot to ask, did you recognize the woman in the Marie Antoinette costume who won the dance with you?" Honey inquired.

Terry shook his head. "I have no idea. She didn't say one word through the entire dance."

"Well, she certainly wanted to dance with you. That was the largest bid of the evening," Woodrow added.

Honey decided to make fresh coffee since it looked as though they were going to be up for several more hours. She raided the refrigerator and made a platter of sandwiches.

"Why did you and Sam leave tonight?" Woodrow asked Hap.

Hap hesitated for a moment before he responded. He felt confident no one in the room had anything to do with Younger's death. "This information stays in this room. While I was at the party someone put a flash drive in my pocket. I showed it to Sam and we went to the office to have a look."

"You could have used one of the computers here," Woodrow told him.

"Sam and I thought it might be related to another case we are working on. Sam's been making some headway on one of our cold cases, shaking a lot of cages, making some people nervous."

"Why would anyone put a flash drive in your pocket?" Woodrow asked.

Hap shook his head. "I have to assume they wanted to keep their identity secret."

"Is it possible someone didn't recognize your costume and dropped it in your pocket by mistake?" Theo asked.

"I don't think I fooled anyone with my costume. Everyone who spoke to me recognized me," Hap replied.

"Why would they do that at a party?" Honey asked.

"I imagine they wanted to remain anonymous," Sam answered.

"Was it helpful to your case?" Woodrow asked.

Hap looked at each of them. "No, it had nothing to do with that case. It held some damaging information about our gubernatorial candidates."

"Was it damaging enough to get one of them killed?" Honey asked.

CHAPTER THIRTEEN

O LIVER AWOKE AT THREE IN the morning and quietly walked downstairs to raid the refrigerator. He was surprised to see Woodrow, Theo, and Honey gathered around the kitchen table still dressed in their costumes. Dressed in pajama bottoms, he stopped at the doorway. "I feel underdressed."

Woodrow waved him into the room. "You're fine. Come in and join us."

"I was going to raid your refrigerator, Woodrow. I didn't know you guys were still partying."

"Help yourself to whatever you want," Woodrow told him, pointing to the platter of food.

"We're not partying, Ollie. There's been another murder," Theo said.

Oliver jerked his head around and looked at Theo. "What? Another murder? Are you joking?"

"Hap and Sam are outside with the other officers going over the crime scene right now," Woodrow told him.

Oliver plopped down in a chair. "How terrible." It took a moment for his attorney brain to kick in. "Was it one of the guests at the party? Another shooting victim?"

"It was Mr. Younger. You know the man we met here the other day, the man who was drinking in excess. Hap said he wasn't shot, his head was bashed in," Theo answered.

"I remember him, he was Napoleon tonight. I saw him with another man, in what looked to be a rather heated conversation tonight." Oliver glanced at his watch, and amended his statement. "Or should I say, last night."

"Do you remember who he was arguing with?" Woodrow asked.

"It was Paul Revere."

"I take it you would have known if that Paul Revere was Jacob," Theo stated.

"It wasn't Jacob, but one of the other men."

"There were definitely a lot of Paul Revere costumes at the party," Honey stated.

"It might have been the most popular costume, but it wasn't the most memorable," Oliver said. "Who was that…"

Before he finished his question, Sam opened the patio door and walked inside. Oliver directed his question to him. "Sam, who was that half-naked woman with you tonight?"

Sam's eyes darted to Honey. She wasn't looking at him, her eyes were focused on the bottom of her coffee cup. He wished he'd stayed outside with the dead body. "My best friend's fiancée." He glanced Honey's way again. She was totally ignoring him.

"That was some costume, and she had the figure to pull it off," Oliver added.

Honey left the table to grab the coffeepot. She remembered all too well how Liz had her body pressed to Sam's in the library. "Oliver, would you like coffee?

"No, I think I'll have milk. I have my eye on that chocolate cake on the counter."

"I'll cut you a slice."

Noticing how Honey was slighting Sam, Woodrow asked, "Sam, would you like anything?"

"No, thanks. I've had my fill of coffee. I'm going home. I came in to say good night. Hap told me to tell you he would see you later. He left to go see Mrs. Younger. I'll be back at dawn to have a look around." He glanced Honey's way. "Don't let Elvis run around back there. The crime scene investigators will be out there for a while. If you don't mind, maybe Elvis can help us out in a few hours."

She didn't look at him, but simply said, "Sure."

Sam pushed open the patio door. "Honey, could I speak with you for a few minutes?"

Honey didn't want to talk with him, but if she didn't, Woodrow would think she was being rude. "Of course."

Closing the door behind them, Sam walked a few feet from the door so they wouldn't be overheard. "Honey, I don't want you to be alone. If you're returning to your cottage, I could crash on your sofa for a few hours."

Honey laughed. "Not a chance. I imagine someone is waiting for you at home."

Sam took a step closer to her. "I know you are upset with me, but I didn't kiss her, she kissed me."

Honey held her hand in the air. "It's not about that. At least, not only about that. Sam, you never mentioned a fiancée, not once in all of the time we've been together. And it looks like the two of you have some unfinished business."

"She might, I don't." Sam lowered his head, looked at his shoes and expelled a deep breath. "I should have told you. But everything seemed so right between us, and it wasn't something I enjoyed discussing. Liz was unfaithful when we were engaged. We lived together for a year in Texas, she complained constantly about my job, the long hours, my dedication...you name it...she didn't like it. I told her I was a cop when we met, and I had no intention of changing professions. One day I came home from work and found her in bed with a guy from her office."

"Seems like she's not faithful to anyone." Honey shook her head. "It doesn't matter, you should have told me before tonight. It wouldn't have made a difference between us. We both had a life before we met, but I shouldn't have found out about your relationship from her. And tonight of all nights. I had really looked forward to spending time with you at the party."

"You're right. I should have told you." Sam stared at her, looking miserable. "You look beautiful tonight, and I intended to spend time with you, but you didn't leave Theo Parker's side."

Honey glared at him. "What was I supposed to do? Wait for you to stop kissing Liz?"

Sam threw his hands in the air in frustration. "She kissed me just as you walked in. I didn't have time to react. I was as surprised as you were."

"I doubt that."

"Do you have something going with Theo?"

Honey stuck her chin in the air and glared at him. "That's none of your business."

Sam turned and walked a few steps away. He looked back and said, "Stay with Woodrow. I don't think you should be alone until we figure this thing out."

"I have Elvis, I'm never alone." Honey opened the patio door and walked inside.

Theo walked with Honey to her cottage so she could rest for a few hours. After a long soak in the tub, she climbed into bed and glanced at the clock. Four thirty. Elvis jumped on the bed beside her. "Don't be a bed hog tonight, and you better let me sleep a few hours."

She tried to fall asleep, but she couldn't stop thinking about Sam, Liz, and Theo. Before tonight, she thought their relationship might get back on track after they spent some time together at the party. With everything that happened tonight, she no longer thought things would ever be right between them again. But one thing was certain, she wasn't going to jump into another relationship so quickly. As attracted as she was to Theo, she needed time to make certain the next man in her life was one that she could trust.

Her thoughts drifted to Mr. Younger. Sad as his death was, considering his personality, it didn't surprise her that he must have made enemies. Did the killer choose tonight to do his dirty deed so there would be many suspects? Was Younger's death related to Trey Sullivan's? Was the killer a woman? Had Mrs. Younger reached the end of her rope? Why were both murders committed on their property? Honey didn't remember falling asleep, but she awoke to Elvis barking.

Grabbing her robe, she hurried to the door. Glancing out the sidelight, she saw Sam standing there. She pulled open the door, and Sam held out a bag from the bakery. "Please tell me you have coffee."

Honey tightened the belt of her robe around her. "I was in bed."

Sam's eyes glided longingly over her, and he didn't say what he wanted to say. "If you invite me in, I'll make the coffee while you get dressed."

Snatching the bag from his hand, she peered inside. "Don't think chocolate glazed donuts will get you out of the doghouse."

He had hoped chocolate would help his case. "I know." He followed her inside and kneeled down to give Elvis some attention. "I'll let Elvis out."

Detouring toward her bedroom, Honey heard him talking to Elvis as he opened the patio door. Sam knew their routine. He would fill Elvis's bowl with dog food and give him fresh water while Elvis was outside. They were comfortable together, and her heart ached over the loss of her trust in him.

When Honey joined them in the kitchen, Sam held a cup of coffee out to her. He'd placed the donuts on a plate, and when Honey picked one up, she was happy to see they were drenched in chocolate and still warm. "These are so fresh."

"Yeah, I waited for them. I know how you like the chocolate warm."

Honey found herself trying to think of something to say. She'd never felt that way with him before, and the thought that their relationship had irrevocably changed broke her heart. Unable to finish her donut for the lump in her throat, she dropped it on the plate.

"Don't you like it?" Sam asked.

"I guess I'm not very hungry."

Sam had seen her polish off three chocolate donuts without taking a breath. He knew what was on her mind. "Honey, I want to try to explain why I didn't tell you about Liz."

Honey thought he deserved a chance to explain—after all, he did bring chocolate donuts.

"I planned to tell you…" Sam hesitated, then amended what he was going to say. "I wanted to tell you, but I guess I thought you might think my job would keep me from being a reliable partner. We get along so well, and I just kept putting it off. Not only that, but it's not very flattering to say your girlfriend had an affair with another man."

Eyeing him skeptically, Honey asked, "So, your ego was hurt?"

"Hell, yes." He shrugged. "I think any man would react the same way if they found their girlfriend in a compromising situation. First of all, I didn't ask her to move in with me. I came home one day and there she was. She'd pressured me into proposing, and I knew right away I'd made a mistake. I don't know why I didn't break it off immediately. When I found her with her co-worker, it solved my problem. It was insulting, but the truth was, I was relieved to be out of that situation."

As much as she didn't want to give him any quarter, she couldn't help but think he was telling her the truth. It didn't mean she agreed with his decision not to tell her before now.

Sam reached over and placed his hand over hers. "Honey, I would have told you."

She wasn't quite ready to be forgiving. "I guess we'll never know." She could tell by the look in his eyes that she had wounded him. "Why didn't you call me before the party?"

"Cam and Liz were late getting in town. Of course, I didn't know Liz was coming with him. I think I was so shocked that I forgot about everything else. We returned to my house, and Liz went to bed, so I sat with Cam, trying to find a way to talk him out of marrying her. He was concerned I might still have feelings for her. I tried to tell him he was making a huge mistake, but I didn't want him to think I was jealous."

"Are you jealous of their relationship?"

Sam expelled a noise, something between a snort and a laugh. "No. Because Liz doesn't love anyone but herself. Cam will be miserable if he marries her."

"Why don't you tell him what she did last night if you want him to end it?"

"I thought about it, but I know it would be my word against hers, and he's a man in love. He told me he fell in love with her when she was with me, but he never acted on his feelings."

"Didn't he know you found her with another man?"

"I never told him."

"Gallant."

Sam shook his head. "Maybe just embarrassed." He squeezed her hand. "I'm sorry, Honey."

Honey believed him, but resuming their prior relationship was going to take some time. "Are you going to look for the murder weapon?"

Sam removed his hand, disappointed that she didn't seem more receptive to his sincere apology. "Yes. If you don't mind, I might come back and get Elvis if we don't have any luck."

"How did Mrs. Younger take the news?"

"Not good. Hap said he had to call Dr. Morgan to come to her house and give her a sedative."

"I feel sorry for her, even though I didn't care for her husband."

Sam arched his brow at her. "Not many people cared for him."

CHAPTER FOURTEEN

"**E**LVIS FOUND OUR MURDER WEAPON," Hap announced, taking a seat at Woodrow's kitchen counter.

"Really?" Woodrow handed Hap a cup of coffee and grabbed a treat for Elvis, his reward for a job well done. Woodrow glanced at Hap and saw the angst on his friend's face. "What's wrong, Hap? I would think you would be happy having made that discovery."

Hap sighed and leaned back in his chair. "Because I'm going to have to ask to see your golf clubs."

Woodrow gave him a puzzled look. "My golf clubs? Whatever for?"

"It looks like the putter Elvis found is the murder weapon. I'll know for certain when the testing is done."

"The murder weapon was a putter?"

"Yep. Question is, did the murderer bring his own weapon, or did he conveniently use your putter?" Hap took a drink of his coffee. "I'm thinking if he brought his own putter, then the murder was premeditated."

"I understand. I'd like to know the answer to that question myself. It's unsettling to know we had a murderer in this house last night. Finish your coffee. We can go to the garage to see my clubs."

Woodrow pointed to the second set of clubs in his garage. "Those belong to Theo. He brought them with him."

Hap saw that both bags held putters. "Any other clubs around here? Does Honey play?"

"This is all we have. No, Honey's not a fan of golf. Says it's too slow for her."

They returned to the kitchen where Theo, Oliver, and Jacob were having a cup of coffee and discussing the murder.

"I can't believe I slept through all of the action," Jacob said. "Why didn't you guys wake me?"

"We knew you needed your beauty rest," Theo teased.

"Elvis found the murder weapon," Woodrow told them as he and Hap joined them at the counter.

"Was he shot?" Jacob asked.

"No, someone bashed his head in with a putter," Hap responded.

"A golf putter?" Oliver asked.

"Yes."

"Hap and I were in the garage looking at our bags, Theo. Our putters are still there," Woodrow told him.

"So someone brought a putter with them to the party specifically to kill Mr. Younger?" Theo asked incredulously.

"Looks that way." Hap accepted a fresh cup of coffee from Woodrow. "I don't guess any of you saw someone walk in with a putter?"

"With some of those costumes, it wouldn't have been difficult to hide a cannon," Oliver replied.

"True. One exception was the woman who arrived with your detective," Jacob commented wryly to Hap.

"Yeah, I doubt she was our murderer." Hap started to say something else, but Sam tapped on the patio door.

Woodrow motioned him inside. "Want some coffee?"

"No, thanks. I wanted to tell Hap I'm taking off."

Hap motioned him inside. "Wait just a minute, let me finish my coffee and I'll walk out with you. I already looked at Woodrow's clubs. All accounted for."

Sam pulled out a chair and sat down. "The murderer has good taste. He used an expensive putter."

"What kind of putter?" Woodrow asked.

"A Titleist Scotty Cameron," Sam answered.

"Oh, that was what..." Theo started.

Always the lawyer, Oliver kicked Theo under the table. "Yeah, our friend back home has one of those. Great club."

Theo gave him a questioning look and Oliver shook his head. Theo glanced at Woodrow and to see if he was going to mention Terry's club.

"Before I forget, Woodrow, I'll need a copy of your guest list," Hap said.

Sam pulled a sheet of paper from his jacket. "Honey gave me a copy this morning." He glanced Theo's way to make certain he was listening. He wanted him to know he was still in the picture when it came to Honey.

Hap looked at Sam and said, "It's probably not necessary, but we need to interview your house guests, Sam."

"I'm ahead of you. I told them to be at the station at three today. They're leaving town in the morning. I thought you could interview them." Sam hoped to avoid Liz until he drove them to the airport.

"Jacob, I guess you are the only one we haven't asked if you saw anything unusual last night," Hap said.

"I guess you mean as it relates to Mr. Younger. I saw him exchanging some words with John Wilkes Booth and with Mr. Lincoln."

Hap looked at the others at the table. "Now, who was John Wilkes Booth?"

"His campaign manager, Aaron Branson," Woodrow answered.

"And Lincoln was Will McNeal," Sam added.

"That's right." Hap finished his coffee and stood. "Sam, we're going to have our work cut out for us on this murder."

"It's going to be an unusual investigation, that's for sure."

Once the two men were outside, Sam said, "That cell phone I found near the bench was charged."

"Any good information on it? Please tell me Younger recorded his killer's voice."

Sam chuckled. "Dreamer. The phone didn't belong to Younger."

Hap stopped and looked at Sam. "Don't leave me hanging. Who owns that phone?"

"Terry Meiners."

Hap expelled a loud breath. "I didn't expect that."

"Me neither."

"Has Trey Sullivan's cell phone turned up?" Hap asked.

"Nope, and Younger didn't have a phone on him."

"Oliver, I appreciate your quick thinking. I certainly didn't want to throw suspicion on Terry because of his golf club," Theo said.

"I saw no reason to reveal that bit of information at the moment," Oliver responded.

"Truthfully, I didn't know if I should say something or not. Of course, I know Terry didn't have anything to do with Younger's death. However, I feel a bit guilty not revealing what I know to Hap and Sam," Woodrow said.

"Those chaps are decent fellows. I'm certain you could trust them to do the right thing," Jacob added.

"For now, let's keep this to ourselves until we see what develops," Oliver suggested.

"Perhaps you are right. No need to give them a reason to suspect Terry at this point. I think that's the best course right now," Woodrow agreed.

Sam and Hap were on the phone for hours talking to the guests who attended the party. It was nearly eight o'clock when Sam walked in Hap's office and slumped into a chair.

"This is the craziest case I have ever worked. When I ask the guests if they saw anyone interacting with Younger, they say, "Well, I saw Younger spill his drink on Mary Lincoln, or he had one of the saloon girls pinned to the wall." Sam expelled a loud breath. "My favorite response so far, 'I saw Winston Churchill go into the lavatory after Napoleon.'"

Hap rubbed a hand over his scruffy face. "I'm getting the same kind of information. That woman…who did Honey say she was?"

"Which one?"

"You know, Napoleon's mistress."

"Oh, her name was Maria…something or other. I left my notes in my office."

"No one seems to know who she is," Hap told him.

"I haven't been able to reach Aaron Branson. I'm sure he'll know her."

"Yes, well, I talked to Bunny Spencer, and she said she saw a saloon girl talking to Younger. Apparently, the conversation didn't look pleasant, but she didn't know the saloon girl's identity."

"There were a few women dressed as saloon girls," Sam commented.

Hap picked up his pen and started tapping his desk. "I'm getting confused with all of these costumes."

"We need help. Let's get with Honey and Woodrow and try to match the guest list with the costumes," Sam suggested.

Hap nodded. "Good idea. We can stop by the distillery in the morning."

Sam stood and headed to the door. "I'll call Honey and ask if she'll be available early."

"How are things going with you and Honey?"

"Things aren't going." Sam hesitated and turned back to Hap. "I screwed up big-time."

"I'm hungry. Tell you what, I'll buy us dinner and if you want to talk about it, I'll listen."

Over dinner, Sam told Hap about his previous engagement to Liz, and the fact that he'd never told Honey.

"Well, that was before you even met Honey," Hap mused. "Was it that bad of an omission?"

"We had discussed previous serious relationships. I told her my profession didn't seem to coincide with a long-term connection. And she had to hear about it from Liz at the party."

"As I see it, you were truthful." Hap picked up his beer and took a big gulp. "But, I can also I can see why Honey is upset. You didn't actually lie, you omitted the full story. Why didn't you tell her about Liz? You don't still have feelings for her, do you?"

"No, no, that relationship was over a long time ago." Sam told him the same thing he'd told Honey. "I guess I hate to admit failure."

"I don't see it as a failure. It was a learning experience. From the sound of it, you jumped into that relationship without giving it a lot of thought. While men are in the heat of the moment, they should step back and take things slow. Men aren't nearly as smart as women."

"Yeah, you can say that again." Sam gulped his beer and ordered them another round.

Hap studied Sam for a moment, then said, "There's something you aren't telling me."

Leaning back in the booth, Sam said, "I can see why you're a good cop. There's more."

Sam told him about the scene in the library during the party.

Hap let out a low whistle. "Boy, Honey may never talk to you again."

"Well, she is talking, but not very cordially." Sam finished his dinner and beer. "Let's go back to the office and solve some murders. That, I'm good at. Relationshipsnot so much."

"I don't imagine she understands why you haven't had a lot of free time lately."

"I told her I'm busy working cold cases," Sam replied.

"Maybe you should tell her everything."

"I'm afraid that might really scare her off. I've been told many times that my profession doesn't mix with a relationship."

Back in the office, Hap asked Sam if he had time to look at the flash drive again. "Maybe we'll notice something we didn't before."

The video was filmed in Younger's campaign office. Jeff Younger was lying on the sofa across the room. The back of a nude woman comes into range of the camera. They could see Younger watching her every move. When the woman reaches the sofa, Younger pulls her to him. Her long hair covers the side of her face as she leans down to Younger, preventing Hap and Sam from identifying her.

"I wish we could see her face," Hap quipped.

"Guess we could have a lineup and tell the suspects to show us their backsides."

Hap laughed. "What I can't figure out is why Younger would be so stupid. He had a beautiful wife, and he had a lot to lose if this got out." As he looked at the screen, Hap shook his head. "If that man had a thought in his head, it would have died of loneliness."

Sam snorted. "Yeah, I got that feeling, particularly when he's drinking. I wonder if the voting public knew what an idiot he was."

The liaison on the screen didn't last but a few minutes, and the woman stood and walked out of view.

Younger got to his feet and adjusted his clothing. "That was great."

Hap and Sam could hear the woman's sultry voice.

"I know," she replied confidently.

Sam pointed to the computer screen. "I'd bet we just got to see Maria's backside."

"Maria?" Hap questioned.

"Napoleon's mistress. Maria Walewska."

The scene on the screen changed to another office. By the signs on the walls, there was no doubt it was Will McNeal's headquarters.

A man had his back to the camera, and Sam asked Hap, "You're sure that's Will McNeal?"

"It's him."

They could hear a woman's voice, but she was standing in front of McNeal and they couldn't see her.

"Why did you come here?" McNeal asked her.

"Why do you think?"

"It's not wise for you to be seen here," McNeal told her.

For the second time, Sam and Hap watched the screen in silence. The couple stopped talking, but they watched the woman put a hand around McNeal's neck and pull his head down. McNeal leaned over, gripped her hips, and walked forward until the woman's back was against his desk.

"We can't do this here," McNeal ground out between heated kisses.

"I know," the woman replied.

The couple continued to kiss, and Hap and Sam heard heavy breathing.

After a few minutes, McNeal took her by the arms and held her from his body. "We can't. Not here."

"Let's go somewhere," she responded breathlessly.

Hap looked over at Sam. "Do you feel dirty, like we're watching porn?"

Sam grinned at Hap's comment. "I haven't spent my time watching porn, but if we sit here much longer, I might need a cold shower."

McNeal said something they couldn't hear, but they clearly heard him say, *"I'll be there at eight."*

"Do you think they both have something going with the same woman?" Hap asked.

Sam jumped from his seat and tapped the screen. "Look! We missed that earlier."

Hap leaned forward. "What? What did you see?"

"Go back a few seconds," Sam instructed.

Hap did as he was told, and when Sam yelled "Pause!" Hap hit the button.

Sam put his finger on the screen. "There—that mirror. We can see her face." They both leaned closer to the computer screen.

Hap slapped his desk. "I can't believe it."

CHAPTER FIFTEEN

"IT LOOKS LIKE THE SAME person was spying on both candidates," Sam mused as he pulled the flash drive from the computer.

"I agree. But why? Blackmail?"

"If it was blackmail, why give it to you?" Sam asked.

Hap nodded. "We need to figure out who put that flash drive in my pocket."

Sam pulled his notebook from his pocket. "Let's list everyone you spoke to at the party."

Hap swiped a hand across his face. "Sam, I talked to just about everyone."

"Did you notice anyone acting unusual?"

"You mean besides all of the people dressed as historical figures?"

Sam shrugged and slammed his notepad on the desk. "There is that." He was quiet for a moment, feeling as though his brain was working at half speed. "Did you dance with anyone? It would be pretty easy to slip it in your pocket while you were dancing."

Hap's eyes brightened. "That's assuming it was a woman who put the flash drive in my pocket. But I did dance several times."

"With?"

Hap held up one finger. "Susan McNeal."

"Will McNeal's wife?"

Hap nodded. "Have you met her?"

Sam picked up his pad and wrote her name down. "I met her for the first time at the party."

"She's a very nice woman." Hap held up a second finger. "I also danced with Bunny Spencer." A third finger popped up. "And that gal who came to the party with Theo's master distiller—Gloria..."

"Gloria Barnes?"

"That's her." Hap gave Sam a sly smile. "She asked me to dance."

"Gloria's not shy." Sam added her name to the list.

"No, she isn't. The more she drank, the more flirtatious she became."

"Anyone else?" Sam asked.

"Your grandmother, but I think we can rule her out."

Sam tapped his notes. "This gives us a place to start." He stood and said, "I'll go make some calls and set up some appointments."

"Before we call it a night, why don't we go see if we can track down McNeal, maybe he's home by now."

"Let's go."

Hap smiled cordially when Susan McNeal answered the door. "Hello, Mrs. McNeal. I'm sorry to disturb you at this late hour."

"Hap, I told you to call me Susan." She motioned for them to come inside.

"Do you remember Sam Gentry?" Hap asked.

Susan gave Sam a warm smile. "Yes, we met last night. What can I do for you?"

"Is Will home?" Hap asked.

"No, he's not. I wish I could tell you when he will be back, but I'm afraid I was out shopping when he left. I've tried calling his cell, but he's not answering. Knowing Will, he's probably out bending the ears of some possible voters."

"When did you last see him?" Sam asked.

Drawing her brows together as if she didn't understand why he asked the question, she hesitated before saying, "This morning. Why do you ask?"

"Did you two come home together after the party?"

"Why are you asking these questions? What's happened? Is it something about Will?"

"No, there was an accident." Hap held up his hand, and quickly added, "Not involving Will. We are trying to see where everyone was at the time of this accident."

"What kind of accident?" Susan asked.

"I'm not at liberty to say right now. Did you two come home together after the party?"

"No."

It was late when Lela Knight's doorbell rang. She pulled the door open and asked, "What are you doing here?"

"Did Younger show up?" Aaron asked, walking inside uninvited.

"No, I've called his cell, but he's not answering." Lela led the way to the kitchen. "Want a drink?"

"Yeah. You have bourbon?" Aaron sat at her counter while Lela pulled out a bottle of bourbon.

Holding the bottle for Aaron to see, she asked, "How about this?"

"Good." He ran his fingers through his hair. "He's probably passed out somewhere. That's what worries me. He can't make a mistake now. What if the press finds him before I do?"

Lela leaned across the counter to set a glass and the bottle in front of Aaron, giving him a bird's-eye view of her lack of clothing beneath her robe. "You mean he hasn't been home since the party? Have you talked to his wife?"

"I called, but no one answered." Aaron poured some bourbon into the glass and took a sip. "Did he call you after I dropped you off last night?"

"No. Like I told you last night, he basically dragged me out to the patio and we walked in the garden. He was drunk and I knew what he had on his mind." She held her glass out for Aaron to pour her some bourbon. "He was pawing me like an animal. I don't like it when he's drunk. It's boring." She tossed back the contents of her glass, picked up the bottle and poured more in both glasses. "How do you put up with him? Especially when he's drunk?"

"I've devoted too much of my time to let him throw away this election now. He's a vehicle to get to where I want to go." He gave her a knowing look. "I could ask you the same thing. You're young and beautiful." He hesitated as his eyes roamed over her body. "Why waste your time on a guy like Younger?"

Lela smiled. "He's just a vehicle to get me to where I want to go. You're young, handsome, and smart. Unlike me, you were smart enough to get a good education; I was a high school dropout. I use what I have to my advantage." She looked at him over the rim of her glass as she finished her drink. "I can't figure out why you don't run for office."

"I don't have old money like Younger and McNeal's wife. Their families know every important person in the state, and a lot of people owe them favors. Running for office takes a lot of money and a lot of contacts. Working for Younger has given me an opportunity to make my own contacts. Many people have told me if I ever want to run for office, I could count on their support and backing. So my time hasn't been wasted."

"I guess we both are using what we have to our advantage."

"Yeah? Well, I don't sleep with him."

Lela walked around the counter until she was standing behind him. She ran her hands over his shoulders, leaned to his ear and whispered, "We don't sleep."

Aaron finished his bourbon and turned to face her. He'd seen her naked before when he'd barged into Younger's office unannounced. He thought Younger intentionally left the door unlocked that day, wanting someone to see him with a younger, beautiful woman. When he saw Lela, he understood Younger's obsession with her. He'd even envied him. Lela was gorgeous, but she wasn't the type of woman men in politics married. She'd made overtures to him several times, but he'd never taken the bait. Until now. Tonight he couldn't seem to ignore her; his willpower had deserted him. "Want to show me what you do besides sleep?"

Hours later, Lela lifted her head from Aaron's chest and gave him a frown. "Is that your phone that keeps beeping?"

Aaron chuckled. "Yeah, but I'm too exhausted to move. It looks like they're not going to give up." He rolled over to grab his jacket that he'd tossed on the chair beside the bed. Pulling out his phone, he glanced at the last call. He scrolled down and saw several different calls and a long list of text messages. "What! I can't believe this!"

Lela sat up and looked at him. "What's wrong?"

"Younger's been found…"

Lela sat up and looked over Aaron's shoulder at the phone in his hand. "Passed out drunk somewhere?"

"Dead."

Twenty minutes later, Aaron was sitting in Hap's office with Hap and Sam questioning him.

"I left you a message two hours ago. I'm surprised you didn't call long ago," Hap commented, taking in Aaron's disheveled appearance.

Aaron shifted uncomfortably in the chair. "I was visiting a friend and didn't answer my phone."

"I see."

"I came as soon as I listened to your message," Aaron added. "What happened to Mr. Younger?"

Instead of answering his question, Hap asked one of his own. "What time did you leave the party last night?"

"The same time most people left. I really didn't check my watch."

"Did Younger leave with you?" Sam asked.

"We took different limos to the party. I didn't see him when I left. What happened to Mr. Younger?"

Hap knew the press had been announcing Younger's death, but they did not yet know he had been murdered. "He was found at Woodrow Howell's estate."

"Heart attack?" Aaron asked.

"Why would you think it was a heart attack?" Sam asked.

Aaron turned his attention on Sam and shook his head. "You saw him at the party. Everyone knew he was drinking too much, he was overweight, had high blood pressure, and he never worked out. I told him to take better care of himself, but he wouldn't listen."

Sam didn't comment on the cause of death. "You spent some time at the dance with a young woman, and I believe you bid on a dance with her."

"Lela."

"Can you tell me Lela's last name?"

"Knight."

Sam scribbled her name in his notebook. "This was the woman dressed as Maria Walewska?"

"Yes."

"And Younger wore a Napoleon costume," Sam commented.

"That's right."

"Interesting," Hap said. "Mrs. Younger's costume was Josephine."

"Yes."

"And you were?" Sam couldn't remember his costume.

"John Wilkes Booth."

"Who is Lela Knight? I don't believe I've met her," Hap asked.

"She works for the campaign," Aaron replied.

"Do you have her address?" Sam asked.

Aaron gave them Lela's address. "I suppose I should call her and tell her about Jeff." He glanced from Hap to Sam. "You have notified his wife, haven't you?"

"Of course," Hap responded.

Sam found it interesting that Aaron thought of contacting Lela before Younger's wife. "I noticed last night that Younger was bidding on Lela Knight, but you took over the bidding. Why did you do that?"

Aaron looked down at his hands, debating on what to reveal. He didn't worry about Younger's reputation now, but he had to consider his future role in politics. He was known as a man who could be trusted, and he couldn't tarnish that image by being a gossip now. "I guess since Mr. Younger is dead, I can say certain things that will be kept in confidence."

"Whatever you tell us stays in this room," Sam assured him.

"Mr. Younger had a...I guess a polite way of saying it would be a *special* relationship with Lela."

"By special relationship, I assume you mean they were having an affair," Sam stated bluntly.

"Exactly."

"How long had this special relationship been going on?" Hap asked.

"Several months."

Sam jotted down some more notes. "Is Lela Knight married?"

"No."

Sam then asked Aaron if he'd seen any unusual interactions between Younger and any of the guests at the party.

"I'm sure you know Mr. Younger drank too much, and he had a habit of being confrontational when under the influence."

"We're hoping you might be able to shed some light on that. We are interviewing everyone who attended the ball. Did you see anything unusual?" Sam asked again.

"You mean besides Mr. Younger trying to embarrass his wife in public?"

Sam and Hap exchanged a look.

Without waiting for a reply, Aaron went on to say, "I did see Mr. Younger talking with Paul Revere. I was too far away to hear their conversation, but it looked rather heated."

Sam focused on Aaron's face. "How could you tell it was *heated*?"

"I've worked for Mr. Younger long enough to know when he was angry. His face was red and he was poking the man in the chest."

Hap leaned forward on his desk. "There were several men dressed as Paul Revere."

Aaron nodded. "I thought it was Terry Meiners. He was tall and looked to be in good shape. Mr. Younger recently had words with him, so I assumed it was a continuation of that same disagreement."

"What can you tell us about this disagreement?" Sam didn't need to ask the question; he was aware of Younger's animus toward Terry.

"Mr. Younger thought Meiners was giving Will McNeal more time on the radio. Terry is always telling his listeners he wants them to hear both sides of the issues, but Mr. Younger didn't see it that way."

"You're the campaign manager. What was your opinion?" Hap asked.

"I do think Meiners is more supportive of McNeal. I don't know if it is intentional, but that's my opinion."

"You bid on Lela to dance, but you didn't dance with her. Who did you dance with?" Sam asked.

"I won the bid on Mrs. McNeal."

Sam realized he'd hardly been paying attention during the bidding. He'd been too worried about Honey. "Where was Mr. McNeal during that dance? Didn't he bid on his wife?"

Aaron shook his head. "I don't know. All I know is when Hap bid on Mrs. McNeal, I thought I would give him some friendly competition."

Sam's eyes traveled from Aaron to Hap.

Hap shrugged. "He's right, I did bid on her. That was before we had to leave."

Sam didn't comment. "Aaron, why would you want to dance with McNeal's wife? Wouldn't Younger be angry about that? Why not dance with Mrs. Younger?"

"I figured I would let Mr. Younger figure out how he was going to dance with two women. I like Lela, but Mr. Younger was promising her things he was never going to deliver. And I didn't see Mrs. Younger during that dance. I've met Mrs. McNeal on several occasions and she's a very gracious lady. When Hap dropped out of the bidding, I won the dance with Mrs. McNeal. I thought a dance with her would be rather humorous. You know, John Wilkes Booth dancing with Mrs. Lincoln." He hesitated a moment, then added, "To be honest, I like both Mr. and Mrs. McNeal. But you know politics."

Sam and Hap stared at him, waiting for him to say more.

Aaron shrugged. "You have to pick a side."

Hap arched a brow at Sam before he asked, "Did you arrive alone to the party?"

"No, Lela and I rode together in a limo."

"Did you see Mr. and Mrs. Younger leave?" Sam asked.

"No, I didn't see either one, so I assumed they'd already left before we did."

"And you and Lela Knight left together?" Sam asked.

"Yes."

"Let me get this straight. You won the bid on Lela, but Younger danced with her. You also won the bid on Mrs. Younger as well as Mrs. McNeal. You danced with Mrs. McNeal."

"Right."

"Then where was Mrs. Younger?"

Aaron shook his head. "As I said, I didn't see her during the dance."

Sam decided to share how Younger died, to gauge Aaron's reaction. "Younger was murdered on Woodrow's property."

Aaron's mouth dropped open, and it was several seconds before he collected himself. "Murdered? I can't believe it. Who would murder a man running for governor?"

CHAPTER SIXTEEN

S AM, HAP, HONEY, AND WOODROW were sitting in Woodrow's office trying to match the people on the guest list with the costumes they were wearing.

"Some of the guests didn't want to reveal their identity, but I think we know most of them," Woodrow answered.

"We have a good start," Sam replied. "By the way, do either of you know Lela Knight?"

"The name is not familiar," Woodrow answered.

Sam glanced at Honey and she shook her head. "She was the woman dressed as Maria Walewska."

Honey didn't have to check the guest list to know that name wasn't there. "She wasn't invited to the party."

"She works for Younger, or she did. She accompanied Aaron Branson to the party," Sam told them.

"I did forget to tell you something last night," Woodrow said. "It may not be important, but when I returned from driving Virginia home, a limo was sitting in front of the house. The driver said he was waiting for a guest, but I told him everyone had left. I assumed whomever he was waiting for found another way home."

"Did he mention who he was waiting for?" Sam asked.

"No, he didn't."

"Do you know how many people came in limos?" Hap asked.

"We informed everyone alcohol would be served, so they were

welcome to use a limo service we provided. Judging by the number of limos, I assumed that's the way most people arrived."

Sam looked at the list in his hand. "I guess we should start with the guests who wore Paul Revere costumes. That costume was the most popular of the night."

Honey pulled up her list on her laptop and started typing the costume beside the name of each guest. "Of course, Terry Meiners was Paul Revere."

"Cullen Webb was another Paul," Woodrow told them.

"Does anyone know how many Paul Reveres there were?" Hap asked.

"I'm not certain, maybe five or six," Woodrow said, glancing at Honey.

"I don't know either. Every time I turned around I saw another one. The only three I knew were Terry, Jacob, and Cullen. And their costumes were very similar."

"Let's move on to everyone else," Hap suggested.

As they moved through the list, Honey saw Sam's friends were next on her page. "Liz Simmons was Josephine Earp, and Rick Cameron was Doc Holliday." She glanced Sam's way. He was staring at her, and she was the first to look away.

Once they assigned names to the various costumes, Honey told them the names of the remaining guests. "I don't know the costumes of these guests: Jack Cleary, Mitch Janes, Thomas Grayson, Dr. Morgan and…" Honey hesitated.

"And?" Sam asked.

"I almost said Trey Sullivan," Honey answered.

"Do you think these two murders are related?" Woodrow asked.

"We don't have proof, but I'd say they are in some way," Hap responded.

"No headway on Trey's murder?" Woodrow asked.

"We can't find a single person who had an ax to grind against that young man. He was well-liked by everyone who knew him. And we still haven't found his cell phone." Sam's phone rang, and when he glanced at the screen he excused himself and walked out of the office to take the call. When he returned to Woodrow's office, he told Hap that they needed to stop at the coroner's office.

"We can ask Mitch if he was one of the Paul Reveres when we see him.""Have we accounted for everyone at the party?" Hap asked.

"Not necessarily. Some people brought dates, and I'm not certain we met everyone," Honey replied.

Sam and Hap stood to leave. "If you think of anyone else, give us a call."

Sam hesitated in the doorway. He had a legitimate reason to go back to Woodrow's house, but he hoped to see Honey alone while he was there. "Woodrow, I need to go back to the crime scene later and have a look around. Elvis seemed particularly interested in an area near that bench. I didn't see anything, but I'd like to have another look around. We haven't found Younger's cell phone either."

"You have the code to the gate. Feel free to come and go as you need," Woodrow responded.

Sam nodded, and gave Honey one last long look before he walked out the door and caught up with Hap.

"I thought you guys would want to see what was in one of Mr. Younger's pockets," the medical examiner, Mitch Janes, said to Hap and Sam when they walked into his office. Mitch led them to another room and pointed to a table. "Take a look."

Hap pulled a ballpoint pen from his pocket and used it to lift the sliver of red material. "Wow, I've never seen underwear this tiny."

Mitch laughed. "It's a thong."

Hap whistled and winked at Sam. "Not much there. You think we could use the thong like Cinderella's slipper? Have all of the women who were at the party try it on, if it fits, we found our suspect."

"Now that would be interesting," Sam replied on a grin.

"I'd pay to see that," Mitch added.

"Does this evidence mean what I think it means?" Sam asked.

"Yes. It seems Mr. Younger really enjoyed his evening," Mitch said.

"You mean right up to the time his head was bashed?" Sam asked.

Mitch nodded. "Yeah, right up until then."

"DNA?" Hap asked.

"Oh, yeah, on Younger's white pants," Mitch assured them.

Hap slapped Sam on the back. "That's the best news we've had all day. Let's go start interviewing our large pool of suspects."

"Mitch, were you Paul Revere?" Sam asked.

Mitch nodded. "As it turned out, it was not very original. I counted at least five."

"Did you know who they were?" Hap asked.

"Terry Meiners and one of those English chaps I spoke to. I don't think I spoke to the others."

"Did you notice anything unusual at the party?" Sam asked.

"Unusual?"

"Anyone arguing, particularly with Younger," Hap added.

"I did notice a saloon girl getting pretty chummy with you, Hap," Mitch teased. "I didn't know you were such a good dancer."

Hap chuckled. "I used to be a pretty good dancer in my day."

Sam inclined his head toward Hap and grinned. "Other than twinkle toes here, did you see anything else?"

"I saw some woman go out to the patio with Will McNeal, and it wasn't his wife."

"Who was it?"

"I was on the other side of the tent, so I only saw her costume. I know Mrs. McNeal was dressed in black as Mrs. Lincoln. This costume was more colorful."

Before they left the coroner's office, Sam had another question. "Mitch, are you convinced the putter was the murder weapon?"

"No doubt about it."

"Would the person who wielded that putter have blood on their clothing?" Hap asked.

"I'd say it's a given."

"There was blood on the bench and grass. We should look at every costume when we interview the guests on our list," Sam told Hap.

That afternoon, Sam and Hap split up to interview some of the guests. After several hours, Hap called Sam. "Have you found out anything interesting?"

"Not yet, but I've only seen five people on my list."

"Yeah, me too. Are you still going to Woodrow's before it gets dark and have a look around?"

"Yeah."

"Call me later and let me know if you find anything. I'm going to stop back by the McNeals'."

"Hello again, Susan," Hap said when Mrs. McNeal answered the door.

"I'm afraid Will has not returned, Hap."

Hap thought Mrs. McNeal looked as though she'd been crying. "Would you mind if I asked you a couple of questions?"

"Not at all, please come in." Susan led him to the sitting room. "Please, have a seat. I imagine Will is still at his headquarters."

Hap sat in a chair across from her. "Do you spend much time there?"

Susan glanced away. "Not really. They are usually so busy, and to be honest, I don't really enjoy campaigning."

"I see. Did you hear about Jeff Younger?"

"Yes, I did. While I didn't care for the man, it is so sad that he's dead. Did he have a heart attack?"

"No. He was murdered."

Susan's eyes widened. "Murdered? At Woodrow's? The news said he was found on Woodrow's property, but I didn't hear he was murdered." She looked down and linked her fingers together. "How sad."

"Did you know Younger well?"

"At one time, Paige and Jeff were good friends. That seems like a lifetime ago."

"Susan, when we danced at the party, did you happen to drop a flash drive in my pocket?"

She gave him a puzzled look. "A flash drive? No, I didn't."

Hap thought her reaction seemed honest. "I found one in my pocket and I'm trying to find the owner." He decided to change the subject. "How well did you know Trey Sullivan?"

"Not very well. As I said, I don't spend much time in the campaign office." She gave him a slight smile. "It's odd that I married a politician when I don't like politics."

Hap nodded. "I can understand your feelings. Had you heard of anyone who didn't like Trey, or didn't get along with him?"

She shook her head. "Will said everyone really liked him."

Hap didn't want to be offensive, so he approached his next question carefully. "Susan, is everything okay? You seem to be upset."

"I'm tired. It's seems like this campaign has gone on forever." She looked Hap in the eyes. "Truthfully, I just want it over with and maybe our lives can get back to normal."

"It seems to me if Will becomes governor, nothing will ever be normal."

"That's probably true. Although if Will wins, I may get to see more of him."

Hap wasn't so sure about that, but he didn't think now was the time to give her his opinion. While she was thinking about that question, he hit her with the one he really came to ask. "Would you show me the costumes you and Will wore to the party?"

"Of course."

Sam walked slowly around the area that was thirty yards from the bench where Younger was found, and out of view of the pathway. The private alcove was surrounded by tall bushes, making it a perfect place to hide. The lawns were beautifully manicured, so the crushed grass in that area indicated someone or something had been there recently. Considering what was found in Younger's pocket, Sam hypothesized it was possible Younger had a sexual encounter on the grass. While DNA would be uncovered on the red panties, that didn't mean they would know the identity of the person wearing them unless she had previously committed a crime. He walked back to the pathway leading to the bench where Younger had been murdered. There was no way Younger could have seen anyone lurking about, particularly with no light. Even without a broken light, there were several little hidden areas off the pathway where one could hide if one was so inclined. Did Younger break the light so anyone walking that way would turn around, assuring he and his girlfriend would go unobserved? Or, did the person with the putter break the light so he, or she, wouldn't be seen as they committed murder?

"Can we talk?" Sam asked Honey when she opened the door to her cottage.

Honey didn't think she had much of a choice since her traitor dog was already in Sam's arms. "Come in. I was going to make myself something to eat. Would you like to join me?"

"That sounds good." Sam and Elvis followed her to the kitchen.

"Don't you want to know what I'm cooking?"

"It doesn't matter. If you make it, it'll be good."

"We're having hot browns. Would you like a drink?"

"I'll have a bourbon, but I can handle the drinks while you cook."

"It won't take long. I already have the sauce simmering."

Sam carried their glasses of bourbon to the kitchen. "Has Elvis had dinner?"

"Not yet."

Sam set the glasses on the counter, walked to the pantry and grabbed the canister of dog food to fill Elvis's bowl.

Covertly, Honey watched Sam as he moved around her kitchen. It almost seemed as though they were back to the same routine before Sam became too busy at work, before Liz…before Theo. She was comfortable with Sam, but then again, she was comfortable with Theo. Elvis loved them both. Honey tried to think of something to say to fill the awkward silence. "Did you find anything outside?"

"No, there's one area that I wanted to check out, but I didn't find anything. Elvis can go back there now; the area is cleared."

Honey placed the turkey on the toasted bread, smothered them with sauce, and slid them under the broiler. "How's the investigation going?"

Sam walked over to the range and leaned his hip against the counter and snagged a piece of bacon Honey had just pulled from the oven. "Slow."

"I remember you told me once that most people know their murderer."

Sam noticed she wasn't really looking at him when she spoke. "Murder is rarely random."

"Did they find fingerprints on the weapon?"

"Don't know yet. But we have DNA from the crime scene."

Honey looked up at him. "That's good news, isn't it?"

"It is, if the person is on file. If they haven't previously committed a crime, it won't be of much help right now."

"True." Honey thought about the area where Younger was sitting. "I guess Mr. Younger was meeting someone at that bench."

Sam stared at her. "Good guess."

Honey smiled at him. "You know something you aren't telling me."

"Some things I'm not at liberty to talk about yet."

"Trey and Younger's deaths must be related," Honey suggested.

"Seems logical."

"What can you tell me?" Honey pried.

"I'll just say that Hap and I are going to be visiting all of the guests and looking at their costumes."

"Why don't you ask them to come to the station so you don't have to drive all over the place?"

"We didn't want to give them advance warning that we are interested in seeing their costumes. I want to observe their reaction when I ask them."

Honey arched her brow at him. "Is that why you stopped by? You want to see my dress?"

Sam picked up his glass and took a sip of his bourbon. "No. I wanted to see you." He winked at her. "Besides, I saw your dress after you found Younger."

Honey pulled the dishes from beneath the broiler. She started to reach around him for the plate of sliced tomatoes. Sam caught her hand and pulled it to his chest. "Honey, I'm really sorry. I should have told you I had been engaged. I was wrong. Will you forgive me?"

"Of course, I forgive you. But that doesn't mean I can forget."

"Is this something we can get past?"

"I don't know."

"Honey, I wasn't kissing her. I told you the truth. She'd just wrapped her arms around me and locked her lips onto mine when you walked in."

"Why were you in the library?"

"I was looking for a restroom that wasn't occupied. I had been in the bathroom in the library before. I had no idea she followed me. When I came out of the bathroom, she said she wanted to talk." He shrugged.

"Next thing I know she walked right up to me, wrapped her arms around my neck and kissed me."

"You didn't know she still had feelings for you?" Honey asked incredulously.

"I had no idea. I hadn't spoken to her since I moved to Kentucky. When Cam and Liz arrived I told them both about you. I don't think she could stand the thought that I broke it off with her and found someone who made me happy. Liz is competitive, she never did like to lose. I don't think she really cares for me, she just wanted to be the one to break it off." Sam put this finger under Honey's chin and urged her to meet his eyes. "I care about you."

CHAPTER SEVENTEEN

"How was your day?" Hap asked Sam when they spoke on the phone later that night.

"Not productive. But I did check all of the costumes while I was at Woodrow's tonight. No blood on any of them."

"I checked Mr. and Mrs. McNeal's costumes. Nothing there. I still haven't spoken to Will yet."

"Sounds like the missus hasn't seen much of her husband since the party," Sam remarked.

"I know, and today she seemed upset about something."

"Hap, we are two idiots!" Sam shouted into his phone.

"What do you mean?"

"McNeal. I bet he was at Younger's home visiting with Mrs. Younger." Hap expelled a loud breath. "I bet you're right."

"Okay, you want to interview Younger's wife, or his girlfriend, in the morning?" Sam asked.

"I'll take Mrs. Younger," Hap answered.

"I doubt we'll have time to meet at the station, so I'll call you between interviews." Sam clicked off, glanced at his watch, and decided it was too late to call Honey. He knew it would take her some time to forgive him for not telling her about Liz. As much as he wished he could blame Liz, there was no one to blame but himself. He had to find a way to build Honey's trust again. There was no way he was going to lose her to Theo.

"Are you Lela Knight?" Sam showed his identification as he introduced himself.

"Yes." Lela motioned him inside her condo with the cup of coffee she was holding. "I guess you're here about Jeff."

"Yes, ma'am." Sam couldn't help but notice the slinky little robe she was wearing.

"Oh, you don't have to call me ma'am. Lela is fine. Please have a seat. Could I get you some coffee?"

"No, thank you." Walking to a chair, Sam looked around the room, taking note of the expensive furnishings. "How did you hear about Mr. Younger's death?"

"Aaron told me. He was here when he found out."

"Are you two good friends?" Sam asked.

Lela smiled. "I guess you could say we are very close."

Sam read between the lines. "I want to ask you some questions about the last time you saw Younger."

Lela tucked one bare leg beneath her as she took a seat on the sofa. "Sure. What do you want to know?"

"Let's start off with Mr. Younger bidding on you for the dance," Sam started.

Lela smiled at him. "Actually, Aaron won the bid, but I danced with Jeff."

"Why did he dance with you and not his wife?"

"Detective, I'm sure you already know Jeff and I had a thing going."

"A thing?"

"We were having an affair."

Sam arched his brow at her. She was direct, so he would be as forthright. "Was it just sex, or was it more? Were you in love with him? Was he in love with you?"

"I wasn't in love with Jeff, but he was good to me. He bought me lots of gifts, paid for this condo, as well as a new Mercedes."

"What about him? Was he in love?"

"Jeff loved himself. But he did say that when he became governor, he was divorcing his wife and marrying me."

"Did you believe him?"

Lela shrugged. "Who knows?"

"How did you meet him?"

"I was waitressing at a restaurant and he introduced himself one night. One thing led to another and I invited him to my apartment after my shift was over. We hit it off."

Sam asked what restaurant, and he wrote down the name, then he asked, "What did you do for his campaign?"

"I kept Jeff happy."

Sam had already figured that one out on his own, but he appreciated her honesty. "Did you and Mrs. Younger ever cross paths?"

"Not really. She never confronted me, if that's what you're asking. Jeff said she argued with him all the time about me. He said she threatened to leave if he didn't stop seeing me." She took a sip of her coffee, then added, "He thought she was bluffing because she wanted to be the first lady. He also told me she didn't like…well, you know, so I saved her the trouble."

"How did you get to the party?"

Lela told him about attending the party with Aaron. "Aaron is always my date. We went in a limo."

Sam asked her if she mingled with other guests. Lela responded by naming all of the men she danced with besides Younger and Aaron.

Sam wrote down the names. "Which Paul Revere?"

"I don't know. I don't think I recognized any of them."

"Was it the master of ceremonies?"

"It could have been. By that time, I'd already had several bourbons. I do remember he was quite tall and had beautiful blue eyes. Later on, I saw Jeff arguing with him when I was dancing with Aaron."

"How did you know they were arguing?"

"I could tell when Jeff was angry."

"Are you sure it was the same Paul Revere?"

Lela looked away and frowned. "Well, he was tall, but I guess I couldn't swear it was the same one."

"What else happened that night?" Sam asked.

She arched her brow at Sam. "Detective, are you asking if Jeff and I had sex?"

He appreciated the way this gal cut to the chase. Saved him a lot of dancing around the subject. "Did you?"

"Yes. He said he wanted to go for a walk to sober up, but I knew what he had in mind. We stopped at a bench and had sex."

"Weren't you worried someone would see you?"

"We were pretty far from the ballroom, and it was so dark I could hardly see anything." She gave him a smirk. "It didn't take long."

"Was he alive when you left him?" Sam asked bluntly.

Lela chuckled. "I'm good, Detective, but I've never killed anyone with sex."

Sam tried not to smile. "What happened after your, ah…encounter on the bench?"

"I told him I wanted to go back in and dance. He said he was going to sit out there and sober up."

"Can I see the costume you were wearing?"

"Sure."

While he was waiting for her to return with the costume, Sam walked around the room, looking at photos she had displayed on various tables. Most photographs were of Younger, Aaron, and herself. He didn't see family photos, or other friends.

When she returned holding her costume, she walked up and stood directly in front of Sam. It took him all of two seconds to notice she was standing there in her bra and thong, minus the robe. Judging by the size of the thong, the red panties the medical examiner found in Younger's pocket belonged to her.

She held the costume away from her so he could have an unobstructed view. "Did you want me to model it?"

"If you don't mind, I'll take the costume with me." He took the costume from her and folded it over his arm.

"No problem. Jeff paid for it, and I won't be wearing it again."

"Why Maria Walewska?"

"Jeff knew a lot about history, and he told me about her."

"Did you wear it to embarrass Mrs. Younger?"

Lela shrugged. "It was Jeff's idea. He said he told his wife someone was coming as Napoleon's mistress. I imagine he'd been drinking when he told her. I think he enjoyed embarrassing her."

Sam thought Younger was a real jerk. "Did you see Younger when you left the party?"

"No, I assumed he was with his wife. I knew he would call me later."

Sam walked toward the door. "I appreciate your honesty. That's all I need right now."

Lela held the door open for him, but she placed her hand on his arm. "Detective, if you find a pair of red panties, they're mine. I think Jeff tucked them in his pocket when we were on the bench."

"I'll make a note of that."

Giving him a seductive smile, she said, "Come back anytime, Detective."

As soon as Sam reached his car, he called Hap to tell him about the owner of the red panties.

"That must have been one interesting conversation," Hap managed to choke out when he stopped laughing. "Saved us some time, I guess."

"She's a real piece of work. But I'll say this for her, she puts it all on the line. She readily admitted to her affair with Younger."

"Did they argue over anything at the party? Did Mrs. Younger confront her?"

"She said Mrs. Younger never spoke to her. Younger wanted to go outside, he said for a walk, but she knew he wanted sex." Sam thought about his conversation, and added, "Lela said Younger told her that his wife didn't like sex."

"You mean she didn't like to have sex with him," Hap commented.

"Yeah, I'd say that's more accurate."

Hap told Sam he was headed to another interview, and planned on stopping at McNeal's campaign headquarters to have a talk with him. "I haven't been to Mrs. Younger's yet. Do you have time to stop by and get her costume? Anyway, you're obviously more persuasive with the ladies."

"I don't know about that. For whatever reason, Lela Knight wanted everyone to know about her relationship with Younger. Why else would she wear that costume to the party? Though she did tell me it was Younger's idea."

"Hmm. Good question. I see what you mean. Do you think Mrs. Younger was angry enough to kill her husband for embarrassing her?"

"Wouldn't be the first time a woman killed her husband for cheating."

Sam thought in Younger's case there could be several suspects. "We should keep her on the suspect list."

"Yeah, too many suspects in Younger's case. I'd be happy to have one suspect in the Trey Sullivan case," Hap told him.

"Sullivan's case is a puzzle, but something will turn up. His cell phone will be the key to that puzzle." Sam sounded more confident than he felt at the moment.

"Let's talk later."

Sam pulled up in front of Younger's home just in time to see a man walking to the front door. Thinking he recognized the man, he hurried to the door before Mrs. Younger answered.

"Are you Dr. Morgan?" Sam asked.

"Yes, and call me Mike, Detective," Mr. Morgan replied.

Sam extended his hand. "Sam Gentry. Sorry we didn't get to meet at the party the other night."

Dr. Morgan shook his hand and gave him an amiable smile. "Nice to officially meet you. I'm afraid I didn't stand out with my costume since I was one of many Paul Reveres. But your Wyatt Earp costume was very convincing."

"Thanks. Is Mrs. Younger okay?"

The doctor rang the doorbell. "That's why I'm here. I wanted to check on her."

"I don't know many doctors who make house calls anymore." Sam was paid to question everyone's motives. Mrs. Younger was an attractive woman, and the doctor wasn't wearing a wedding band.

"I've been her doctor for several years. I care about my patients, and it's not every day one of my patients has a spouse murdered. I wanted her to know I'm here for her."

"That's admirable."

The door opened, and Mrs. Younger looked surprised to see both men standing there.

"Hello." She glanced from the doctor to Sam. "Please come in."

Once inside, Sam flashed her his identification. "Mrs. Younger, I'm Detective Sam Gentry."

"Yes, I know. What can I do for you?"

"You may want to talk to the doctor before you speak with me since I have some questions that might take longer."

The doctor reached out and took her hand in his. "Paige, I just came by to see how you're doing. I wanted to see if you needed help with anything...the arrangements. I'll be more than happy to offer you my services."

Paige smiled at him. "Mike, that is so thoughtful of you, and I really appreciate your concern. Jeff's campaign manager has been very helpful. He's handled everything."

Sam thought the doctor had the look of a love-struck puppy. It reminded him of the way Elvis gazed at Honey. Or maybe it was the way he looked at Honey.

The doctor leaned over and kissed Mrs. Younger's cheek. "I'll call you later. Now get some rest." He looked at Sam and extended his hand. "Nice to meet you, Sam."

"Doc, I'll be by your office tomorrow to talk with you. We are interviewing everyone from the party."

"Come early before my day starts. I make hospital rounds before my appointments."

"Then I'll stop by your home." Sam thought that would be the best way to see his costume.

The doctor's eyes slid to Paige, before he said, "Make it about five a.m."

When the doctor left, Sam politely asked Mrs. Younger if she felt like answering questions.

"Yes, I know you want to find my husband's murderer." She directed him to the sitting room.

As Sam took a seat in a large overstuffed chair, he said, "First, I'd like to know how you got home from the party."

"I took the limo. I couldn't find Jeff, so I left and sent the limo driver back for him."

"Did you consider waiting for him?"

Mrs. Younger gave him a slight smile. "If you knew my husband, Detective Gentry, then you would know if he was talking politics, I couldn't have pried him away with a crowbar."

"So you weren't worried about him?"

"No, why should I have been worried? We were at a party, and I certainly didn't imagine something like this could happen at Woodrow's."

She didn't seem to be very upset, so Sam moved on to more intrusive questions. "Even though your husband bid on you for the dance, he didn't dance with you. Where were you during that dance?"

"I was outside with a friend."

"Who is this friend?"

"I'd rather not say."

"Why?"

"It might be embarrassing for my friend."

Sam stared at her.

"Since my husband had a partner for that dance, I guess that would indicate he was alive at that time."

"True. The problem is, no one remembers seeing you for quite some time after that dance."

"As I said, I was with my friend. I didn't look to see how long I had been gone."

"Mrs. Younger, it will most likely be necessary for you to reveal your friend's name."

Mrs. Younger met his eyes. "If you decide I'm a suspect, I'll deal with that problem then."

Sam had one last question before he left. "Did you know who your husband danced with when you were outside with your friend?"

"Yes, as I'm certain you do as well."

"Did that trouble you?" Sam asked.

"If you're asking if I killed my husband over infidelity, then the answer is no."

Sam stared at her a full minute before he stood. "If you don't mind, I'd like to take the costume you wore with me to the station."

CHAPTER EIGHTEEN

HAVING TIME BEFORE HIS NEXT interview, Hap called Sam to see if he could meet him at the diner to compare notes. He slid into the booth opposite Sam, asking, "Have you eaten?"

"Nope, and I'm starved." Sam reached for the menu resting between the napkin dispenser and the condiment caddy.

"The club sandwiches are good here if you haven't had them. And they come with a huge stack of the best fries you'll ever eat."

"I see you're watching your diet," Sam quipped, but he also ordered the club sandwich when the waitress appeared.

Over their sandwiches, Sam told Hap about his meeting with Mrs. Younger.

"What's your gut tell you? Should we keep her on our suspect list?"

Sam took a drink of his coffee as he thought about his answer. "She's a cool number, and she definitely knew her husband was with Lela. She also didn't shed one tear over his death while I was there. I don't think she'll be mourning him."

"But would you consider her a suspect?"

"Yeah, thinking about the odds, I can't rule her out. I also have her costume in the car."

"So we have the girlfriend's and the wife's costumes?" Hap asked incredulously. "The girlfriend didn't object?"

"Nope. She offered to model it for me when she lost her robe."

Hap had taken a big bite of his sandwich and he nearly choked. "Are you serious?"

Sam laughed at Hap's disbelieving expression and nodded. "Oh, I'm serious."

"Nothing like that ever happens to me," Hap complained as he wiped his mouth with his handful of napkins. "These sandwiches are good, but messy."

"Worth it." Sam pulled more napkins from the stainless container and tossed some to Hap. "Tell me about McNeal."

"Interesting. When I asked him where he was while his wife was dancing with Aaron Branson, he said he was talking to a friend. He didn't reveal the name of that friend. He's bringing his costume to the station later."

"What do you think of him?"

"He seems like a genuinely nice guy. I know the ladies think he's handsome, and he's intelligent." Hap frowned and shrugged. "At least that's what everyone tells me."

Sam grinned. "Jealous?"

Hap spread his hands wide. "Who me?" He smacked his protruding belly. "Didn't you know I'm described as having a *dad bod*? I've been told that is like catnip to the ladies. At least, that's what one of the saloon girls told me at the party." He chuckled. "Look at all that time you've wasted exercising. I didn't see you dancing with anyone at the party."

"You might have a point." Sam had given a lot of thought to Theo dancing with Honey at the ball.

Growing serious again, Hap leaned back in the booth. "By the way, I didn't spot a camera in McNeal's office. But that little romantic scene on that flash drive was definitely taken in his office."

"Interesting. You think he found the camera and had it removed?"

"I don't know, but I thought we'd hold that card until we need to play it." Hap picked up his sandwich, preparing to take another bite. "I haven't told you the best part of my visit with McNeal. You're gonna love this."

Sam arched his brow and waited for Hap to continue.

Hap took a huge bite of his sandwich and smiled as he chewed, making Sam wait for his big revelation. After he took a drink of his iced tea he gave Sam a mischievous grin. "You'll never believe who was working tonight at McNeal's campaign headquarters."

Sam shook his head. "No clue."

"Honey and Georgia."

The french fry Sam was holding dropped to his plate. "Tell me you're joking."

"Yep, the dynamic duo. I asked what they were doing there and Honey said they'd volunteered." He leaned over the table and lowered his voice. "You and I both know why they are there. Honey has called me every day to find out if I knew why Trey Sullivan was killed on that road."

"This is like the last dead body Honey found. She couldn't stay out of that case either. I saw her last night and she didn't say one word about volunteering at McNeal's," Sam muttered.

"Yeah. I halfway understood why she wanted to get involved in K. C. Cleary's murder. They had been good friends since childhood. She didn't even know Trey Sullivan, but it doesn't matter to her. If she finds a corpse, she determined to get involved."

"She finds too many corpses to suit me," Sam grumbled. "I guess I should go talk to her in the morning and tell her..."

Hap's phone rang and when Hap looked at the screen, he held one finger up to Sam and answered the call. "Hi, Honey."

Sam tried to hear what Honey was saying, but all he could hear was Hap's one-sided conversation.

"Where did he find it? Did you call him? No, don't call. I'll stop by in the morning."

Honey said something else, and Hap replied, "That'll make the trip even better." Hap hung up and looked across the table at Sam. "Elvis found a wallet tonight as they were taking a walk on the property. "Honey says it belongs to McNeal."

Sam was disappointed that Honey had called Hap and not him. "You want me to pick it up in the morning?"

"I'll go since she called me. You two haven't patched things up?"

"Nope, she says she forgives me, but she can't forget. I've apologized over and over, but I'm not making any headway."

Hap nodded his understanding. "I figured since she called me she's still miffed at you. Give her time."

"It hasn't help that I haven't spent any quality time with her in weeks."

"Why haven't you told her what's going on?" Hap asked.

"I don't want her to worry."

"Yeah, I get that, but you run the risk she might think you are no longer interested," Hap replied.

"True enough. And Theo Parker is all too available to step in and take my place."

"He's seems like a real gentleman," Hap teased.

Sam expelled a loud breath. "Thanks a lot. I thought you were on my side."

Laughing, Hap said, "I am, but you have to be on your toes around these Englishmen. All of the women at the party were talking about them. Too bad we missed the bidding dance on the men. I was told Theo drew one of the largest bids of the evening."

"So I heard," Sam growled.

"Did you also hear who won the bid?"

"Yeah, I did. Don't rub it in."

"Since you're so down in the mouth, and you obviously need my help mending your fences with Honey, you can go get the wallet in the morning. She'll be at Woodrow's house. I want you to know I'm giving up her homemade cinnamon rolls. She told me she'd make extra for me, so you'd better bring me some." Hap jabbed his fork in Sam's direction. "You owe me big for that. Don't lose that gal, she's a keeper."

"Since the women are so hot for you, maybe you have some suggestions as to how I can manage to do that."

Hap chuckled. "If you're desperate enough to take tips from me, you're in real trouble. I haven't even had a date in over a year. I only know one way of eliminating the competition."

Sam's eyebrows went up in interest. "What's that?"

Hap gave him a wide grin. "It involves parting with a lot of cash on something that you can see sparkling from the space station."

Before he made it to Woodrow's front door, Sam could smell the cinnamon in the air. He chuckled to himself, thinking that his nose was almost as good as Elvis's. It wasn't necessary for him to ring the doorbell since he spotted Elvis watching him through the glass oval in the door. He knew Honey wouldn't be far behind. Through the glass he saw her hurrying to the door, wearing a light pink sweater and jeans. He thought she slowed a step when she saw him. He hoped it was just his imagination.

Once she opened the door, Elvis leaped on him.

"I thought Hap was coming," Honey said.

"Good morning. Hap had some early interviews, so I came instead. I hope you don't mind." Sam bent on one knee and rubbed Elvis affectionately.

Honey closed the door, gave him a slight smile and asked, "Have you had breakfast? I'm making cinnamon rolls."

"I smelled them when I got out of the car. I'm starving."

She finally smiled at him. "Aren't you always?"

Sam thought that was a good sign. "When you're cooking I am."

"Come on, I need to get them out of the oven." Honey turned toward the kitchen, and Sam and Elvis followed.

Reaching the kitchen, Sam saw Woodrow at the counter talking with Oliver and Jacob. Theo was peeking inside the oven.

"Are they ready?" Honey asked him.

Theo turned and grinned at her. "I hope so. I can't wait any longer."

Everyone said hello to Sam, and Woodrow invited him to sit at the counter as he poured him a cup of coffee. After he placed the pot back on the burner, he slid a baggie toward Sam. "Here's McNeal's wallet. Honey can show you where they found it after breakfast."

Honey pulled the rolls from the oven and placed them on a huge platter when Elvis ran from the kitchen.

"Honey, were you expecting anyone?" Woodrow asked as he stood to follow Elvis.

"Not unless it's Hap."

Woodrow returned with Terry Meiners. "Honey, we need another plate."

"Good morning, Terry." Honey walked over and gave him a hug. "What brings you out so early?"

"Someone told me you were making cinnamon rolls," Terry teased.

The men shook hands with Terry, and Woodrow poured him a cup of coffee. "Have a seat, Terry."

"Are you guys having a party this morning?" Terry asked, looking at everyone at the counter.

"Looks like it," Woodrow answered.

Everyone filled their plates with cinnamon rolls and the room grew quiet as they ate. The men kept adding more rolls to their plates, and when they finally slowed down, Terry said, "I almost forgot that I did come here for a reason. I wanted to see if anyone turned in my cell phone. I think I left it on one of the tables when I was getting a snack at the party."

Everyone but Sam responded, saying they hadn't seen his phone.

"The servers didn't turn in a phone. But I will check with them," Honey told him.

"Thanks, Honey." Terry glanced at Woodrow, and added, "I also left my putter here the other day."

The room went silent, and Woodrow, Theo, Oliver, and Jacob exchanged glances.

Sam noticed. "You left a putter here?"

"Yeah. I brought it over to show Woodrow, and we all practiced with it the other day. When I got home, I remembered I had left it here."

Sam hadn't called Terry yet to tell him he'd found his phone. Now, for the first time, he was hearing Terry had left a putter at Woodrow's house. "What kind of putter?"

"A Titleist Scotty Cameron. Did you see it?"

Sam glanced at every face at the counter. Everyone but Honey looked guilty. No one had told him that Terry brought a putter over to show Woodrow, and it just happened to be the same brand of putter that was used in a murder. "Yeah, I've seen it. It was used to kill Jeff Younger."

Terry thought Sam was joking. "Right. Seriously, did you see it?" Terry glanced at Woodrow.

"Sam isn't teasing, Terry," Woodrow replied.

Terry stared at Woodrow, expecting him to burst out laughing. When no one laughed, Terry said, "You're serious? My new putter killed Jeff Younger?"

"Not the putter, but it was the weapon of choice wielded by the murderer," Sam replied.

"I thought he was shot," Terry said.

Arching one brow, Sam directed his attention on the others. "What I would like to know is why no one told me about that putter."

Woodrow was the first to respond. "We knew Terry wasn't involved."

"That's beside the point," Sam countered. He looked directly at Theo. "Did you use Terry's putter?"

"I did."

"And you didn't think to say something?"

"I also hit a few balls with the putter," Oliver spoke up.

"I hit a few as well," Jacob added.

"The least you could have done was tell me so we could have fingerprinted each one of you." Sam turned to Honey. "I guess you hit some balls with it too."

"No, I'm not a golfer," she replied coolly.

"I don't suppose any of you have any objections to giving us fingerprints." Once he received unanimous agreement, he then asked, "What about DNA?"

No one objected, so Sam said, "Terry, I need to speak with you."

"If you want some privacy, feel free to use the library, or if you prefer, the patio," Woodrow offered.

"Let's go to the patio." Sam stood and headed to the patio door. As he slid it open, he turned to back to the rest of the group. "I'll see the rest of you in my office at six p.m. sharp."

"Why do you need to see me? I didn't use Terry's putter," Honey asked.

"I have another reason I need to speak with you."

"I can't be there until eight thirty."

"I'll see you then." Sam's jaw was twitching as he walked outside and slid the door shut behind him.

"That's the first time I've seen Sam that angry," Honey told them. She watched Sam through the glass, and that's when she realized he was wearing his bulletproof vest under his shirt again.

"He has a reason to be upset with us," Woodrow replied.

Terry took one last gulp of coffee before he stood to follow Sam.

"Terry, would you like me to go with you? I can't practice law in your country, but I can advise you," Oliver offered.

"Thanks, Ollie, I appreciate your offer. I have nothing to hide, but I guess it can't hurt to have you as a witness to what I have to say."

"I'm here if Terry needs me," Oliver said to Sam once they joined him on the patio.

Sam nodded. "That's fine. I wanted to tell Terry that I found his cell phone. It's at the station."

"Great! Where did you find it?"

"Near Younger's body." Sam watched Terry's reaction.

"But wasn't he found outside in the garden?" Terry asked.

Sam nodded.

"I wasn't outside. I walked to the door leading from the tent to get some air, but that's as far as I went."

"Tell me exactly where you left your phone," Sam told him.

"I think I left it on one of the tables when I got something to eat."

"We've found two sets of prints on your phone. I'll need your fingerprints."

"No problem."

CHAPTER NINETEEN

"**W**HY DIDN'T YOU TELL ME you were volunteering at McNeal's headquarters?" Sam asked Honey when she took a seat in his office later that night.

Honey tossed her purse in the vacant chair. His greeting didn't engender tender feelings toward him. "I didn't know I was required to tell you my schedule."

Sam braced his elbows on his desk and pinched the bridge of his nose. It had been a long day, and he didn't intend to start off the conversation this way. Start over. "Where's Elvis?"

"He's with Woodrow."

"Would you like to grab a bite while we talk?" Sam already knew she'd been to McNeal's campaign headquarters after she left the distillery, so she hadn't had time to eat dinner.

Honey stared at him. "Oh, right, I forgot you like to take women to restaurants to interrogate them." Honey wasn't subtle reminding him that she had seen him at a restaurant a few months ago with a woman he was supposedly *questioning* in a murder investigation.

Sam groaned. "I'm not interrogating you. I only want to talk."

Honey silently acknowledged that she was being petty, reviving an old argument, so she acquiesced. "We can go to the diner."

Sam stood and reached for his jacket before she changed her mind. "Good, I'm starving."

For the second time in as many days, Sam slid into a booth at the diner. "Hap and I ate here last night. The club sandwich was delicious."

"We could have gone somewhere else if you preferred. I suggested it because the food is good and it was close."

"This is fine with me." Sam ordered two iced teas and sat back in the booth. "Honey, I didn't know you were interested in politics."

"I'm not particularly. You know why Georgia and I volunteered to work there."

"I figured as much. What have you learned?"

"Everyone said Trey was a nice guy, but he was also very ambitious. I did hear one thing that was surprising..." Honey hesitated when the waiter reappeared with their tea.

They placed their order, and when the waiter walked away, Honey said, "A couple of people mentioned that they thought Trey was friends with Mr. Younger."

"Really? I hadn't heard that." Sam thought he should put her on the payroll.

"I'm not certain it's true, you know how the rumor mill can be."

"I don't have to remind you that we have two murders on our hands, and it's very likely they are related in some way. Please promise me you'll be careful. Remember the last time you interfered in a murder investigation, someone threatened your life."

Honey frowned at him. "I wasn't interfering then, and I'm not interfering now. I want to know why Trey was killed on our property."

Sam lowered his head and sighed loudly. He knew no matter what he said it would just fall on deaf ears. "Be careful."

Honey's phone rang, and seeing the name on the screen, she said, "It's Georgia. She's at the campaign headquarters. I want to make sure she doesn't need anything."

Sam nodded his understanding.

"Hi, Georgia." Honey listened as Georgia started talking.

Sam could hear some of Georgia's conversation. "She said he was dating Gloria. You remember Gloria, big store-bought boobs, small brain."

"Uh-huh." Honey eyes were on Sam, wondering if he could hear what Georgia was saying.

Sam didn't crack a smile.

Honey hung up and looked at Sam. "Georgia heard tonight that Trey dated Gloria."

"Gloria?"

Honey rolled her eyes at him. "You know darn well I'm referring to Gloria Barnes. I know you remember her. The woman you *questioned* over lunch."

Sam wanted to ask if she was ever going to let it go, but he just shook his head.

"Didn't you see Gloria at the party? She was dressed as a saloon girl. I'm certain you recognized her."

Sam held his hand in the air. "I saw her." He remembered all right. Gloria's costume was very revealing, but he was smart enough to know whatever his response, it was going to be the wrong one. Although he did find that tidbit of information about Gloria Barnes dating a murder victim interesting. First thing tomorrow morning, he'd find out if that was credible information. Instead of telling Honey she might have helped his investigation with this new lead, he changed the subject. "How long are you going to volunteer for McNeal?"

"We are only volunteering a few hours a week. I guess it depends on what we find out."

"Have you noticed any cameras in the office?"

"No, but I can't say I've looked for cameras. Why?"

"That flash drive Hap found in his pocket had videos from McNeal's office. I was curious who placed the camera in his office."

Honey eyes widened. "What kind of videos?"

"I can't tell you right now."

"I'll look for cameras."

"Be careful. The murderer might work for McNeal. For all we know, it could be McNeal himself," Sam warned.

"Why didn't Hap ask Mr. McNeal about the camera?"

"We aren't revealing everything we know just yet, so keep this information between us."

Honey looked at his chest. "Why are you wearing your vest again?"

"I'm trying to break it in. They're stiff and uncomfortable."

Sam dropped Honey off at her car and followed her home before he drove back to the station. Seeing Hap was still in his office, he walked in and sat across from his desk. "Honey found out some interesting news at McNeal's headquarters. It seems Trey was dating Gloria Barnes."

Hap dropped his pen to his desk and leaned back in his chair. "You're kidding. That seems like an odd pair."

"From what I've found out about Trey, I would agree with you. I thought he was a conservative type of guy, rather straight-laced. Gloria Barnes is the exact opposite."

Hap shook his head and grinned. "I'd say you're right about that. She's definitely not a conservative kind of gal. She's the one who told me I was catnip to the ladies."

Sam rolled his eyes. He couldn't help but think of Georgia's description of Gloria. "If she was dating Trey, maybe she slipped that flash drive in your pocket when you were dancing."

"In the morning, I'll go to Cleary's Distillery and have a talk with Gloria."

Sam nodded his agreement. "One more thing. Honey said there's gossip that Trey knew Younger. It seems that Trey was an ambitious young man, and I've been wondering if he had something to do with that flash drive. He could have had the opportunity to install the camera, and considering what was on it, he would have had a lot of leverage if he wanted to use that information against someone."

"You could be on to something," Hap agreed. "Maybe Gloria can shed some light on Trey's ambition, and what he was willing to do to get ahead."

Gloria was late for work, and when she arrived the receptionist informed her that the chief of police was waiting for her in the conference room.

Hap stood when she entered the room. "Gloria, please have a seat. I need to speak with you."

Gloria dropped her purse on the table as she took a seat. "Chief, I'm already late this morning."

"I won't take long. I'm interviewing everyone who attended Woodrow's party."

Leaning forward in her chair, Gloria asked, "Do you think someone who attended the party killed Mr. Younger?"

"That's why we are interviewing everyone. Did you speak with Mr. Younger that night?"

"He asked me to dance."

Hap wasn't surprised by her response. Younger had danced with several women. "Had you met him before?"

"Yes."

Hap observed how tightly she was gripping her hands together. "Can you tell me when and where you met Younger the first time?"

Gloria hesitated, then said, "Someone introduced us at a restaurant in Louisville about six months ago."

"Who introduced you?"

"My date."

Hap arched a brow at her. "His name?"

"I really don't see why that matters," Gloria hedged.

"Was it Trey Sullivan?"

"Chief, what difference does it make?"

"Why are you afraid to tell me? The man is dead. I assure you, he won't mind."

Gloria crossed and uncrossed her legs nervously. "That's the problem."

Hap thought about her response. "Are you telling me that you're worried about your safety?"

Gloria glanced over her shoulder as if she thought someone might overhear what she had to say. "He told me to stay away from Younger."

Hap stood and closed the door. "Who told you to stay away from Younger?"

"Trey," she whispered.

Pulling a chair next to Gloria's, Hap sat back down, leaned close to her, and lowered his voice. "No one can hear us. Why don't you start at the beginning and tell me why you're afraid."

"Trey and I had dated for a few months. He wasn't at all what I expected when we first met."

"Everyone tells me Trey was as straight as an arrow," Hap interjected.

Gloria nodded. "That's what everyone thought about Trey, but he had a wild side. He made certain we'd always go to out-of-the-way places where he could relax and not be *on* all of the time. He was planning on running for office one day."

"You said Trey introduced you to Younger?"

"We saw Mr. Younger at a bar in Louisville one night."

"Did they seem to know each other well?" Hap asked.

"Yes. They knew each other very well."

"Do you remember anything they discussed that night?"

Gloria took a deep breath. "Mr. Younger had too much to drink that night. He sat down at our table, uninvited. Trey tried to get rid of him, but Mr. Younger wouldn't leave. He made inappropriate advances toward me right in front of Trey."

"How did Trey react?"

"We just got up and left. He told me that Mr. Younger didn't respect women. He warned me to stay away from him, he said he wasn't to be trusted."

"Did he explain why he thought he couldn't be trusted?"

"No, but he did tell me that he did some work for Mr. Younger."

That was news to Hap. "Did Trey work for Younger before he joined McNeal's campaign?"

Gloria leaned closer to Hap. "He didn't say, but he must have. One night at my apartment, Trey had several drinks and he told me he was spying on the McNeal campaign for Mr. Younger."

"You mean Trey was on Younger's payroll?"

Gloria nodded. "That's what Trey told me. He said he took steps to protect himself because he didn't trust Mr. Younger to live up to his end of the deal."

"Did McNeal know Trey had worked for Younger?"

"Trey said Mr. McNeal had no idea. I asked him if he felt guilty about that, and he told me it was politics."

"Was Trey good with computers?" Hap asked.

"He was a genius with computers."

"You put that flash drive in my pocket."

Gloria hesitated momentarily before she nodded. "Trey gave it to me for safekeeping. He told me what was on that flash drive was his ticket to a lot of money."

"Did you know what was on the flash drive?"

Gloria shook her head. "He didn't tell me, and I didn't look. He said the less I knew the better."

"Did Younger mention Trey to you at the party?" Hap asked.

"He asked me who I thought killed Trey. I told him I had no idea, I assumed it must have been a random robbery, or something like that."

"Is that what you believe?"

"No. Trey told me politics was the dirtiest business there is, and never trust anyone, especially Mr. Younger. He said they were all crooks, and they would do whatever it took to obtain power and keep power. I asked him if that included murder." She hesitated a moment, then added, "I was only teasing, but when I saw the look on his face, it scared me."

"What did he say?"

"He said they would certainly commit murder without giving it a second thought. He wasn't teasing. We were together the last few days before he was killed, and he seemed nervous about something."

"Did he say what was wrong?"

"I asked him a few times, but he wouldn't tell me."

Hap finished with his notes, then stood. "We haven't found Trey's cell phone. You don't happen to have it, do you?"

Gloria shook her head. "Trey was never without his phone."

CHAPTER TWENTY

HAP WAS DRIVING BACK TO the station when his phone rang. "Sam, where are you?"

"At the station, and you need to get here as soon as you can."

"I'm headed there now. What's up?"

"McNeal and Mrs. Younger are in my office right now."

Hap expelled a breath. "Did you bring them in?"

"No, McNeal wasn't there when I stopped by his headquarters this morning. I still have his wallet. They walked in and said they needed to talk to us. I thought you might want to hear this conversation."

"You bet I do. Be there in five."

Hap said hello to Paige Younger and Will McNeal when he entered Sam's office and took a seat.

McNeal was the first to speak, and he directed his comment to Sam. "I know you were at my office today, Detective Gentry. I think I know what you wanted, and that's the reason Paige and I decided to come here to talk to both of you."

"Why do you think I was at your office?" Sam asked.

"I imagine you found my wallet." McNeal's eyes bounced from Sam to Hap, waiting for one of them to confirm his hunch.

"Go ahead and tell them everything, Will," Paige Younger encouraged.

Will nodded, took a deep breath and said, "Paige and I are lovers." His eyes met Paige's and he reached out and covered her hand with his own. "It's not just an affair. We fell in love from the first moment we met. It was like destiny."

Sam could see tears forming in Paige's eyes as she gazed at Will. He remained silent, waiting for Will to continue.

"Of course, we couldn't tell anyone. Her husband, my wife, the election…we agreed to wait until after the election before we made some changes."

"By changes, do you mean you were both going to divorce your spouses?" Hap asked.

"Yes, that was our plan," Will replied. "Anyway, the reason I'm telling you this…well, at the party Paige and I were in the garden together…and…well you can guess what we were doing. That's where I think I lost my wallet."

"Where exactly in the garden were you?" Sam asked.

Will described the area where Sam had searched. "I searched that area and I didn't see your wallet there." He didn't mention Elvis found the wallet.

"I hung my jacket on a limb not far away, and I assumed it fell out when I took it off."

"Did either one of you have anything to do with Younger's murder?" Hap asked bluntly.

"No," Will answered quickly.

"Of course not," Paige replied a second later.

Hap glanced at Sam before he added, "You know you two are the most likely suspects considering what you've told us."

Will nodded his understanding. He glanced at Paige, squeezed her hand again and gave her a reassuring smile. "That's why Paige insisted we come and talk to you. She thought we would be implicated if our affair was discovered. We want to be together, but we would never have solved our problem by killing Jeff, even if he deserved it."

"Do you think he deserved to be murdered?" Sam asked.

Will gave Sam a steady look. "I'm not sorry he's dead, if that's what you are asking. He deserved it for the way he treated Paige."

"Are you talking about his affair?" Sam asked.

"I know that sounds rather hypocritical considering we are doing the same thing. But this is not something either of us have done before. Jeff had numerous affairs, and he wasn't in love with any of the women," Will replied.

Sam directed his next question to Paige. "Do you think your husband deserved to be murdered?"

"The truth is, his affairs aside, Jeff was not a nice man. Maybe it was the alcohol, I don't know. But no, I don't think anyone deserves to be murdered."

"You said affairs. How many were there?" Hap asked.

Paige lifted her shoulder and shook her head. "How much time do you have, Chief?"

Hap arched his brow at Sam.

"I'm sure this latest woman he's involved with thinks she's the first, and he'd most likely promised to leave me and marry her. Jeff was good at promises, but he wasn't good at follow-through."

"What if I told you we were already aware of your affair?" Hap said.

"Then I'd say we weren't as careful as we thought," Will answered.

"If we know, do you think anyone else knew?" Sam asked. "How about your wife, Will?"

"I'm sure she knows I've been...different.... She's asked me for months what's troubling me, but I haven't told her. Paige and I haven't seen each other often, and when we have, we've been very careful."

"Jeff and I used to play golf with Will and Susan. We were all friends, and we spent a lot of time together. But Will and I knew we couldn't go on like that. We tried to stay away from each other, and we did for months. Occasionally, when Jeff was drinking, he would ask me if I was in love with Will. For a man who was usually drunk, he seemed to have a sixth sense about some things," Paige told them.

"Paige and I hadn't seen each other for a while until a few months ago. We ran into each other and...we couldn't deny our feelings any longer. We were both miserable."

Sam thought it was time for the question that had been on his mind. "Will, do you have cameras in your headquarters?"

"You mean security cameras? We have some on the outside of the building."

"No inside cameras?"

"No. We saw no reason for cameras inside as long as we have the outside covered."

"Who recommended Trey to you?" Sam asked.

"I met him at one of my functions. He was an impressive young man, a real go-getter. After I met with him a few times, I offered him the position as my campaign manager."

"Did you know Trey worked for Younger?" Hap asked.

Will's eyes flicked from Hap to Sam. "That's impossible."

Hap nodded. "It's true."

Turning to Paige, Will asked, "Did you know?"

Paige shook her head. "No. I had met Trey before, but I can't remember where."

"Not only did Trey work for Younger, he was spying on you for Younger." Sam looked at Mrs. Younger, and added, "I doubt your husband paid Trey through his campaign. If you have no objections, I'll like to see your bank records to see how he was paying Trey."

"I have no objections."

"What proof do you have that Trey was spying for Younger?" Will McNeal asked.

Sam reached in his drawer and pulled out a plastic bag holding the flash drive. He tapped it with his forefinger. "We have video of you and Mrs. Younger in...let's say, an intimate moment. It was taken in your office."

Paige dropped her head into her hands. "I can't believe this."

Will stood, walked to Paige's chair and placed a comforting hand on her back. "There's nothing we can do about it now, Paige. I'm certain they will keep what's on that flash drive confidential."

Paige pulled a tissue from her purse and dabbed at her eyes. "But if this gets out, there goes your chances of becoming governor."

"Will is right, this is confidential. There's no reason anyone should see this. As far as I know, other than Trey, Sam and I are the only two who know what's on this drive," Hap told them.

After Paige and Will left Sam's office, Hap flopped back down in a chair. "You have any bourbon in that desk?"

"Yeah, you left your bottle in here a few weeks ago." Sam opened a drawer, pulled out the bottle of Woodrow's Devil's Due along with two glasses. After he poured a hefty amount in each glass, he leaned over and handed one to Hap.

Hap took a drink, leaned back in the chair and closed his eyes as the bourbon slid down his throat, savoring the slight afterburn. "So what do you think about those two? You think they're being truthful?"

Sam took a drink as he replayed the interview in his mind. "I believed them." After he took another drink of his bourbon, he added, "Honey said something to me the other night and I think she was on to something."

"What was that?"

"She said that she saw McNeal dancing with Mrs. Younger. As she watched them she said McNeal looked at Mrs. Younger like a man in love."

"So you actually believe what they said about falling in love at first sight?" Hap asked, skepticism lacing his words. "Is there really such a thing?"

Sam thought about the first time he saw Honey. He'd been with Hap when they stopped by to see Woodrow, who was at Honey's cottage having dinner. When Honey opened the door, he remembered thinking she was the most beautiful woman he'd ever seen. From that first night, he was hooked. He looked at Hap and held his glass in the air. "Yeah, I guess I do."

Hap took another drink of bourbon. "I thought detectives were more cynical."

"You think I'm wrong?"

Hap shook his head. "Nope. I think you're right. I believed them."

"I know they both have a motive for wanting Younger dead, but..." Sam couldn't explain that sixth sense he had about murderers. It doesn't feel like they are our culprits."

"Yeah, I know what you mean. That piece of the puzzle just doesn't fit," Hap agreed. "But one thing you should know: Jeff Younger was old money. And Will McNeal married into money. Susan McNeal inherited a fortune when her father died."

Sam leaned back in the booth. "And you don't think he'll divorce his piggybank if he becomes governor."

"I hate to be so cynical, but I doubt it. It's possible he thinks he will, but reality will set in if he wins the election, and he'll find that people might frown on leaving the wife for a more attractive version. But then, Mrs. Younger will inherit her husband's fortune and be one wealthy widow," Hap responded.

"Meaning Will wouldn't have anything to lose financially if he divorced and married Mrs. Younger," Sam replied.

Sam looked out the window, thinking about all of the suspects in the case. "Hap, we can't lose sight of motive. We have so many choices in this case: money, lust, love, or plain old hate. Someone who knew Younger killed him. I'd say that someone had a lot of pent-up anger."

"You know, even though Younger ticked off everyone he knew, he seemed to save most of his animosity for one person—Terry Meiners."

Sam nodded. "Yeah. But everyone, including Woodrow and Honey, says Terry displayed considerable restraint with Younger. He could have easily punched Younger one time and he would've been on his butt, which I would have been inclined to do."

Swallowing the remainder of his bourbon, Hap set his glass on Sam's desk. "Maybe Terry had finally had enough of Younger's insults. Every man has his limits, and it's entirely possible Terry reached his." Hap leaned back in his chair and shared a possible theory. "Younger pushed Terry over the edge with his smart mouth, and in a moment of rage, Terry whacked him with his golf club."

Sam arched his brow at Hap. "You don't really think Terry had anything to do with this, do you?"

Hap stood and walked to the window. "Heck, I don't know anymore. This is one strange case. I mean, how many times do you hear comments during an interview like Paul Revere was arguing with Napoleon; Lincoln looked like he was ready to challenge Napoleon to a duel, Mary Todd was dancing with John Wilkes Booth, Buffalo Bill Cody was seen in a heated discussion with Napoleon, Josephine was seen going out the door with Lincoln, or Napoleon was chatting it up with a saloon gal, and a woman dressed as a high-class French prostitute." Hap turned back to Sam and shook his head. "Geez, I'm beginning to feel like I just fell down the rabbit hole."

Sam couldn't help but chuckle at Hap's view of the case. "When you think about it, we have no shortage of suspects." He leaned forward in his chair. "Wasn't Gloria Barnes one of the saloon girls?"

"She was, and she seemed scared to death of Younger."

Sam polished off his drink and set his glass by Hap's on the desk. "Nothing about this case is easy."

Hap sat down again and glanced at his glass, thinking about having another. "And you're not convinced Terry should be a suspect?"

"I can't see it, but no one is totally off my radar." Sam pulled the bottle of bourbon from the drawer again and poured another two fingers in each glass. "Not even Paige Younger, no matter if I believe their love story. If she inherits Younger's fortune that could solve a lot of problems for them if they decide to marry."

"I asked Officer Reed to find out all he could about Terry's confrontations with Younger. I have a feeling there's more there than we know."

"I guess it's possible, Hap. Yet, I've seen no evidence that Terry has that kind of pent-up anger."

Hap swirled the bourbon in his glass as he considered Terry as a suspect. "Maybe he hides his anger better than most. No one can be as calm as he seems all of the time." He looked at Sam and said, "Changing the subject, I haven't had a chance to tell you that Gloria Barnes told me that Trey gave her the flash drive the morning he was murdered. Apparently, he'd spent the night at her home, and before he left that morning, he told her he was going to have a meeting with Younger."

"Considering that, Younger would be our number one suspect in Trey's murder."

"Yeah, but can we prove it?" Hap asked.

"I bet Lela Knight knows about that meeting."

CHAPTER TWENTY-ONE

Early the next morning Hap was at Mrs. Younger's door to pick up her husband's financial records. At the same time, Sam was at Lela Knight's door planning to ask her questions about Younger's relationship with Trey Sullivan.

Sam wasn't surprised when Lela opened the door dressed in a nearly transparent short nightgown.

"Detective, I didn't expect to see you again so soon."

"I apologize for the early hour, but I have a few more questions."

Lela motioned him inside. "Please have a seat. Could I get you some coffee?"

"No, thank you." Sam followed her to the living room. He thought he heard a shower running, but when she didn't leave the room to turn it off, he assumed she might have been doing laundry. Maybe that was the reason she was half dressed—well, almost half.

Lela took a seat across from him and crossed her bare legs. "What can I do for you, Detective?"

Sam tried to keep his eyes above her neck. "I can wait if you'd like to dress."

She smiled at him. "I'm fine. Go ahead and ask your questions."

He no longer heard water running. "What can you tell me about Younger's relationship with Trey Sullivan?"

"Lela, what did you do with my shirt?"

Sam turned to see Aaron Branson towel-drying his wet hair. When Aaron pulled the towel from his head, he saw Sam sitting there. Sam almost smiled when Aaron quickly wrapped the towel around his waist. *She definitely wasn't doing the laundry.*

Aaron inclined his head at Sam. "Detective, I apologize, I didn't realize you were here."

Sam arched his brow at him. "Branson. Why don't both of you get dressed. I have a few questions for you as well." He watched Aaron's eyes slide over Lela's nightgown.

"We'll only be a minute," Aaron said.

Lela expelled a loud breath as she stood. "If I must." She leaned over and placed her cup on the coffee table in front of Sam. "If you want coffee, help yourself."

"Thanks."

Three minutes later, Aaron took a seat on the sofa and asked, "What's on your mind, Detective?"

Sam waited until Lela was seated before he started his questions. "What can you tell me about Younger's relationship with Trey Sullivan?"

"I know they were acquainted," Lela answered first.

"Lela's right, they knew each other," Aaron said.

"Did Trey work for Younger?"

"I don't think so." Lela glanced at Aaron. "Did he?"

Aaron shook his head. "I'm really not sure. I was with Mr. Younger several times when we ran into Trey, and I could tell they knew each other well. I asked Mr. Younger how he knew Trey and he just said they'd met on several occasions."

"The initials TS were on Jeff's cell phone contact list," Lela told him.

Sam couldn't confirm her information since they hadn't found Younger's cell phone. "Did you ask him about it?"

"He told me it was a business contact."

Sam looked at Aaron. "What did Younger and Trey discuss when you saw them together?"

"Nothing of consequence. I did overhear Trey tell Mr. Younger one time that he needed to talk to him."

"Did either of you know that Trey was supposed to meet Younger on the day of his death?"

Lela shook her head. "Jeff didn't mention a meeting to me."

"Why would they meet? Did they meet on Woodrow's property?" Aaron asked.

Instead of answering, Sam asked, "Did either one of you notice a camera in Younger's office?"

"I did," Aaron answered. "I pointed it out to Mr. Younger, and he was surprised it was there. We had no idea who put it there."

Sam reached his car and called Hap. "Hap, Lela said she thought Younger and Trey were acquainted, but that's all she knew. Aaron was the one who spotted the camera in Younger's office. He said Younger didn't know it was there. We need to find Trey Sullivan's phone and Younger's phone."

"You're think Younger is responsible for Trey's murder?"

"Yeah, I have a feeling when Younger saw that camera in his office, he probably figured out that Trey was responsible. I imagine Trey was planning on a little blackmail."

"I have Younger's bank records; I'll go back to see Mrs. Younger and see if she has her husband's phone." Hap turned his vehicle around.

"Why don't you ask if she has any laptops that don't belong to her husband? Trey might have downloaded the video to a computer. You might look at any computers while you're there."

"I will, but have you seen Younger's house? It looks like the White House, it'd take her a month to find her husband's phone if it was hidden." Hap glanced at his watch. "Give me thirty minutes and I'll buy you a club sandwich for lunch and we'll compare notes."

Sam laughed. "I have to stop eating with you or I'll have a dad bod before I know it."

"See you at the diner."

Theo tapped on Honey's open office door and Elvis ran to greet him. "I stopped by to see if you had time for lunch."

"I have an appointment at one thirty, so it will have to be somewhere close by."

"Woodrow told me the diner has great club sandwiches with lots of bacon."

Honey laughed at his newfound love of bacon. "They're very good." She opened her desk drawer where she kept treats for Elvis. After she placed a couple of bones in his bowl, she stroked his head. "You'll have to stay here and wait for me."

Theo petted Elvis goodbye. "Wish we could take him with us."

"Me too." Honey grabbed her handbag.

"I'll bring you some bacon, buddy."

Theo and Honey slid into a booth just as Sam and Hap walked through the door. As was his habit, Sam surveyed the room as he walked to his table, and his eyes locked onto Honey.

Hap saw Honey at the same time. "Let's go join them." Before Sam could comment, Hap told the waitress they saw some friends at another table. Reaching their table, Hap nodded to Honey and shook Theo's hand. "Good to see you again." He motioned for Theo to move over. "How are you two doing?"

Following Hap's lead, Sam sat down beside Honey, but unlike Hap, he didn't ask her to move over. When his thigh touched hers, she moved closer to the wall.

Sam moved his long leg to the side until his knee was still touching hers. "What are you two doing here?"

"We were going to have lunch," Honey replied.

"Sam and I had the same idea. Do you mind if we join you? I have a few more questions for you."

"We didn't plan on a business lunch," Theo replied, none too pleased with the interruption.

"Theo, Sam enjoys interrogating his suspects over lunch." Though Honey was smiling, her tone was dripping with sarcasm.

Sam turned and looked at her. "There's a difference between interviewing individuals who can provide information and interrogating suspects."

"Oh, that's right, you only interview *certain* people over lunch. What do you do afterward, take them home with you?" Honey asked sweetly.

"No, I'm more thorough. It generally involves taking suspects to the station, shining a bright light in their face, turning up the heat, and screaming in their face."

Theo's and Hap's eyes bounced from Honey to Sam.

Before Honey could form a snappy comeback, the waitress appeared, and they all ordered club sandwiches. Theo ordered extra bacon.

"Their club sandwiches come with a lot of bacon, Theo," Hap told him.

"The extra bacon is for Elvis."

Sam noticed Honey gave Theo a warm smile. Theo had already figured out the way to Honey's heart was straight through Elvis. Sam glanced across the table at Hap, but Hap's reply was a slight shrug. Still, Sam felt like he could hear Hap's thoughts. *Well, son, you got yourself a big problem here.* Sam didn't know what questions Hap had for them, so he was interested to hear how he was going to improvise. To his surprise, all throughout lunch Hap managed to ask questions as though they were planned. Sam was impressed.

"Sam and I are looking for Younger's cell phone. If Elvis happens to find it on his outings, let me know."

Honey started to respond, but Sam's phone rang. He'd placed his phone on the table when he sat down beside Honey.

Honey automatically looked at the screen. Liz Simmons. She glanced up at Sam, whose eyes were also on the screen. "You should answer that call."

Sam stared at her. "I have no interest in that call." Sam wasn't about to tell her that Liz had been blowing his phone up since she'd left Kentucky. He hadn't answered one call, nor had he listened to one voicemail. He told himself he didn't have time nor the desire to deal with Liz's manufactured dramas. He'd even considered changing his number.

Honey was the first to look away. She wondered how many times he'd spoken with Liz since their encounter in the library. She didn't think Sam was lying to her, but she also thought he must have some unfinished business with Liz.

Hap made a comment to Theo, and Honey turned her attention on their conversation, ignoring Sam, which she continued to do for the remainder of their lunch.

After Honey and Theo left the restaurant, Hap gave Sam an apologetic look. "Sorry, I thought I was helping when I interrupted their lunch." When Sam didn't reply, Hap changed the discussion to their case. "I found out something new from Mrs. Younger. It seems her husband's car is also missing."

"His car?" Sam thought about that for a moment. "Since he was the victim, and we had nothing to tie him to Trey's murder before, we had no reason to search his car. Does she think it was stolen?"

"She said she didn't know. I've already checked to see if Younger called in a report. He didn't."

"I'll call Aaron and Lela. They might know where it is."

Hap waggled his eyebrows at him. "Better not let her invite you in this time."

"Oh, I forgot to tell you, Aaron was taking a shower at her condo first thing this morning." Sam went on to tell Hap about his early morning meeting, and how Lela was dressed when she answered her door.

When Hap stopped laughing, he said, "That is one busy gal."

"Seems that way."

"I wonder what she'll do now that Younger's dead."

"I think she's already hooked her wagon to Aaron. I imagine he'll be running for some office before long."

Hap's phone buzzed and Hap read the text. "The boys matched up some of the prints on Terry's putter. All but one thumb print match Woodrow's guests, no hits on that one."

They stood to leave and Sam said, "I'll stop by the McNeals' after my other interviews, to find out if his computer turned up. I should be back at the station around nine tonight."

Sam had an exhausting day, but he still had to stop by the McNeals' and meet Hap at the station. He hoped he wasn't too late because he wanted to call Honey on his way home. After her comments at lunch, he didn't know if she would want to talk to him or not. But he wasn't ready to wave the white flag yet. If he lost out to Theo, it wouldn't be because he quit making an effort.

Will McNeal wasn't home, and his wife said he was attending a fundraising event that didn't require her attendance. Susan McNeal invited Sam inside and politely answered his questions.

"Mrs. McNeal, I understand that you and your husband were close friends with Younger and his wife."

"Yes, at one time. Will and I used to play golf with them every week."

"What happened?"

"Jeff was a heavy drinker, and the more he drank, the more outrageous he became. He would become flirtatious and Will grew tired of his antics."

"Younger flirted with you?"

She gave Sam a slight smile. "Does that surprise you, Detective?"

It did surprise Sam, but he was gracious enough not to admit that fact. He figured Younger flirted with her to get under Will's skin. "Is Will normally jealous?"

Susan looked away. "No, not really, but Jeff was obnoxious when he drank. It got out of hand."

"Are you and Mrs. Younger still friends?"

"No, we no longer see each other. I imagine she was tired of Jeff's behavior as well."

Driving to the station, Sam replayed their conversation in his mind. One thing he had to say about Younger, he seemed to have a preference for attractive women. His wife and Lela were both very attractive women. Susan McNeal was a nice woman, but she wasn't exactly the type of woman who would have interested Younger. Sam thought if Younger made advances toward her, he was trying to anger her husband.

Sam had removed his jacket when an officer popped his head in his office door and told him a woman was in the lobby asking for him.

Sam hoped whoever wanted to see him would make it quick. He wanted to grab some food on his way home, have a hot shower, and call Honey. On reaching the lobby, he heard the door open and when he glanced that way, he saw Honey walking inside. He altered course and headed in her direction.

Honey drove to the station to apologize in person for the way she'd treated him at the diner. "Sam..."

"Oh, Sam!" Liz Simmons was sitting in the lobby, and as soon as she saw Sam she jumped from her chair and ran to him, throwing her arms around his neck. "I've been calling and calling. I had to see you."

It took Sam a couple of seconds to figure out what was going on. One minute, he was surprised to see Honey walking through the door, and a heartbeat later, Liz, the octopus, was clinging to him. He saw the look on Honey's face as she did an about-face and hurried out the door. Sam pulled Liz's arms from his neck, shoved her aside and ran after Honey.

Honey had opened the door to her Jeep when Sam caught up to her. "Honey, wait!" He grabbed the door before she could slam it in his face.

"Did you need something? Is something wrong?" Sam asked.

Honey stared at him a moment, reminding herself to stay calm. "No, nothing's wrong. I just came by to apologize to you about the way I behaved at the diner this afternoon. I had no reason to be unpleasant."

Sam was surprised and relieved by her admission. "I was going to call you on my way home to ask if you were ever going to forgive me."

Honey pointed to the station lobby. "You better go back, I'm sure she's waiting for you."

"Honey, I don't know why she's here. I haven't talked to her since she left. She's called several times and left messages, but I didn't listen to them."

"Well, she's here and not in Texas, so I guess you're stuck with her."

"No, I'm not. There is nothing between us. I'll call Cam to find out what's going on."

Honey saw Liz walk out the door, headed in their direction. "She's coming to get you. Three's a crowd, so I'm leaving." She pulled the door closed and backed out of the parking lot. As she drove away, she looked in her rearview mirror and saw Liz reach for Sam's arm.

Exasperated, Sam shook off her hand. "Liz, why are you here?"

"I broke my engagement with Cam."

"I would ask why, but I don't care. That still doesn't explain why you're here."

"I told Cam about us. I had to be honest about my feelings for you."

Sam's patience was exhausted. "There is no us."

Liz gripped his arm again. "Sam, you know you still care about me."

Sam sighed loudly. He didn't want to be cruel, but she left him no choice. "No, I don't care about you. You need to go back to Texas, there's nothing for you here."

"Sam, talk to me. We've had too much between us, I know you care about me."

Sam turned away and walked toward the station. Liz followed him. He didn't stop until he reached his office. He took a deep breath, trying to calm down before he turned to face her. "I will get someone to drive you to your hotel."

"I thought I would stay with you," Liz responded.

"You are not staying with me."

"Sam, are you ready to go over our notes?" Hap was looking at some papers when he entered Sam's office and didn't notice Liz at first. When he saw her, he looked at Sam. "Sorry, I didn't know you were with someone."

"Liz is leaving. I'm going to find someone to drive her to a hotel."

"Sam…" Liz started, but stopped when he gave her a stern look.

Hap thought Sam looked as though he wanted to strangle the woman. "We can do this in the morning. I can drive her to a hotel."

"I appreciate that, Hap." He walked over to Liz, leaned down until he was mere inches from her face. "I'm going to call Cam. I want him to hear it from me that there is nothing between us. I don't know what game you're playing, but it's not going to involve me. I've known Cam since kindergarten, and I will not allow you to destroy our friendship."

Liz glared at him. "If you don't still care about me, why didn't you tell your current girlfriend about our past?"

"Liz, I didn't tell Honey because I was embarrassed that a woman I was engaged to had such low moral standards that she would sleep with another man in my bed." Sam didn't worry about embarrassing Liz in front of Hap. It was the truth. "I'm in love with Honey. Now, you'd best get the next flight back to Dallas. This is the last time you'll see me. If you come here again, I'll find some reason to arrest you."

Hap escorted Liz out the door, and Sam sat at his desk and pulled out Hap's bottle of bourbon. He poured a healthy shot into his empty coffee cup. He tossed it back, then poured another. He needed to call Cam. He wanted to call Honey. Pulling out his phone, he pushed Honey's number, but it went directly to voicemail. He left her a message saying Hap was driving Liz to a hotel, or the airport. He asked her to call him when she felt like talking. His next call was to Cam. He explained to Cam the real reason he'd broken his engagement to Liz. "Cam, she doesn't love me. She resented the fact that she didn't break it off with me first. I'm sorry you're upset, but I think one day you'll be glad that she walked away."

On his drive home, Sam thought about his conversation with Cam. He was thankful Cam believed him, and he knew he'd get over his broken heart. Sam didn't think it would be as easy for him to get over Honey if she didn't forgive him.

CHAPTER TWENTY-TWO

Honey was walking out the front door of her cottage when Sam pulled up the next morning. As usual, Elvis ran to him as soon as he opened his car door. Relieved to see Elvis wasn't mad at him, he pulled a big bone from his pocket. Glancing at Honey, he said, "Can I give this to him?"

"Sure." Even though she was upset with Sam, she wouldn't deny Elvis his treats.

Once Elvis trotted off with a big bone between his teeth, Sam got out of his car. "Can we talk?"

"I was just leaving for work."

Sam walked to her Jeep and leaned against the door. "Please give me a minute."

Honey looked at him. He looked so tired that she felt a pang of guilt, mixed with regret. "You look like you've had a long night."

"Well, it isn't for the reason you're probably thinking. I told Liz if I saw her again, I would find a reason to arrest her. Hap took her to a hotel, and that's the last I will ever see of her."

"So you said in your message."

"I talked to Cam and told him the reason I broke it off. I told him he was better off if he didn't take her back."

"Is he upset with you?"

"No, we're good friends, and he believed I didn't encourage her in any way. I hope you believe me too."

"Sam, I do believe you. The only thing I can't understand is why you didn't tell me in the first place about Liz."

Sam reached for her hand. "Do you forgive me?"

"There's nothing to forgive. I came by the station last night to apologize to you for being so obstinate."

Sam brought her hand to his lips. "We're both obstinate."

"I guess that's true."

"Will you give me a chance to make it up to you?"

"There nothing to make up. You know how I feel, and I do believe that you would have told me...eventually."

"Where do we go from here?"

Honey thought about his question for a minute. "We'll take it slow and see what happens."

"Guess I'll have to compete with Theo."

"It's not a competition."

Sam smiled, thinking she didn't understand men at all if she thought Theo wasn't planning on being stiff competition for her affection. "Of course it is." He thought he should remind her of what they had between them. He leaned down, placed his palm on the back of her neck, gently urging her closer. Then he kissed her. It was a long, intimate kiss, one they hadn't shared in way too long. When his mouth left hers, he found it encouraging to feel the pulse in her neck kick up a few beats. *Game on, Theo*. He said goodbye to Elvis and walked back to his car.

When he snapped his seat belt in place, he looked at her through the window. He couldn't help but smile at the dazed look on her face. He didn't want to walk away after that kiss, but he would take it slow, like she suggested. He waved and drove off.

By noon, Sam had interviewed five people, and he decided to stop by Lela Knight's house to see if she knew anything about Younger's car. He called Hap on the way to tell him where he was and they agreed to meet back at the station after their interviews.

"Son, be careful if she opens her door in her nightgown again, you might want to back away, or call me."

Sam laughed. "I think I can handle it."

To Sam's surprise, Lela answered her door fully dressed in jeans and a sweater. "Hi, Detective, you're the best thing that's happened to me today." She invited him inside, but Sam declined.

"I have one question for you. It seems Younger's car is missing. You wouldn't happen to know where we can find it, do you?"

Lela's eyes widened. "I totally forgot about it. It's in the back of the condo in the parking lot."

"Are you sure?"

Lela nodded her head. "He came by the morning of the party. We stayed in bed all morning, then after lunch we had a few drinks and he didn't want to drive home. Aaron had arranged to have a limo available for him for the day, so I called the service to pick him up and take him home."

"You wouldn't happen to have the keys, would you?"

Lela smiled at him, walked to the kitchen and opened a drawer. "Yes, I have his second set."

On the way to the car, Lela apologized again for forgetting that Jeff had left it there.

"No problem, a lot has happened in a few days." Sam believed she actually did forget about the car. "Is there any way that Aaron knew the car was here?"

"No, Aaron parks in my garage. It's a two-car garage and I only use one spot. Aaron is always worried someone will see him here. Jeff never worried about being seen."

They reached the car and Sam told Lela not to touch anything. He unlocked the door and looked inside, but there wasn't anything on the seats or floorboards. When he popped open the trunk, he smiled. Lying in plain view was what he assumed was Trey's missing laptop and also a cell phone.

Lela was standing to the side and pointed to the phone. "That's not Jeff's phone."

Sam glanced at her. "You're sure?"

"Yes, I was with him when he bought a new phone a couple of months ago. It was gold, not silver."

Behind the laptop, Sam saw a jacket rolled up in a ball. He pulled a pen from his pocket, unfurled the jacket and found a pistol tucked inside. What looked to be dried blood stains covered the front of the jacket.

Lela backed up a step. "Is that...blood?"

"I'd say that's a good guess."

Sam pulled out his cell phone and called Hap. When he ended the conversation, he closed the trunk, locked the car and walked back with Lela to her condo to wait for the team.

While they waited, Lela poured Sam a cup of coffee. "Do you think Jeff killed Trey Sullivan?"

"I don't know."

"Jeff met me the day Trey Sullivan was killed. I remember because he'd played golf, then called me late and asked me to meet him at a restaurant."

Sam pulled out his notepad. "What did he talk about that night?"

"He was late and I almost left. He said he'd played golf, and that he and Will McNeal argued on the golf course. He also told me he stopped by Woodrow's to apologize for his behavior on the golf course. He told me Terry Meiners was there and he exchanged words with him. Of course, he'd been drinking, as usual." She stopped and thought back to that day. "He told me about Trey's murder, and I remember he said Trey got what he deserved." She looked at Sam, and added, "I thought that was an odd statement since I didn't think he knew him well."

Sam made a note to check the time Trey's murder hit the news. "Can you remember anything else? Did he seem nervous?"

"No, I could tell he'd been drinking, but he wasn't nervous. He wanted to hurry back to my condo. The first thing he did when we got here was make himself a drink. I'm not even certain why he even came home with me. He'd drunk so much that he passed out in my bed. I told him he could drink at home and not to waste my time. His wife called his cell phone several times while he was here."

Once Sam showed Hap the contents in the trunk, Hap said, "It looks like you were right about Younger committing the first murder. I'd say we just found the murder weapon."

One of the officers searching the car walked over to Hap and Sam and held up a plastic bag. "This was wedged between the front seat and the console."

Hap noted the bourbon bottle was half empty. "The man knew good bourbon."

Lela says the phone is not Younger's. My guess is it belonged to Trey Sullivan. Let's get it charged to see what it tells us."

Back at the station, Hap discussed his morning interviews with Sam. "Sam, I had three people tell me today that they witnessed Terry, or a blue-eyed Paul Revere, and Jeff Younger in an argument."

"I had two people tell me the same thing. I asked how they knew it was Terry, and they both said they were close enough to see his blue eyes."

Hap threw his pencil on his desk. "I know you don't think he's a potential suspect, but we need to interview him."

Sam didn't think Terry was involved, yet he had to interview him to eliminate him as a suspect. "I'll call and have him come to the station. We'll keep it quiet, make it appear to be a social visit."

"Sounds good."

Honey begged off having dinner with Woodrow and his guests. It had been a long, tiring day, and she wanted some time alone to think. Specifically, she wanted to think about the kiss she'd shared with Sam that morning. Though she couldn't forget he'd omitted telling her of his engagement, she couldn't deny she still had strong feelings for him.

After a long walk with Elvis, she made herself a salad for dinner, then decided to relax in a bubble bath. She'd almost dozed off in the tub when Elvis ran from the room and headed to the front door. Jumping from the tub, Honey tied her robe around her without toweling off and hurried to the door. Before she reached the door, she figured it was Sam by the way Elvis was jumping around.

Through the sidelight, Sam saw she was wearing a silk robe and he thought he might die of a heart attack. She'd obviously been in the tub and hadn't dried before donning her robe. It was clinging to her in all of the right places. "I hope you don't answer the door like this for just anyone." He was thinking specifically of Theo.

"I was in the tub."

"I'm not complaining, I'm happy it was me at the door." He leaned over and kissed her cheek. Since he knew he was still more than halfway in the doghouse, he thought he should change his focus before he said or did something really stupid. He kneeled down and rubbed Elvis's back.

Honey looked down to see her robe was now completely wet. "Excuse me, I'll get dressed. You know where everything is if you want something."

Sam watched her walk away. "Elvis, are you saying good things about me? Let's go find you a bone." Elvis trotted along beside him to the kitchen. "If you promise to be on my side, I'll buy you a year's worth of your favorite bones." Sam reached into the pantry and pulled out some treats. "I know I haven't been around much lately, but I hope to make it up to you and your master."

Elvis looked up at him with his big dark eyes, cocked his head and emitted a forlorn sound.

Sam handed him a treat and rubbed his head. "I've missed you too."

Elvis licked his hand before accepting his bone.

"You know, Elvis, I think I'm going to need your help."

"Are you trying to bribe my dog?" Honey asked.

Sam whirled around to see her standing there in yoga pants and a tee shirt. "How long have you been listening?"

Honey arched her eyebrows and smiled. "Long enough."

"At least I can score points with him. Can I bribe you?"

"Flowers work," Honey teased and walked to the refrigerator. She looked up at him and asked, "Need a snack?"

"What do you have?"

Honey opened the refrigerator and pushed containers around on the shelves. "Sushi?"

"You're not serious. That's not food, that's fish bait."

Honey smiled at him. "Elvis doesn't like it either."

"Do you have any bourbon balls?"

She saw the hopeful look on his face. "Sorry to say, not one bourbon ball. Theo ate them all."

Sam looked at Elvis and whispered in his ear, "Another reason to kick his butt."

Honey stuck her head in the freezer. "Ice cream?"

"Yes, if you have chocolate syrup." Sam knew she always had vanilla ice cream in her freezer.

Pulling out a tub of ice cream, Honey turned to him. "And I do have chocolate syrup."

As she was scooping ice cream into a bowl, Sam leaned over and kissed her behind her ear. "I've missed you and nights like this."

"I was beginning to think you were avoiding our evenings here," Honey admitted.

Sam shook his head. "That will never happen."

Honey turned to look at him, and she noticed he was wearing his vest under his shirt again. "Would you like a drink?"

"Do you have some iced tea?"

Opening the refrigerator, Honey pulled out a pitcher of tea. Sam filled two glasses with ice and poured the tea.

They sat at the counter sharing a big bowl of ice cream, and Honey asked him about the investigation.

"I'm questioning Terry tomorrow."

Honey stopped eating and frowned at him. "Why on earth are you questioning Terry? Surely, you don't suspect him of anything."

"No, I don't, but I'm not certain Hap is convinced. We have so many people who witnessed arguments between Younger and Terry, that we have no choice but to interview him. Several people say they saw Paul Revere arguing with Younger, and while they didn't identify Terry specifically, they said he had blue eyes."

"Terry does have blue eyes, but he wasn't the only Paul Revere that night with blue eyes."

"Really? Do you always notice a person's eye color?"

Honey smiled at him. "Georgia asked me the same question the first night I met you. She was looking to see if you were wearing a wedding ring, and I told her you had the most beautiful blue eyes I had ever seen. Haven't you heard a person's eyes are the window to their soul?"

"I have, but I can't say it's the first thing I notice."

"Well, there are so many different colors of blue. Maybe they need to be a bit more specific. Terry's eyes are light blue." Honey looked into his eyes. "Yours are turquoise, like the Caribbean waters. Some people have dark blue eyes."

"Windows of the soul, huh? What do you think they tell you about the soul?"

"When I looked into your eyes that first night, I remember thinking I would be scared to death if you interrogated me. While your eyes are striking, you have a steely stare that would intimidate the most hardened criminal. Your eyes look softer when you look at Elvis."

Sam smiled at her. "And what about Terry?"

"I already know that Terry's a genuinely good person. He has the kindest heart of anyone I know." She took another bite of ice cream before she asked, "Haven't you ever noticed how a dog will stare into your eyes? Elvis does it all of the time. I think he sees the soul."

"Maybe that's how he detects criminals," Sam suggested.

"It's possible. Some people are afraid to look a dog in the eye. I think they're afraid of what a dog might see."

"I've heard a dog will feel threatened if you look into their eyes, but I'm not certain I believe that." Sam thought about something she said earlier. "Since you notice everyone's eyes, other than Terry, what other men have blue eyes who wore a Paul Revere costume?"

"Dr. Morgan and Jack Cleary both have blue eyes. The doctor's eyes are a medium blue, and Jack Cleary's eyes are a deep dark blue. I consider both of them friends too, so I hope they don't become suspects."

"I'll go where the evidence leads."

Honey frowned at him. "The next time I find a dead body, I think I'll bury it to keep my friends from going through so much trouble."

Sam stopped eating long enough to grin. "I hope you're teasing, but on the bright side, I'll be the one searching you if I have to arrest you."

Honey smacked him on the arm with her spoon. "You're impossible. I understand interviewing everyone who attended the party, but shouldn't you focus on the ones who golf?"

Sam swallowed a big bite, then asked, "Why just the ones who golf?"

"Well, it was so dark in that area that I thought someone who found the club had to be sure of their skills to hit him in the back of the head and make contact. A golf club certainly wouldn't have been my weapon of choice. Not being a golfer, I would have whiffed the target, particularly in low light." She drew her brows together. "Of course, I guess they could have used it like a club."

Sam knew the details of the injury to Younger's head. "There was only one blow to the head. But if I only considered golfers, Terry would still be on that list."

"You still haven't told me why you might need Elvis's help."

Sam told her about finding Younger's car and his laptop. "But we haven't found his cell phone. If you don't mind, Elvis and I will search around here tomorrow. I'll pick up something belonging to Younger to give him the scent. Has he ever found a cell phone before?"

"Yes, he finds mine for me all of the time."

"How did you train him to do that?"

"I taught him cell phone first, then I trained him as he was trained for other scents."

Sam saw Honey's phone lying on the counter. "Could he tell yours from mine?"

"Of course, by your scent."

"I want to see this. Will you take him in the other room while I hide our phones?"

Honey stood and motioned for Elvis to follow. "Come on, Elvis, let's show Sam how smart you are."

They left the room and Sam tucked Honey's cell phone in his back pocket, and placed his phone on top of the refrigerator. He called out for them to come back in the room.

Before Honey reached the kitchen, she gave Elvis his instructions. "Find my cell phone."

Sam watched Elvis sniff the air in the living room. He held his nose in the air as he made his way to the kitchen where Sam was standing, leaning against a counter. Within seconds Elvis walked up to Sam, put his nose on his back pocket. He barked and looked at Honey.

Sam pulled Honey's phone from his back pocket and held it for her to see. He reached down and rubbed Elvis's back. "Elvis, you are one special dog. That deserves a big treat." Once he pulled another bone from the pantry, he grabbed a jar of peanut butter and spread a healthy portion on the bone. Elvis was drooling before Sam handed it to him.

"Now you've done it. He'll want to find things all night for more peanut butter," Honey teased.

"I'll stay all night and feed him," Sam replied, grinning at her.

Honey shook her head at him, but she was smiling. "Finish your ice cream."

"Aren't you going to help me?"

"I'm trying to lose a few pounds."

Sam eyed her curves. "You look perfect to me."

"Just for that, you get more chocolate." She picked up the syrup and drizzled a healthy portion on the remaining vanilla.

They sat back down at the counter and Sam asked, "Would it be okay if I come by in the morning to search for the phone?"

"Sure, you know Elvis loves to be with you, whether he's playing or working." She watched Elvis nudge Sam's arm, his way of telling him he wanted more peanut butter. Honey realized how much he'd missed Sam. Problem was, Elvis liked Theo too.

CHAPTER TWENTY-THREE

Terry Meiners arrived at the police station carrying two huge boxes of donuts. Sam met him in the lobby and laughed when he saw the boxes from one of the best bakeries. "I guess you believe the stories you've heard about cops and donuts."

"I've interviewed a lot of cops and not one has ever turned down a good donut."

"They don't have to be good. Come on back to my office. I made some fresh coffee, and I even washed the cups." Sam made sure anyone overhearing their conversation would think Terry's visit was strictly personal. When they reached Sam's office, Sam pointed to the boxes and said, "You better have something in there with a lot of chocolate icing, or I might have to put you in the slammer."

Terry opened one of the boxes as Sam poured the coffee. "You're in luck. Lots of chocolate in here."

Once they'd polished off several donuts, Sam stood and closed his office door. "As far as anyone knows, this is a personal visit."

"I appreciate that."

"Terry, nearly everyone we've spoken to who attended the party have told us they saw you and Younger arguing. Now, for the record, I don't think you had anything to do with his murder, but I want you to fill me in on what was going on with Younger that night."

Terry leaned back in his chair and shook his head. "Each time I left the stage, Younger would approach me complaining about the same thing he's complained about for months. He said I gave more airtime to his competitor. He was drunk, as I'm sure every guest can corroborate."

"Did you argue with him?"

"Not really. The last time he approached me, I told him that he needed to stay off of the sauce because his arguments were getting stale."

"How many times did the two of you exchange words?" Sam asked.

"I lost count. The man was irrational when he was drinking, and lately that seemed to be his usual state. I've smelled alcohol on him when I've interviewed him in the middle of the day. I guess you could say he was a functional drunk, but he was still irrational and argumentative. I've tried to ignore him."

"Do you have any idea who hated him enough to want him dead?"

"I can't see any reason for anyone to want him dead, but I wasn't married to him." Realizing what he'd said, Terry held up his hand and added, "I'm not saying his wife wanted him dead. She is a nice woman who didn't deserve the way he treated her."

"Did you give more airtime to McNeal?"

"Absolutely not. Younger was delusional. He'd convinced himself I was going to vote for McNeal. I told him I have listeners who were fans of McNeal's who say I gave Younger more time when I interview him. I try to be fair to everyone. I want my listeners to hear both sides, and it's not about my opinion."

"Did you like Younger?"

"I interview a lot of people who I wouldn't socialize with," Terry replied evasively.

Sam arched a brow at him.

"He wasn't my favorite guest."

"What about McNeal?"

"He's a much more pleasant politician, and seems like a nice guy, but I don't know him as well as Younger thought."

"Why did you take your putter to Woodrow's?" Sam asked.

"I was going to his house to check out the ballroom. He told me earlier in the day he'd like to hit a few balls with it, so I brought it along with me."

"Who was at Woodrow's house when you arrived?"

"Woodrow, his guests from England, Honey, and then Younger showed up. As I was leaving, I saw McNeal at Woodrow's gate."

This was new information to Sam. "Are you certain it was McNeal?"

"Yes. I waved to him."

Sam made a note on his pad to ask Woodrow why McNeal was there.

"Did you ever find out whose prints were on my phone?" Terry asked.

"Not yet."

Terry took a drink of his coffee. "Looks like I could be your number one suspect considering the golf club was mine and I lost my phone. Is it possible someone wanted to frame me?"

"Do you have any enemies besides Younger?"

"I wouldn't have considered Younger an enemy. In my profession, I often have people who disagree with me, but I can't think of anyone who I would consider my enemy."

"Younger's campaign manager, Aaron Branson, told me that he also thought you were partial to McNeal."

Terry's eyes widened in surprise. "You're kidding? I thought he had more sense than that."

Sam silently wondered if Branson might have a reason to throw suspicion on Terry.

Setting his coffee cup aside, Terry leaned forward and looked Sam in the eye. "Sam, I know you don't know me well, but do you think I killed Younger?"

Sam didn't hesitate to answer honestly. "No, I don't."

Terry took a deep breath and leaned back in his chair. "Thank you for that."

"When you were in the tent having something to eat that night, do you remember who was in the room at that time?"

"I spoke to Honey and Theo. I also talked with Georgia and Preston. I saw Younger again, and I thought he might have followed me in there to continue his tirade. Fortunately, Annie Oakley and Buffalo Bill Cody joined me, and Younger turned his attention on some saloon girl."

Sam rubbed his forehead and groaned. He didn't feel like referring to his notes to see who was wearing those costumes. "Now who were Annie Oakley and Buffalo Bill Cody?"

Terry laughed. "Sharon and Rudy Lewis. I didn't recognize the saloon girl. Mrs. Younger talked to me for a while, and I figured I'd be safe from Younger's venom as long as his wife was around."

"Why do you say that?"

"It seemed he was trying to stay far away from his wife. I noticed he didn't even dance with her once."

"Anyone else talk to you while you were in the tent?"

"Susan McNeal."

"What about her husband?"

"I saw him several times, but I didn't see him in the tent. I also spoke with one of the Paul Reveres. It was Theo's friend, Jacob. We compared our costumes, and they were surprisingly similar even though his was made in England."

"And you're certain you left your phone on the table in the tent?"

"I guess I can't swear to it, but I remember it vibrated in my pocket. That's the only time I remember looking at it that night. I didn't realize I'd lost it until I got home."

Sam was silent for a moment, absently tapping his pen on his notepad, trying to make sense of Younger's anger toward Terry. Finally, he asked, "How long had you known Younger?"

"Years. In the past, we've played in some golf tournaments, always opposing teams, but we were friendly enough."

"When did his attitude toward you change?"

Terry looked at Sam and furrowed his brow. "Good question." He grew quiet as he thought about his relationship with Younger through the years. "I never really thought about it, but I guess it was a few years ago when I saw a change. We were playing in a tournament for charity, and Younger and his partner were leading most of the time. As it turned out, my partner and I both had a good day on the course, and we came out on the winning end. Younger wasn't a gracious loser that day, not to me or to my partner."

"Why do you think he was so angry that he lost?"

"He was never at his best when he lost, but that day he was worse than ever. Later, there was talk around the golf course that he'd made a large wager on the game. He bet on himself to win. Word was, he'd been drinking heavily and he bet large that day."

"How big a wager?" Sam asked.

"I heard it was a twenty-five-thousand-dollar gamble."

Sam let out a low whistle. "I guess that could make someone a bit angry. Who bet against him?"

"I heard it was Jack Cleary."

"Jack Cleary of Cleary's Distillery? K. C. Cleary's brother?" Sam asked, thinking about the first murder he investigated when he came to Bardstown. K. C. Cleary was the victim.

Terry nodded. "That's the one."

"Was Younger that good of a golfer?"

"He was before the booze got the best of him."

"How did you manage to keep your cool with Younger? I might have been tempted to punch his lights out." Sam chuckled and added, "But you didn't hear that from me."

"It would take more than Younger to get under my skin. I guess I felt sorry for him. I knew it was the alcohol, and there was no reason for me to respond in kind."

Sam nodded. Honey was right. Terry was a genuinely good guy. "You're a better man than most."

Not long after Terry left Sam's office, Hap walked in carrying the laptop found in Younger's car. "How did the interview with Terry go?"

"Good. He spoke to a few people in the tent, and he thought he'd left his phone on the table while he was eating."

Hap pulled a chair close to Sam's desk and situated the laptop so they could both see the screen. "You still think Terry's not involved in any way?"

"There is no way Terry is involved with this murder." Sam gave Hap the highlights of his conversation with Terry. "I've talked to several of his lifelong friends who said they have only seen Terry angry one time in all of the years they've known him."

Hap arched his brow. "Only once?"

"Yeah, and it was a long time ago. He was in college playing a pickup basketball game with friends. One guy they didn't know was playing on the other team, and he apparently thought Terry fouled him. The guy cold-cocked Terry from behind and took off running. That's the only time Terry's friends could recall seeing him angry."

"Did Terry go after the guy?"

"No, he was dazed and the guy ran off."

"I still say it's possible Terry finally had enough of Younger's insults. I'm not ready to eliminate him from our list." Hap tapped the laptop. "The boys pulled Younger's prints from the laptop, as well as Trey Sullivan's. They told me the password to Trey's email account, so let's see who he was corresponding with."

Within a few minutes, they found emails that Trey had written to Younger. Trey's last email to Younger said he had something on video that he definitely wanted to see, which would force McNeal out of the race for governor. Sullivan told Younger to bring the cash with him to their meeting. Younger replied to the email, instructing Trey to meet him on the service road behind Woodrow's estate that afternoon, saying he had to visit Woodrow after their meeting.

Sam opened the file that held the videos from the cameras. They were the same videos that were on the flash drive Hap found in his pocket. "It seems Trey was getting paid for his surveillance work for Younger. Do you think he upped his price once he saw his camera had captured McNeal with Mrs. Younger?"

"No doubt. I'd bet Younger didn't know Trey installed a camera in his own office until he opened this file."

"Maybe Trey had an accomplice in Younger's office," Sam suggested.

"Could be. We need to talk to those folks."

Hap handed Sam a piece of paper. "Here's the numbers pulled from Trey's phone. Some of the numbers were saved by name, but there's a few we need to identify."

"I'll do it later. I need to swing by Mrs. Younger's home and grab something of her husband's for Elvis to use for a scent. I'm searching Woodrow's property tonight for Younger's phone. Assuming Elvis doesn't find the phone, I'll ask Mrs. Younger if she has any objections if we search her home. If she agrees, I'll take Elvis with me to make our life easier. I have a feeling when we find that phone, we'll have the answers to our questions."

"Elvis can find a cell phone?"

Sam told Hap about his cell phone experiment the night before. "He is the most amazing dog."

"You really think the information on Younger's phone will help solve this case?"

"Absolutely. If we can't find it, I think we should subpoena the phone records. If there wasn't incriminating evidence on the phone, why would someone take it?"

"Maybe Younger just lost it," Hap theorized.

"I guess that's possible, but I can't see a politician going without a phone for a day."

Hap closed the laptop and stood. "Let's make some calls, then grab some lunch later. I'll go with you to see Mrs. Younger, and then join you and Elvis for the search."

On the way to see Mrs. Younger, Hap turned on Sam's radio. "Let's hear what Terry has to say today."

The first thing they heard was Terry commenting on the local news, specifically Younger's murder.

"I've been reading comments on social media about the murder of Jeff Younger. Some of you think it's taking the police too long to solve his murder," Terry stated.

Sam glanced at Hap. "Great, that's all we need. The public telling us how to do our job." He turned up the volume.

Terry went on to say, "As sad as it is that Mr. Younger was murdered, you have to understand what a difficult investigation this must be for the police. I'm sure most of you know that I was the master of ceremonies at the masquerade ball that night. The costumes were fantastic, but this is probably the reason it's been difficult for the detectives to narrow down the suspects. Even with the experienced police chief, Hap Nelson, and the infamous detective, Sam Gentry, this case has to be frustrating.

"Can you even imagine the witnesses accounts of what happened that night? The first witness would say something like, *I saw Paul Revere arguing with Josephine Bonaparte.* The second witness might have a different account. *No, it was Buffalo Bill arguing with Doc Holiday.*"

The more Terry joked about the make-believe questioning, the man in the studio with Terry was laughing so hard that he was snorting. Sam and Hap both chuckled.

Terry was on a roll as he continued his mock account of the investigation. "Another account of a witness related that *Queen Victoria and Prince Albert had a tiff in the middle of a waltz.*"

More laughter from the man in the studio with Terry.

Terry didn't slow down. "Napoleon's paramour, Maria Walewska, was seen flirting with George Washington."

Hap chuckled. "It is pretty funny when you think about it."

"It gives me a headache," Sam retorted.

Terry spoke in a falsetto voice for his next rendition of his imaginary witness account. "I saw that floozy Belle Brezing making eyes at Abraham Lincoln." Terry explained to his listeners, "For those of you who don't know, Belle Brezing was the infamous madam whose house of ill repute was located in Lexington. She was said to have owned a very successful high-class establishment. While her costume was intriguing, it failed to come close to Wyatt Earp's girlfriend then wife, Josephine Earp."

Terry's studio companion said, "After your description of Josephine, I wish I had seen that costume."

"You wouldn't have believed it. If you've seen Josephine Earp's photo on the internet, then you know what costume I'm talking about. I think Wyatt Earp spent some time with her."

Hap and Sam exchange another look.

"He's not doing much to help your cause with Honey," Hap commented sheepishly, trying to hold back a laugh.

The man in the studio said to Terry, "I checked Facebook, and someone posted photos of that night. Wow! That Josephine Earp's costume was really something."

Terry laughed. "Wyatt Earp called out Wild Bill Hickok for flirting with his Southern belle, and Annie Oakley had to break up the fight." Terry and his cohort couldn't stop laughing at this point.

Hap couldn't help himself, he laughed along with them.

"Who would have won that gun battle between Wyatt Earp and Wild Bill?" Terry's friend asked.

"Might be a toss-up. Wild Bill looked like he could handle himself. Guess we'll have to wait and see," Terry replied.

The man asked, "Didn't you say that detective handling the Younger murder investigation was Wyatt Earp that night? I bet he liked Josephine's costume. Maybe that's why he didn't notice a man being murdered right under his nose."

Sam reached over and turned off the radio. He wasn't laughing. He hoped Honey wasn't listening to Terry's show today. *Fat chance.*

Hap glanced over at Sam, and seeing his jaw muscle twitching, he prudently decided now was not the time to tease him.

Mrs. Younger opened her door to Hap and Sam and invited them inside. Sam went straight to the purpose of their impromptu visit. "Have you found your husband's cell phone?"

"No, I haven't."

"I'd like to bring a dog with me to search your home," Sam told her.

"I thought dogs found drugs," Mrs. Younger replied.

"This dog can find a cell phone. Of course, you're welcome to watch us the entire time," Sam replied.

"We think if we find your husband's phone, the information on there could help us solve his murder," Hap added.

"Do what you need to do, Detective," Mrs. Younger said.

By her response, Sam didn't think she was trying to hide anything, or perhaps she already knew they wouldn't find anything. "I'd like to borrow one of Mr. Younger's shirts or jackets, something that hasn't been washed."

Mrs. Younger left the room and returned a few minutes later with one of her husband's jackets. "I'm afraid all of his shirts were laundered by my maid, but I remember he wore this jacket recently."

After they scheduled a time for their return, Sam and Hap drove to Honey's.

It was dark by the time Sam, Hap, and Elvis finished searching the grounds for Younger's phone. Having no success, they walked back to

Honey's cottage. Sam tapped on the patio door and slid it open. It didn't improve his mood to see Theo and Chance McComb sitting at the counter talking to Honey while she tossed a salad.

Honey turned and smiled. "Just in time. I've made a huge grilled chicken salad."

Hap and Sam acknowledged the men. Hap walked over to Honey and looked over her shoulder. "Smells good and I'm starving."

"Good, I also have dessert in the oven."

Honey glanced at Sam at the sink washing his hands. She noticed both men were wearing their bulletproof vests under their shirts again. "Any luck?"

"No, it looks like I'll need Elvis tomorrow." Sam opened the pantry and grabbed Elvis's food. After he poured some food in his bowl, he said to Elvis, "Dinner first, before you get a special treat."

Hap took a seat at the counter beside Theo. Seeing a set of architectural plans on the counter, he asked, "Are you building a home, Theo?"

"Yes, Chance and I were going over the drawings."

Hap leaned over and pointed to an area on the drawing. "Is that a wall of glass doors?"

"Yes, they'll open to an outside patio area that will overlook the land."

"You must have purchased a pretty piece of land to have a view like that. Where's it located?" Hap asked.

"Right here. I purchased twenty-five acres from Woodrow."

Sam was in the process of placing his firearm on top of the refrigerator, but he stopped in mid-motion and turned to look at Honey. "Woodrow sold some of his acreage here?"

"Yes, he thought it would be good to have someone else on the property for safety reasons, particularly when he starts traveling," Honey replied.

Though he had more questions, he asked Honey what he could do to help.

"You can pour the wine."

Two bottles had been uncorked, so Sam pulled wineglasses from the rack beneath the counter. "Just five of us tonight?"

"Yes, Jacob and Oliver decided to have dinner in Louisville, and Woodrow is having dinner with your grandmother."

"Did you happen to hear Terry on the radio today?"

"Yes, I did." To his surprise Honey chuckled. He glanced at Hap, but he was conversing with Theo and Chance.

"I thought it was pretty funny. It gave me a new perspective on what you must be dealing with when you interview people," Honey told him.

Sam slid the filled wineglasses in front of the men, then turned back to Honey and casually leaned against the counter. "It's been an unusual investigation."

Elvis walked over to Sam and nudged his hand, letting him know he'd finished his dinner and was expecting his treat.

"Good boy. No, I didn't forget." Sam pulled out some bones and peanut butter. After he smothered the bones in peanut butter, he dropped them in Elvis's empty bowl.

"You're spoiling him," Honey told him as she pulled the freshly made bread from the warming oven.

"He's a hardworking guy who deserves a special treat tonight."

When Sam and Honey sat down at the counter, Theo turned to Sam and said, "Did you hear Terry's program today?"

CHAPTER TWENTY-FOUR

Sam and Mrs. Younger followed Elvis from room to room as Elvis searched for the cell phone.

"Do you remember the last time you saw your husband with his phone?" Sam asked.

"I know he had it at the party, because I saw him texting." She followed Sam and Elvis from room to room. "Hap called me and told me you found his car. Where did you find it?"

Sam saw no reason to keep the truth from her. "Behind Lela Knight's condo."

"I'm not surprised. She doesn't have Jeff's phone at her condo, does she?"

"She said she hasn't seen it, but I plan to take Elvis there if we don't find it here."

By the time Sam returned Elvis to Honey's cottage that night, both he and Elvis were tired. Honey was getting out of her Jeep when Sam pulled into her driveway.

Sam opened his car door and Elvis jumped out and ran to her.

Sam held a bag in the air. "Elvis has worked hard today, so he told me to stop and buy burgers."

"They smell wonderful." Honey gave Elvis a kiss on the top of his head, which perked him up.

"Where's my kisses?" Sam asked.

Taking the bait, Honey reached up and pulled his face down to her level and kissed his cheek.

"Is that the best you can do?"

Honey cupped his face and kissed him on the lips. Sam dropped his bags on her car and wrapped his arms around her. When the kiss ended, he said, "Much better."

She smiled at him. "Long day?"

"Yeah, and we didn't find the phone." He retrieved the bags and followed her inside.

Honey tossed her purse on the counter, opened the refrigerator and pulled out the pitcher of iced tea. "You want something stronger to drink?"

"No, tea sounds good."

"What are you going to do now?" Honey asked.

Sam washed his hands and pulled the food from the bags. "I'd like to take Elvis to Lela Knight's condo and have him search there. It's a small place and it won't take him long. Younger's home is about eight thousand square feet."

"That is a large area to search." Honey placed the plates on the counter and unwrapped the burgers.

Sam cut up two hamburgers, tossed them in Elvis's bowl, and refreshed his water bowl while Honey filled their glasses with ice.

Once they sat at the counter, Sam asked, "How close is Theo's home going to be to your cottage?"

"As you drive through the front gate, Theo's home will be up a long drive to the left. I guess it's about a half mile to his building site."

Sam didn't think that was far enough away from Honey. "Did you mind Woodrow selling some of the land?"

Honey shook her head. "Not at all, there's more than enough here. It's not like he plans to build subdivisions. Gramps wanted to make sure I wasn't on the property alone when he travels. I know he would be more comfortable knowing I'm not as isolated."

"If I'd thought of it, I would have asked him to sell me some acreage."

Honey looked at him. "Are you serious?"

"Yes, I love this land."

"Gramps would probably agree to sell you some land if you would want to live here." Honey's phone rang, and she reached over for her handbag. She looked at the screen and said, "It's Georgia."

"Hi, Georgia." She listened for a minute, then said, "I'm sitting here with Sam and Elvis, eating burgers."

Sam watched her expression while she listened to whatever Georgia was saying.

"Let me ask Sam." Honey muted the phone and said, "Georgia, Preston, my mom and dad want to stop by. They picked up pizza, and Georgia said Preston was going to call you and see if you could come here."

"Why?"

Honey shrugged. "I have no idea. Do you mind if they come by?"

"Not at all. Does Preston need my help with something?"

Honey unmuted the phone, and asked Georgia, "Tell Preston Sam is already here. Did Preston need Sam's help?" Honey listened again, and said, "Okay, we'll be waiting."

"What did she say?"

"She said Preston will tell you when they get here." Honey left her chair and opened the patio door. "Elvis, do you need to go outside?"

Elvis trotted to the door and Honey instructed, "Don't go too far. Come right back."

Sam picked up his glass of tea and carried it to the door to watch Elvis. "If you want to change clothes, I'll watch him."

"Thanks, I would like to put on something more comfortable. Maybe expandable if I'm going to eat pizza on top of burgers."

Honey had returned to the kitchen when Elvis ran to the front door. "I guess they're here."

Sam followed Elvis to the door while Honey retrieved more plates from the cabinet.

After everyone greeted Sam and Elvis, they all walked to the kitchen, and Honey kissed her mom and dad. "What's going on, guys?"

Lorraine opened one of the boxes. "First, let's open these pizza boxes. I've been smelling them all the way over here."

Preston held up the beer he was carrying. "I brought beer, Sam. I thought you might need a couple."

"Is something wrong?" Sam asked Preston.

Preston slapped him on the back. "No, everything is perfect."

"We have tea or wine if anyone wants something other than beer," Honey said. "Just grab what you want. I think we should go to the dining room."

"Good idea." Honey's father grabbed one pizza box, and Sam carried the second box to the dining room table.

Everyone sat around the table and piled their plates with slices of pizza. Honey and Sam exchanged glances, silently questioning what was going on. Then Honey spotted Georgia's hand. A very large, blindingly white diamond solitaire ring was on her finger.

"Georgia!" Honey exclaimed, reaching for Georgia's hand.

It took Sam a full five seconds to realize what was going on. *Some detective I am*, he thought.

Honey jumped from her chair and ran to hug Georgia. "What great news! This is why you guys came over? When did this happen?"

Georgia laughed. "An hour ago, and yes, this is why we came over."

"Isn't it wonderful?" Lorraine beamed. "I can't wait to be a grandmother."

Preston rolled his eyes. "Now, Mom, give us some time to be alone before we start having your grandbabies."

Sam extended his hand across the table to Preston. "Congratulations."

"Did you set a date?" Honey asked.

"December nineteenth," Georgia replied.

"Next year?" Honey asked.

"No, this December," Preston answered. "We saw no reason to wait."

"That's not a lot of time for planning," Honey told them.

Preston laughed. "What are you talking about, Honey? Mom arranged everything while we were waiting for the pizza."

Lorraine frowned at Preston. "Very funny. All I did was make a few calls to get things started."

Honey started to walk back to her seat, but Georgia reached for her hand. "Honey, I wanted to ask if you would be my maid of honor."

Honey was thrilled by her request. "Of course, I will."

Preston looked across the table at Sam. "That's the reason I wanted you here, Sam. I want you to be my best man."

Sam's first thought was his best friend, Cam, had asked him the same thing, and look how his relationship turned out. Yet, he thought Georgia and Preston seemed meant for each other. "I would consider it a privilege."

After everyone finished eating, Georgia was helping Honey in the kitchen and asked, "Honey, are you surprised?"

"Yes. Preston hasn't said one word. I didn't know he was even considering getting married right now."

"Do you think we are making a mistake? I know it seems sudden, but we love each other."

"That's what's important. You two seem to be genuinely happy together." Honey wished she was as content in her love life.

Preston and his parents were sitting in the living room with Sam, and they asked him about the Younger case. Sam told them as much as he could, then asked if they had thought of anything they hadn't mentioned before.

"I did remember that I saw Younger arguing with Terry Meiners that night," Thomas interjected. "At least, Younger looked like he was arguing. His face was red and he was waving his arms around like a crazy person. I'm sure it was the alcohol talking."

"Are you sure it was Terry, Dad? There were so many Paul Reveres that night. At one point, I thought I was speaking to Terry, but it turned out I was talking to Jack Cleary," Preston added. "I saw Younger with one of the saloon girls, and they looked to be in deep conversation about something. I don't know who she was."

As soon as Sam left Honey's, he called Hap, and when he answered, he said, "I want to run something by you."

"Shoot."

"Several people have told me they saw Younger arguing with a saloon girl at the party. You interviewed Gloria Barnes and she was dressed as a saloon girl. She admitted that she put the flash drive in your pocket, and she had a relationship with Trey Sullivan. Tonight, Preston told me he saw Younger arguing with someone in a saloon girl costume. Do you think it's possible she could have been blackmailing Younger?

It's possible they got into an argument and one thing led to another? She did have the goods on both Younger and McNeal on that flash drive."

"It's possible, I guess. She told me she didn't know what was on the flash drive. Do you think we should interview her again?"

"I think you should ask her down to the station to interview her, but I can't be there tomorrow. In the morning, I'm taking Elvis to Lela Knight's condo to have a look around. If we don't find Younger's phone there, I may take him to Aaron Branson's house and see if he will give me permission to search. And don't forget, I'm scheduled on Terry's show tomorrow afternoon."

"You're still convinced Terry Meiners is not involved?" Hap asked.

"Terry is not our murderer," Sam answered with conviction. "He invited me on the show, and who knows, someone listening may remember something useful. It can't hurt."

"What in the heck are we missing?" Hap asked.

"The way I see it, we need to focus on the ones who benefited from Younger's death. Mrs. Younger would be at the top off that list, followed by Will McNeal."

"But Mrs. Younger planned on a divorce," Hap reminded him."So she says. I checked their insurance policies; she is going to be even wealthier now. He had a ten million dollar life insurance policy. That's a whole lot of motive. There's also McNeal. He wanted Younger's wife, and he wanted to be governor. It seemed Younger was leading the polls by a slim margin."

"What about Lela Knight? Is she a possibility?" Hap asked.

"Why would she want him dead? He was her meal ticket," Sam replied.

"Aaron Branson?"

"I see no benefit for him if Younger was killed. He was using Younger to further his own career," Sam answered.

"What about the plain old *hate* motive? There's Mrs. Younger, for the obvious reason that her husband fooled around on her. McNeal, if for no other reason than Younger had the woman he loved. And you can't convince me Terry Meiners didn't seriously dislike Younger. He was always bad-mouthing Terry to anyone who would listen," Hap theorized.

CHAPTER TWENTY-FIVE

Sam and Elvis had no luck finding Younger's phone at Lela Knight's home. Aaron Branson gave his permission for Elvis to search his home, but again, no luck. Realizing how short he was on time, Sam called Honey to ask if she would object if he took Elvis with him to do Terry's radio show. He promised he'd have Elvis back by seven o'clock and bring dinner.

Sam took a seat next to Terry, and Elvis sat in the chair beside him. "I didn't think you would mind if I brought Elvis along. He's been helping me out today."

"Is it anything we can talk about on air?" Terry asked.

"I don't want to discuss specifically what we were investigating today."

"Did you want to discuss other investigations, or just the Younger murder? What about Trey Sullivan?"

"We've solved that one," Sam answered.

"Really? Have you made an arrest?"

Sam leaned forward in his chair and looked around to make certain they were alone. "I won't discuss this on air right now, but we are confident Younger murdered Sullivan."

The commercial ended and Terry announced his guests. "Not only do we have Bardstown's infamous detective, Sam Gentry, with us, but he also brought along the best detective of all, Elvis. Everyone in Kentucky knows Elvis as the bloodhound who not only assists the police in solving murders, he helps to find missing persons.

"Sam and Elvis are here to discuss the shocking murder of one of our gubernatorial candidates, Jeff Younger. As you all know, we often had Mr. Younger as a guest on our program. This tragedy has garnered a considerable amount of national attention, and we all want to have this case solved quickly for Mr. Younger's family." Terry went on to remind the listening audience that Younger was murdered the night of the Masquerade Bourbon Ball. "I was honored to be the master of ceremonies that night, and I was dressed as Paul Revere. As it turned out, I wasn't the only one who thought of Paul Revere as the perfect costume. But Sam, your costume was most appropriate for the ball, the legendary lawman Wyatt Earp."

"Not too original, but I couldn't think of anyone else," Sam responded.

"I'm sure you didn't have to buy a new hat since I've never seen you without a Stetson. It was a very entertaining evening with all of the historical costumes, and we raised a lot of money for charity."

"It was a nice evening," Sam concurred. "Right up to the point when Mr. Younger was found murdered."

"I guess it stands to reason with so many in attendance that evening that you have a considerable list of suspects."

"In cases like this, we initially cast a wide net, but it doesn't take long to narrow the list of individuals who had motive and opportunity," Sam answered.

"How difficult has it been to identify all of the guests, since everyone was in costume? I didn't even recognize some people."

Sam nodded at Terry, confirming that he'd zeroed in on the difficulties with this investigation. "That's been a challenge, but we've managed to get it done. As a matter of fact, there were five Paul Reveres, and unfortunately it was difficult to tell them apart. Like you, the men were tall, and the costumes were very similar."

"Yeah, several people who spoke to me thought I was one of the other Pauls. I understand you found the murder weapon."

"Actually, Elvis found the murder weapon for us."

Terry leaned over and gave Elvis a pat on the head. "He's a smart bloodhound." Terry described Elvis for his audience. "He's a beautiful animal. I'd like to hire him to teach my dog some tricks." Terry looked at Sam and asked, "So, is it true that Elvis has identified the actual murderer in other investigations?"

"It's true."

"How does he let you know when he's found the suspect?"

Sam laughed. "Elvis told me not to give away all of his secrets. Let's just say when he identifies a murderer, he's never wrong."

"Tell me, did you bring Elvis down here today to see if he thought I was a suspect in Jeff Younger's murder?"

Sam noticed for the first time, Terry wasn't smiling. Sam chuckled. "As I said, Elvis told me not to reveal all of his secrets."

"Well, folks, since Elvis hasn't taken my arm off yet, I guess I must be in the clear. He's large enough to take a strong man down," Terry commented. "I wouldn't want to make him mad."

"If he doesn't like you, you'll know it." Part of the reason Sam was confident Terry wasn't involved in Younger's murder was due to Elvis's reaction to him. It was obvious he liked Terry.

Terry noticed the way Elvis looked at Sam each time he spoke. "It seems you and Elvis have developed a great bond."

Sam patted Elvis's head. "From the moment we first met we seemed to understand each other."

Terry directed their conversation to an older cold case. "What about the Jim Calhoun case? I know this murder happened before you moved to Kentucky, but I understand you have been looking into all of the unsolved cases. Let me remind our listeners that Jim Calhoun was ambushed and murdered on his own property," Terry said into the microphone. "Sam, I don't suppose you could tell me if Calhoun's murder had something to do with drugs? Wasn't several acres of marijuana found growing on his property?"

"A considerable amount of marijuana was growing on his property, but we know Mr. Calhoun wasn't in the marijuana business. His property covered a vast area, including other counties. Sadly, Mr. Calhoun had no idea what was taking place on his land." Sam leaned forward, closer to the microphone. "You can tell your audience that an arrest is imminent in this case." In truth, Sam wasn't as positive an immediate arrest would be made, but he knew the identity of the perpetrators. His intention was to make them nervous. Real nervous. He'd found when criminals became paranoid, they made mistakes.

"Well, that is good news. I know the family will be thankful to have some answers." Terry and Sam went on to discuss some of the other cases.

"If any of your listeners have any information on any of our cases, we would like to hear from them. They can certainly remain anonymous. They may not even think their information is important, but we will listen," Sam announced.

Terry gave the audience the phone number to the police station, as well as their email address, before pausing for another commercial.

Before Sam realized it, an hour had quickly passed. Commercials were playing when he extended his hand to Terry. "I appreciate your help. You make this pretty easy."

"You're welcome to come back whenever you have time. I want you to solve Younger's murder quickly so Hap will know I'm not the one responsible. I know you guys have been talking to some of my friends."

Sam put his hand on Terry's shoulder. "It's not personal; that's the nature of a good investigation. Hap's under a lot of pressure right now. As you can imagine, the national attention is not making it easy. On top of everything else, he's fielding a ton of phone calls. He'll clear you soon."

"It's still unnerving to think the chief of police thinks you could be a murderer," Terry responded.

"Hap has a hard time wrapping his brain around the fact that you didn't punch Younger in the face, as much as he harassed you. His fuse is not as long as yours." Sam slapped him on the back. "To be honest, mine isn't either. My fuse is shorter than Hap's."

Honey opened the door to the cottage, kissed Elvis on the head, and smiled at Sam. "I heard you on Terry's show. You were wonderful, as usual. Like Terry, you have a great voice for radio."

"Thanks. Terry makes it easy for the guest. He's a real pro. Still, it's rather nerve racking trying to say what you need to say in a clear, concise manner. But right now, I'd do every radio show in town if I thought it would help me solve this case." He held up a large bag for her to see. "I picked up steaks and potatoes for all of us. Elvis has had another long day too."

Closing the door, they walked to the kitchen. Listening to Sam on the radio today, Honey was surprised to hear how many cases he was working. Considering his workload, it wasn't surprising that their relationship had taken a back seat over the past couple of months. She'd felt guilty that she hadn't considered how many hours he was spending on his investigations. She had noticed how exhausted he looked when she saw him; the dark circles under his eyes were always present, just like tonight. "You look tired. Let me fix you a drink. Bourbon?"

"Sounds good."

Sam cut Elvis's steak into bite-size pieces and tossed it in his bowl along with some of his favorite dog food while Honey filled their plates.

"How was your day?" he asked when they finally sat at the counter and started eating.

"Wedding plans occupied most of my day. After hearing your schedule, my days are fairly boring by comparison."

"Not to me. It's nice to talk about subjects other than murder. Isn't a couple of months enough time to plan a wedding? Or, is that a man's point of view?"

Honey shook her head at him. "You men get off easy. There's a lot to plan: the venue, the dinner, the music, the flowers, and of course, choosing the right dress can take forever, not to mention, the dresses for the bridal party. Can you believe Georgia wants a traditional wedding?"

Sam chuckled. "It is kind of hard to believe a gal who has pink streaks in her hair is a traditional kind of girl."

"She's full of surprises, but we did make some headway planning the reception today. Oh, before I forget, can you make dinner Sunday night? Mom and dad have invited Georgia's parents to dinner and they would like to meet you."

"I'll be there. But what about tomorrow night?"

Honey gave him a puzzled look. "Tomorrow night?"

"I'd like to take you to dinner tomorrow night."

Honey dreaded to tell him she couldn't go. "I'm sorry, I can't go tomorrow night."

"Date?" The question popped out before he thought better of asking.

"It's Oliver's last night before he returns to England. Theo invited Woodrow and me to have dinner with them."

Sam didn't comment, but asked another question about the wedding instead. They discussed everything but her plans for Friday night throughout the remainder of their dinner. As soon as Sam finished his drink, he stood and gathered his plate. "I'll help clean up before I leave. Tomorrow is going to be another long day."

Honey reached out and placed her hand on his forearm. Though he tried to hide it, she knew he was disappointed that she couldn't go to dinner with him. "Since I can't go to dinner with you tomorrow, could I talk you into a home-cooked meal on Saturday night?"

He leaned down, cupped her chin and lifted her face to his. "Only if we are dining alone with Elvis."

"I think I can handle that."

"I can take you out if you would prefer," he offered.

"No, I think you need a night to relax."

Sam dropped a kiss on her nose. "Thank you. Your cooking is better than eating out any day."

CHAPTER TWENTY-SIX

U NABLE TO SLEEP, IT WAS three in the morning when Sam turned on the television and channel surfed, hoping he could think about something other than his unsolved cases. He stopped on the Golf Channel and watched a tournament. He couldn't imagine Younger betting twenty-five thousand dollars on a golf game. The man obviously had more money than brains. But was it true? He hadn't confirmed the story with Jack Cleary. He made a mental note to take care of that first thing.

As usual, once he tired of thinking about his cases, his thoughts strayed to Honey. She was going to be with Theo again tonight. No doubt that was part of the reason he was having another sleepless night. He was tempted to crash that party. Maybe he could dog-sit Elvis while Honey went on her date. He smiled. It'd be pretty funny to be there waiting for her to return from dinner with Theo. No way would that Englishman get a kiss good night with him standing there watching. Honey did say Woodrow was joining them. Sam took some comfort in the thought that Theo wasn't really going to be alone with Honey since Woodrow would be with them.

Trying to get his mind off Honey's date, he turned his attention to the guy on the screen stepping up to the tee. He hit a perfect drive down the middle of the fairway about two hundred sixty yards. A camera captured another golfer on the green. He calmly stepped up and sank a difficult fifteen-foot putt. Sam thought about something Honey mentioned. She'd told him he should consider guests at the party who were golfers. She had a valid point. It would take some talent, or a good amount of luck, to hit a man's head with a putter in the dark. The medical examiner said there was only one wound. Problem was, that didn't reduce his suspect list since many of the guests that night were golfers.

Elvis had been close to a few likely suspects, but he hadn't reacted in any way to make Sam suspicious. Sam mentally ticked off the people Elvis had encountered. He hadn't taken Elvis to the campaign offices of either candidate. Later this morning he planned to search Younger's office for his phone. He also planned to call McNeal to find out if he would allow his office to be searched for Younger's phone without a search warrant.

In this case, he had as many motives as suspects. Younger had certainly angered a lot of people. He silently ticked off the list of motives: blackmail, illicit affairs, jilted lovers, powerful positions threatened, and plain old hate.

Tossing his sheet aside, he decided he might as well shower and head to the station. Lying in bed wasn't solving his cases.

Honey left her office early to run to the grocery to pick up everything she needed to make Sam a wonderful dinner the next night. She wanted him to have an evening where he didn't think about his cases. He was under a lot of pressure and she wanted him to relax for a few hours.

Once she arrived at her cottage, she put her groceries away and took Elvis for a walk. She avoided walking in the direction of the bench where she'd found Younger, but that didn't keep her from thinking about the murders. If Younger murdered Trey on Woodrow's property, Honey knew it was deliberate. He probably wanted to punish Woodrow for not declaring his support.

Her thoughts changed course to Sam. She wondered what he thought about Theo building a home so close to her cottage. He hadn't said much when he'd heard Woodrow had sold Theo some acreage. How would she feel if the roles were reversed? Would she approve of a woman who was interested in Sam living near him? Certainly not, she admitted to herself. Yet, it wasn't her land to sell.

Thinking about Sam, she couldn't help but question his motive for the text he'd sent her earlier. He'd offered to stay with Elvis tonight while she was having dinner with Theo and his friends. She told him she'd leave her door open if he wanted to come by and see Elvis. Naturally, Elvis would be overjoyed to see him, and she wouldn't feel guilty for leaving him alone. She didn't question that Sam enjoyed spending time with Elvis, but she suspected he was also hoping to make a point to Theo. She smiled at his tactics. She'd forgiven him for not telling her about his brief engagement to Liz, and she'd even tried to be understanding of his reasons. She didn't want to dwell on it because she was crazy about him. At the same time, it didn't hurt to let him stew a bit about Theo.

While dining with Theo and his friends, Woodrow's phone vibrated at the very same time Honey's phone rang. Honey and Woodrow exchanged a look as they both pulled out their phones.

Honey glanced at her screen. "It's Mom."

Woodrow looked at his phone, and said, "It's Hap."

Honey had spoken to her mother earlier and mentioned going to dinner, so she thought it must be an urgent call. She glanced at Theo and said, "I'm sorry, but I should answer." She then clicked on the call. "Hi, Mom, is everything okay?" She listened and looked into Woodrow's eyes. Honey knew he was hearing the same information. Tears filled her eyes, and she whispered, "Is he alive?"

"Where are you?" Woodrow asked Hap. "We'll be right there."

"What is it?" Theo asked when they both ended their conversations.

Honey stood and gripped her handbag. "Sam's been shot."

"What happened?" Oliver asked.

"Hap said someone ambushed him on his way home," Woodrow replied.

Honey searched her handbag for her keys, but realized she wasn't driving. Theo had rented a limo again tonight.

Woodrow stood and reached for Honey's hand and said, "I'm sorry we have to leave. Sam's in a hospital not far from here."

Theo pulled out his wallet. "Let me pay the check and we'll go with you."

"That's not necessary, Theo. Stay and finish your dinner. He's in surgery right now and no one will be able to see him for hours. You have the keys to the house. We'll call you and let you know what is going on," Woodrow replied.

Theo stood and gave Honey's shoulder a gentle squeeze. "If you need anything, please call me."

As soon as they hurried out the door, Woodrow hailed a taxi.

"Gramps, what happened? You told Theo that Sam was ambushed?" Honey asked.

"Hap just said Sam was on his way home. For some reason he got out of his car on that road that leads to his home and someone shot him."

Honey wiped her tears away. "He was going to go to the cottage and see Elvis tonight."

Woodrow gripped her hand. "Don't cry, Honey. Sam's a strong, determined man. He'll survive this."

The hospital was surrounded by cop cars, and police were posted at every entrance. Hap hurried to greet Woodrow and Honey as soon as they walked through the door. He led them to a private waiting area and directed them to some chairs where Hap could speak freely.

"Hap, did you call Sam's grandmother?" Woodrow asked.

"I sent a car to pick her up. They should be here soon."

"What happened?" Honey asked.

"I'm afraid I don't know much. Sam was out of his car, we think he was removing an obstruction in the road, and someone shot him. My men on the scene think it was a setup. Good fortune had to be smiling down on Sam because a man driving home from work happened by and found him unconscious. The man told us he'd didn't normally travel that road at that hour, but he'd worked late. He recognized Sam, tried to stop the bleeding and called for help." Hap took a deep breath and collected himself before he continued. "Sam was hit three times, but the doctor said the real problem is the loss of blood. He'd lost a lot of blood by the time his savior arrived." Hap took Honey's hand in his, wanting to offer comfort before he told her the worst. "The EMTs told me Sam was near death on the way to the hospital."

Honey gasped.

Hap squeezed her hand. "One of the bullets grazed his head, and he was unconscious when they arrived at the hospital."

"And the other two bullets?" Woodrow asked.

"One went through his shoulder, but it didn't do any major damage. The third shattered his femur, and they are working on that now."

Honey's voice cracked when she asked, "How long has he been in surgery?"

Hap looked down at his watch. "Almost two hours."

Honey remembered Sam had been wearing his bulletproof vest. "Sam and you were wearing bulletproof vests the other night. Didn't he have his on tonight?"

Hap shook his head. "No, he didn't have it on for some reason. I told him…"

When he didn't finish his sentence, Honey said, "What's going on? Why have you two been wearing your vests? Sam led me to believe it was only procedure, but I can tell by the look on your face that there is something he didn't tell me."

Hap saw no reason to lie to her. "Honey, Sam has been working on some unsolved murders. He's investigating some dangerous people, and there have been threats. That's part of the reason he hasn't been visiting lately."

"Are you saying he was worried he was endangering me?"

"Yes, he was worried about being followed, and he didn't want to stick to a regular routine. "

Honey remembered the day at the cemetery when Sam hurried off after a car that had slowly driven by.

"I spoke to our investigators on the scene not long ago, and they told me they are still pulling slugs out of his car. Judging by the cartridges recovered, they think there were at least two weapons used in the ambush."

They sat in silence for another forty-five minutes before Hap's name was called, instructing him to come to the nurses' station. While Honey and Woodrow waited for Hap to return, Sam's grandmother arrived with Officer Reed.

Woodrow stood and hugged Virginia. Before she could ask, Woodrow told her as much as he knew about Sam's condition.

Hap returned to the room with the doctor, and after he introduced everyone, the doctor addressed Virginia. "Do you want to speak in private?"

"No, everyone can hear what you have to say."

The doctor gave her a gentle smile. "Sam is holding his own. No major arteries were involved." He discussed in-depth Sam's injuries and his prognosis. "We had some of the finest doctors working on his leg. He will need weeks of rehab on that leg. He's in a coma, but all things considered he's holding his own. His blood loss was considerable, and he's received multiple transfusions. On the positive side, Sam is a strong man and we are cautiously optimistic because of that fact. We noticed this wasn't the first time he's been shot. He survived before and that will serve him well. He knows what to expect."

"When can we see him?" Honey asked.

"It will be a few hours before family can visit," the doctor responded.

"We are all family," Sam's grandmother informed him in a no-nonsense tone.

The doctor smiled. "That's what I thought. I would tell you to go home and rest for a few hours, but I know you wouldn't listen."

While they waited, they drank coffee and greeted police officers from the surrounding counties who came to express their support. Each one seemed to have a story to share about working with Sam. Honey hadn't realized what an impact he'd made on the community in such a short period of time. Both Honey's parents and Theo called every half hour to check on his condition. When she ended her last call with Theo, she looked up and saw Georgia and Preston entering the waiting room.

Georgia ran to Honey and pulled her in for a reassuring hug. "We couldn't stay away."

When Georgia released her, Preston then wrapped his arms around his sister, and felt her entire body shaking. He kissed her on top of her head and whispered in her ear, "He's going to be okay."

Honey looked up at him and nodded, grateful for their support. "Yes, he will."

Seeing the tears in her eyes, Preston held on to her. "Honey, Sam's the toughest man I know."

One of Hap's officers stuck his head in the door and motioned for Hap to join him in the hallway. After Hap spoke to him for several minutes, he returned to the waiting room and said, "They found some evidence on the scene. We're rushing the DNA."

"I know you have a theory as to why someone ambushed Sam," Woodrow said.

"Sam drew some attention when he was on Terry's show. He intentionally indicated that an arrest was imminent in the Calhoun case."

Honey replayed Sam's conversation on the radio in her mind. He had discussed the Calhoun case, saying he was close to an arrest. "Is he safe here?"

"We have a man posted at every door. No one will get near him," Hap answered.

"I should bring Elvis to stay with him," Honey suggested.

The thought of Elvis by Sam's side protecting him while he was in the hospital appealed to Hap. It would free up a couple of men who could spent more time in the field investigating the attempt on Sam's life. "He's a police dog, he can go where I go."

Preston stood and held out his hand to Honey. "Give me your house key and I'll go get him."

Honey pulled her keys from her purse. "Thanks, Preston. I'll feel better if Elvis is here with him."

Preston leaned over and kissed her cheek. "We'll be back in a couple of hours."

They patiently waited another hour before the doctor joined them once again to give them an update on Sam's condition. "Sam is in recovery, but we hope to move him to intensive care soon. It might be several hours before anyone can see him. If you would like to leave and get some rest, we'll call you if you're needed."

"We'll be staying," Hap replied for everyone.

The doctor nodded at Hap. "There's a diner a few doors down that's open all night if you'd like something to eat. Our cafeteria won't open until six."

When the doctor left, Woodrow and Hap made another trip to the coffee machine. Once Hap made a fresh batch, he dumped several packets of sugar in his cup. "I wonder how long he will be in a coma."

"Let's keep up hope," Woodrow told him.

"It's tough." Hap's voice faltered. He took a deep breath. "I want to be here, but I also want to be out there looking for the SOBs who did this to Sam."

Woodrow put his arm around Hap's broad shoulders. "I know. But I'm sure your men are doing everything they can in your stead. You have a good group of men."

Hap nodded. "I thank God for them every day, and Sam is the best. He's one great detective, and we are fortunate to have him in our town."

"Do you think you know who shot him?"

"Yep, we know the parties responsible. Now, all we have to do is find them. It won't be as easy to track down the man pulling their strings."

"You know, Hap, if you need anything at all, just ask. I don't care what it is, tell me. I will offer a hefty award if you think that will help," Woodrow told him.

Hap stared at him a moment. "Woodrow, you might have come up with a solution."

CHAPTER TWENTY-SEVEN

Sam's doctor was going to allow two visitors at a time in Sam's room for ten minutes. Virginia stood and held her hand out to Honey. Honey hesitated and glanced at Hap. "If he wakes, I'll come get you so you can ask him what you need to know."

"Thanks, Honey. I would like to ask him a couple of questions if he's able to talk."

Honey didn't know if an unconscious person knew what was happening around them, but if he did, she wanted him to know that she was there. As soon as she entered Sam's room she reached for his hand. Lately, there had been moments when she'd thought her feelings for Theo might equal what she felt for Sam. She was wrong. When she'd heard Sam was shot, it suddenly became very clear how much she loved him. What had happened in the past didn't matter; they would work it out. Nothing was more important to her than Sam's survival.

Virginia returned to the waiting room and told Hap that Sam remained comatose. Honey stayed by Sam's side, quietly talking to him. When she became too emotional to continue, she gently pressed her lips to his forehead, then closed her eyes to say a prayer for him. Sam mumbled something and she opened her eyes. "Sam?" But his eyes remained closed. It was disheartening to see him in such a state. Sam always seemed larger than life—so physically powerful and oozing with confidence. It frightened her to see him as he was now. His naturally dark golden complexion was ashen, his lips pale. She smoothed back his dark curly hair and laid her hand softly against his cheek. "Sam, so many people love you, please come back to us." Placing her palm on his chest, she found comfort feeling his strong, rhythmic heartbeat. She kissed his forehead again and her lips lingered on his skin. "Oh, Sam, why did you have to go and get shot?"

He turned his head, giving her hope that on some level he could hear what she was saying. She'd read that people in comas were in somewhat of a twilight state, their thoughts could be dreamlike, unable to maintain a clear mental picture.

Nearly an hour passed before Honey joined the others in the waiting room. "The doctor is with him now."

"Any change?" Hap asked.

"He only mumbled, but he didn't wake."

Elvis ran to Honey as soon as he walked through the door with Preston and Georgia.

"Elvis knew something was wrong. As soon as I opened the cottage door, he ran around me to jump in the car," Preston told her.

Honey stood and grabbed his leash. "I'll take him in to see Sam."

It wasn't necessary for Honey to lead the way, Elvis pulled her to Sam's room as if he had already been there.

"Be careful, Elvis. Sam is sleeping and you must be gentle with him." She almost said Sam was in serious condition, but she didn't want Sam to hear her.

Elvis walked to the bed and gently touched Sam's nose with his own, then softly laid his chin on Sam's pillow next to his cheek. Sam mumbled and tried to raise his hand, leading Honey to believe that Sam knew Elvis was there beside him. Elvis licked Sam's cheek, then jumped up on the bed and settled himself beside Sam.

Honey, Virginia, and Elvis stayed by Sam's side for the next several hours, with Woodrow and Hap relieving them every hour. Elvis stayed with Sam when the doctor came in to examine him. Honey's mother and father arrived at dawn carrying breakfast sandwiches and freshly brewed coffee for everyone.

The doctor joined them in the waiting room. "Sam is awake, but I can't guarantee he will remain so for long. You should be aware that his thoughts are likely disorderly right now. It may take some time before he regains his complete memory of the shooting. "

Hap returned from Sam's room ten minutes later. "He's sleeping again."

"Was he able to help you?" Woodrow asked.

Hap shook his head. "He seemed confused when I asked him a question, then he drifted off to sleep."

Terry Meiners walked into the visiting room with Officer Reed. After everyone greeted Terry and updated him on Sam's condition, he asked if he could see him.

"He's asleep right now, but I'll take you to his room," Hap responded.

Terry and Hap stayed in Sam's room for several minutes, and then Terry hurried to the visiting room and motioned for Honey. When she reached him, he took her by the hand and said softly, "Honey, Sam's blood pressure has increased and the doctor is trying to examine him, but Elvis is not cooperating."

Reaching Sam's room, Honey instructed Elvis to come to her and he reluctantly obeyed. She gave Elvis's leash to Terry, and then she approached Sam's bed, leaned over and brushed a kiss over his lips, then whispered in his ear.

They waited another hour before they received an update from the doctor. Sam was stable, but they wouldn't allow visitors for a couple of hours. Hap and Honey stayed behind while everyone left to go home and get some rest. Honey asked Preston and Georgia to take Elvis home to feed him and give him some outside time. She told them to stay at her cottage to get some rest, and to bring her a change of clothing and toiletries when they returned. Every hour, Hap walked outside to make calls, and Honey sent hourly messages to her family giving them an update on Sam's condition.

"Honey, I need to leave for a couple of hours, but please call me if there is any change or updates," Hap said.

Not long after Hap left, a nurse told her she could sit in Sam's room. Honey didn't know if Sam knew she held his hand, but she was relieved just to sit beside his bed and watch him breathe. She'd almost fallen asleep when Sam finally awoke. He muttered something and Honey lifted her head. Seeing his eyes open, she smiled. "Do you want ice on your lips?"

Sam nodded, and she reached into the pitcher and placed some ice on his parched lips. After a few minutes, she asked, "Better?"

"Yes, thank you." His voice was hoarse and weak, but she was relieved to see he wasn't nearly as pale.

Gently easing her hip on the bed beside him, she ran her fingers through his hair and looked into his eyes. "How do you feel?"

"Probably about the same way I look."

"You look like the same Detective Gorgeous to me."

Her response elicited a chuckle from him. He grimaced and whispered, "Can't laugh."

Honey reached for his hand and laced her fingers through his. "Did you go and get shot to get attention?"

"Ruin your dinner?" he asked weakly.

"Yes," she teased.

"Good."

She leaned over and tenderly pressed her lips to his. Sam fell back to sleep with a smile on his face.

CHAPTER TWENTY-EIGHT

Georgia, Preston, and Elvis returned with an overnight bag for Honey. Once she availed herself of the shower in Sam's room, she changed her clothing. When she walked out, Sam was awake and talking with Georgia and Preston. Elvis was snuggled next to Sam's side.

Georgia turned and smiled at Honey. "Detective Gorgeous woke for Elvis."

"So I see." Honey walked to the bed, rubbed Elvis's back as she studied Sam's face. Much to her surprise, his color was returning. "You look good."

"So do you. Smell good too."

"I used your shower. Does Virginia know you're awake?"

Preston stood and offered Honey his chair. "Virginia kindly left the room so we could visit for a few minutes."

"No more than two visitors at a time," Georgia reminded everyone.

Honey motioned for Preston to sit down. "I'll go to the waiting room while you visit."

Georgia stood and reached for Preston's hand. "We'll go to the waiting room, you stay. I'm sure Detective Gorgeous would rather visit with you."

When they left the room, Honey walked to the side of the bed and pulled the chair close so she could hold Sam's hand. She noticed how dry his lips looked. "Want more ice?"

"The nurse said I could have water."

Honey reached for the cup from the tray, filled it with water, and held the straw to his mouth.

Sam quickly drank the entire cup. "That's good."

"More?"

"Not right now."

Honey set the cup on the table. "I imagine your throat is raw."

Sam nodded. He turned his hand palm up as an invitation for her hand.

Honey gripped his hand and squeezed. "Do you feel like talking?"

"To you."

"I thought you were going to visit with Elvis tonight…I mean last night."

"I can't really remember what happened right now. Everything seems…foggy. But the doc says it will come back to me." He grinned at her. "Who are you?"

Honey narrowed her eyes at him. "You better be teasing."

Sam arched his brow. "Maybe you should remind me with some sort of physical stimuli."

Standing, Honey leaned over and kissed his lips. "How's that for stimuli?"

Giving her a slight grin, he said, "That works for me. I must have had my mind on that when I got shot."

"I'd prefer that you stay sharp and alive." She looked into his eyes, her own filling with tears. "Elvis and I couldn't…"

Hap walked into the room before she could finish what she was about to say.

"Elvis lifted his head, and seeing it was Hap, dropped it back down on his paws.

Hap walked to the bed and patted Sam on the arm. "Good to see you awake."

Sam nodded. "I agree."

Honey glanced at Hap. "Do you need to talk to Sam alone?"

"No, you can hear what I have to say." Hap pulled a chair closer and sat down near them. "We arrested the Harrington brothers, but as you well know, they are just the minions. There was definitely a third shooter. The brothers lawyered up without saying much, except they didn't shoot anyone. Their high-profile attorney happens to be retained by one of the more infamous drug lords."

Sam looked away, trying to organize his thoughts. His mind seemed to be a mass of jumbled memories, and it took some effort to put all of the pieces back into place.

Hap could tell he was struggling to remember. "The state police are helping us out, but it seems the puppet masters have gone to ground. After we destroyed their product on Calhoun's property last year, I thought they would have found a more lucrative territory."

"You can't mean Mr. Calhoun was involved with drugs!" Honey exclaimed.

Hap shook his head. "No, he was a victim. The poor man had no idea that marijuana was growing on his property. Not only that, but his property extends into a couple of counties. It's isolated and not patrolled as much as we would like. At Mr. Calhoun's age, he couldn't get out and survey his property to insure nothing nefarious was going on. I asked him one time why he didn't sell and move closer to town, but like so many old-timers, he couldn't surrender the land that had been in his family for generations. Sadly, since he died last month, his kids listed all of his land for sale. They've all moved to cities around the country and have no interest in the family farm."

A nurse walked in the room carrying a bag of Sam's clothing he had been wearing when he was shot. She placed the bag on a bottom shelf of the open closet. When she left the room, Elvis leaped off the bed, walked to the bag, stuck his nose inside, and sniffed.

"Elvis, get out of there," Honey said.

"He must smell Sam's blood," Hap told her.

Elvis walked back to the bed and started sniffing Sam from head to toe before he settled on the bed again.

Hap laughed. "He must be making sure it's you."

Sam looked off in the distance, a vague memory coming into focus. "Hap, I think one of the men said something to me after I was shot."

"It will all come back to you, Sam." Hap stood and grabbed the bag that held Sam's clothes. "I'm taking this with me for the evidence department."

Once they were alone, Honey asked, "Sam, are you worried what will happen when you leave the hospital?"

"Honey, as we have discussed, my job comes with some risks."

Honey leaned over, bracing her elbows on the bed beside him. "That's not an answer. I know you've been avoiding coming over lately because you want to keep me safe."

Sam lifted his hand and touched her cheek. "You know what I do can be dangerous. I've never lied to you about that. I wanted to see you."

Squeezing his hand, Honey added, "I also know the reason you've been wearing your bulletproof vest. I understand your job is dangerous, Sam, and I would never ask you to change professions."

Woodrow and Virginia walked into Sam's room, and Woodrow shared with Sam what he had planned once he was released from the hospital. "You and Virginia are coming to stay with me."

Sam objected to Woodrow's plan, but his grandmother would not take no for an answer. "I don't want to hear any arguments. You'll need someone to look after you for a couple of weeks. Woodrow was kind enough to invite me and I've already accepted."

Sam didn't argue with his grandmother, but he did ask to speak with Woodrow alone. Once Virginia and Honey left the room, Sam explained his hesitancy to go to Woodrow's home. "Woodrow, you know I was ambushed. It could be dangerous for me to stay at your home until all of the men involved are apprehended."

"Honey and Elvis will also stay with me while the threat is still out there. I've already hired extra security. As you know, the place is almost as safe as Fort Knox with all of the cameras we have. Anyway, Hap told me those men may have moved on since they've drawn so much attention to the area. Like Younger's death, the news of your ambush is all over the news. Of course, the media is trying to connect the two crimes."

Sam was silent as he thought over his options. "I don't want to put anyone in danger. I signed on for this, you and your family didn't. I'd worry—"

Woodrow held his hand in the air, stopping Sam in mid-sentence. "We've already agreed, and unless you want to deal with Honey and your grandmother, I suggest you don't put up a fight. I've also been thinking you might want to consider building a house on the property like Theo. If you have an interest in that proposal, I can part with more acreage."

Sam leveled his eyes on Woodrow. "I appreciate your offer to stay at your home, Woodrow. It will ease my mind to know my grandmother is safe until these men are apprehended. But why are you offering to sell me some acreage now?"

"Your grandmother and I have discussed traveling. Now that Honey is running the day-to-day operations at the distillery, and doing so very well, I might add, it seems like the perfect time to make plans for the future while there is time."

Sam understood what he was saying about time. No one was guaranteed another day.

"I don't want Honey living on that property all alone. Preston will inherit the horse farm, and he's already built a home there. I'd like to know Honey will have people close to her who care about her welfare. After Theo purchased his distillery, and started to look for land to build a home, I thought it was the perfect solution to have someone that we know live there. If you're interested, I think it would also provide you with a safer location than your present home."

Sam agreed that it made sense to have more people on the property. "I'm interested, but I'll have to talk to Honey before I agree. She might not like the idea."

Woodrow knew Honey wouldn't object, but he didn't comment one way or the other. "Of course. Take your time, no hurry to make a decision." Woodrow turned away, shoved his hands in his pockets and walked across the room.

Watching him, Sam thought he seemed nervous about something. "Is something wrong?"

Woodrow walked back to Sam's bedside, cleared his throat, and asked, "Would you have any objections if I asked for your grandmother's hand in marriage?"

Sam couldn't help but smile at Woodrow's worried expression. "I can't imagine why I would have any objections. Do you love her?"

"Yes, I do, and she loves me. We want to spend what years we have left with each other. I haven't asked her yet, I wanted to discuss it with you first."

"Let me be the first to congratulate you in advance."

Woodrow reached for Sam's hand and gently squeezed. "Thank you, Sam. I'm going to wait until you're home to propose so we can all celebrate together."

"This is going to be a big change for you, Woodrow."

"It will be for both of us, but it will be a nice change. We've both been alone way too long."

Honey took Elvis for a walk at a nearby park, and when they returned to the hospital, Susan and Will McNeal were walking into the visiting room. When Honey and Elvis reached the door to the visiting room, Hap was already speaking with the McNeals. Hap glanced her way and waved her over. Honey took a step toward them, but Elvis lurched in front of her and started to growl.

Honey stroked his head. "It's okay, we'll go see Sam in a few minutes." She took a step to walk around him, but Elvis stepped in front of her again. "Elvis, what's wrong with you?" Another step to the side, but again, Elvis prevented her from moving forward. She looked up at Hap and in that instant she realized Elvis didn't want her near the McNeals. By the look on Hap's face, he also guessed Elvis was alerting her to danger.

Hap was cool; he took control of the situation. "I've told Will and Susan they can't visit because they're not family, but we would tell Sam that they were here."

Honey nodded at the couple, and tried to act as though she wasn't holding on to a growling one-hundred-ten-pound dog, who was normally friendly—unless he was near a murderer. "Yes, I'm taking Elvis back to his room now."

"Elvis is protecting Sam, and that is one deputy who takes his job seriously," Hap explained to the McNeals.

Will smiled hesitantly at Elvis. "Looks like he's anxious to get back to his duty."

Honey gave them a little wave. "I'll tell Sam you were here."

"Please give him our best," Will told her.

Honey turned to walk away, but Elvis was not as anxious to move.

He stared at the couple and growled again. Honey pulled him from the room, hoping no one on the staff observed his behavior.

Elvis pulled Honey into Sam's room, and she was forced to release his leash so she could close the door. "Sam, you won't believe what just happened." When she turned around, she saw Cam sitting in the chair beside Sam. "Oh, I'm sorry, I thought you were alone." She turned her gaze on Cam. "Hi, Cam."

"Hi, Honey. How are you?"

"Good, thank you. How did you know Sam was in the hospital?"

"I called the station to talk to him, and Officer Reed told me what happened. I came as soon as I could catch a flight."

Honey thought they might want to have a private conversation. "I'll leave you two alone."

Elvis jumped up on the bed, claiming his spot, and Sam held his hand out to Honey. "Elvis is already comfortable. Don't go."

Just as Elvis plopped down next to Sam, the nurse walked in and told them it was time for Sam to be examined. Sam motioned for Honey to lean down to him. "Give me a kiss, and then you and Elvis get something to eat. I'll see you later."

Honey hesitated, but Cam told her he would stay at the hospital and visit with Sam while she was gone. Honey kissed Sam and said, "I'll be back in an hour."

"What did you want to tell me when you came in?"

"Oh, it can wait."

CHAPTER TWENTY-NINE

LATER THAT NIGHT, HONEY, ELVIS, and Hap were in Sam's room, talking about Younger's murder. Honey told Sam how Elvis reacted to Will and Susan McNeal earlier that day.

Sam shook his head. "Are you sure Elvis was reacting to them?"

Hap set his coffee cup on the table. "Yes, they were the only two people in the visiting room at the time."

"Hap, we need to talk to Mrs. Younger again. Maybe she's so in love she is protecting Will."

Honey picked up a cup of water and held the straw to Sam's mouth. "I can't believe Will would kill Younger."

"Maybe Younger told Will he had photos of him in an indelicate situation with his wife. Maybe he was blackmailing him, or threatening to go to the press if he didn't drop out of the race," Hap theorized.

Sam nodded. "Yeah. Blackmail is a good motive for committing murder. Not to mention that Younger would no doubt garner sympathy as the cuckolded husband."

Honey placed Sam's cup back on his tray. She started to move away, but Sam reached for her hand. "I want you and Elvis to go home and get a good night's rest. You've got a business to run. I'm sure a nurse will be in here soon with another shot to knock me out. And Cam said he would be back early in the morning."

"You have nothing to worry about, Honey. Either I, or one of my officers, will be here throughout the night," Hap assured her.

The nurse came in a few minutes later with Sam's expected shot.

"Everyone can say good night for now. But the good news is the doctors said Sam will be leaving us in a couple of days if he keeps improving the way he has been." She gave Sam a flirtatious grin. "We're calling you Superman around here. We've never seen anyone recuperate so quickly. Of course, you know you are going to need rehabilitation on that leg."

Sam was aware she was flirting with him, but he wasn't going to give her any encouragement. "Well, I have Honey to thank for that." He lifted Honey's hand to his lips and winked at her. "She is my inspiration."

When Honey gave him a smile, he said, "By the way, I told Woodrow I'd stay with you when I'm released."

"Good." She kissed him good night, and she made sure it was a long, lingering kiss. It pleased her to see that she'd left him breathless, and the nurse speechless. She turned and smiled at the nurse. "Take care of *my* Superman."

Hap stood and reached for Elvis's leash. "Sam, I'll walk them to the car. See you tomorrow."

Sam nodded at Hap, but his eyes were following Honey, and his mind was still on that kiss. "I like Detective Gorgeous better," he called after her.

"Is that your wife?" the nurse asked.

"She will be before long," Sam answered, hoping he hadn't read too much in that kiss.

Three days later, Mac, a burly male nurse, helped Sam into a wheelchair, and pushed him from his hospital room once he had been released. Honey and Hap were following behind along with Elvis, listening to Sam grumble about being forced to leave the hospital in a wheelchair.

Mac turned to grin at Honey and Hap, and said, "Is he always this grumpy?"

Hap laughed. "Always, especially this early in the morning."

They passed hospital staff and visitors in the hallway, and Honey saw a man about twenty-five feet away walking toward them, carrying a huge bouquet of flowers. Just as she was about to comment on the lovely flowers, Elvis surged forward, jerking his leash from her hand. He ran full speed down the hallway. Honey zoomed around Sam's wheelchair trying to keep pace with her wayward canine. Elvis charged ahead, and when he was a few feet from the man holding the bouquet, he leapt through the air. In the next seconds, several things happened at once, and Honey felt as though everything was happening in slow motion. The impact of Elvis's body slamming into the man knocked him back several feet. The man's flowers went airborne as his arms flailed, trying to brace for impact. Elvis landed on top of the man and within seconds, his teeth were imbedded into the man's throat. A pistol clattered to the marble floor, its progress halted by a nearby food cart. A colorful array of blossoms floated through the air before landing on the floor around man and beast. By this time, everyone walking in the hallway had stopped to watch the bloodhound take down a two-hundred-pound man, seemingly for no reason.

Seeing her precious bloodhound holding the man by the throat, Honey quickly grabbed his leash.

"Leave him be," Hap ordered. Springing into action, he pulled his revolver, and had it pointed at the man's head.

Sam pulled his pistol from his waistband, backing up Hap. Nurse Mac scrambled to retrieve the man's pistol from the floor.

"Mister, you better start talking fast," Hap said to the bouquet-wielding stranger.

"Get this dog off of me!" the man screeched.

Hap glanced at Honey. "You can take his leash now." He then called one of his officers who was waiting outside the hospital.

A few hours later, Sam was resting in one of the large bedrooms on the main level in Woodrow's home, with a nice fire crackling in the fireplace. It was nearly five o'clock when Theo stuck his head in the open door and asked Sam if he wanted some company.

"Sure, come in."

Theo took a seat next to the bed. "You look good. No one would believe you were shot a few days ago."

"It helps to be out of the hospital. You can't get any rest. They wake you up to give you a shot to put you to sleep."

Theo laughed. "Can I get you anything?"

Sam gave him a sheepish look and lowered his voice. "I'd love a bourbon. I'm off the pain medication."

Theo laughed and walked to the door. "I would too. I'll be right back." He returned carrying two glasses and a bottle of bourbon under his arm. He held the bottle for Sam to see. "Want me to make it a double?"

"A generous one."

Theo poured their drinks before he tucked the bottle in the nightstand. "Don't tell Honey."

Sam held his glass up and clinked it to Theo's. "It will be our secret."

"Good, I don't want to go against doctor's orders."

"He didn't say I couldn't have bourbon." Sam had wanted to speak to Theo about Honey, so he eased into that conversation by saying, "I understand I interrupted your dinner the other night."

"Yes, but under the circumstances, I understand. I hope it's not an experience that you'll repeat," Theo said.

"I'll drink to that."

Both men held their glasses in the air before they took a sip. Theo swirled the contents of his glass as he considered what he wanted to say to Sam. "Sam, I wanted to talk to you about Honey."

Sam rested his drink on his chest and leveled his eyes on Theo. "Good."

"At dinner the other night when Honey received the call about you, it was evident how much she cares for you. I wanted you to know she didn't hesitate in her decision to leave dinner when she found out you'd been shot." Theo took another drink of his bourbon. "I won't deny I wanted to have a fair shot with her, but she's in love with you. I've seen how she looks at you, and I've had enough experience to know it's a look of a woman in love. I wish I could change her mind, but know that I can't."

Sam thought it took one hell of a man to be so honest. Theo was the kind of man he wanted as a friend. "Theo, I can't think of many men who would be so forthcoming with a rival. Thank you for that. I hope we can be friends."

Theo stood and offered his hand to Sam. "I'd like that. You're one lucky man, and if you ever mess up, I'll be there in the blink of an eye."

"I know, and I wouldn't hold it against you."

A few minutes later, Cam walked into the room, and Theo left so the two friends could talk. When Cam left, it wasn't long before Honey, Elvis, and Hap walked in. Elvis jumped on the bed beside Sam, and Honey held boxes from Sam's favorite diner beneath his nose. "I brought your favorite."

Sam gave her a big smile. "Smells like a BLT with home fries."

Honey leaned over and kissed his cheek. "Good guess. I called earlier and everyone gave me their order. I already knew what you would order. Everyone else is eating in the kitchen, so you get the three of us." She opened one box and passed it to Hap. After opening the next box, she placed it on the tray and positioned it in front of Sam. "You have an extra side of bacon for Elvis."

"Great."

"Sam, I did feel sorry that you got shot, but seeing all of this attention you're getting, I'm rethinking my pity party," Hap grumbled as he set the drinks on the bedside table.

"I'll make it up to you by telling you there's a bottle of bourbon in that drawer." Sam pointed to the nightstand. "Help yourself."

Hap opened the drawer and pulled out the bottle. "You're forgiven."

"Clean glasses are on the bureau."

"Honey, would you like one?" Hap asked.

"No, I'll stick with my iced tea."

After they discussed Sam's progress, Hap told them what he'd learned about the man who intended to shoot Sam as they were leaving the hospital. "The flower delivery boy is Clive Barton. He's a cousin of the Harrington brothers. We found his DNA on some cigarette butts and a beer bottle at the scene of the shooting. But here's a surprise for you. There was some of his DNA on the shirt you were wearing that night. I guess that explains Elvis's reaction. The Harrington brothers are singing like songbirds, throwing their cousin under the bus. They're willing to testify that Clive was the only shooter. They told me that Clive walked up to you after you were shot and grabbed your shirt to turn you over. He wanted to make sure you were dead. That part of their story jived with the DNA on your shirt."

Honey shivered at the thought that Barton was so close to Sam that he could have fired another shot point-blank. With that vision in her mind, she lost her appetite. She glanced at Sam to see his reaction and it wasn't what she expected. He stuffed some fries in his mouth, seemingly unconcerned by what Hap was saying.

Sam handed Elvis a piece of bacon and said, "Thanks for saving my bacon, Elvis."

Elvis licked Sam's hand before he took the bacon between his teeth.

After Hap told them everything he knew about Clive Barton, he said, "Now, about the Younger case. Mrs. Younger swears she was with Will in the garden, and he wasn't out of her sight the entire time she was at the party. She believes Will is not capable of committing murder."

Honey was thankful they'd changed the subject. She simply couldn't think about Sam coming so close to death.

"You don't think they could have committed the murder together?" Sam asked as he shared more bacon with Elvis.

Hap shrugged. "Who knows? In our business we can't afford to trust."

"Yeah." Sam looked out the window, thinking about the facts of this case. Finally, he glanced at Hap and said, "I guess you could take Elvis over to Will's home to search for Younger's phone. We've never found it, and that has to be the missing part of the puzzle. We can find out who Younger spoke to once he knew what was on that computer. I have Younger's shirt in my desk drawer at the station. I imagine Elvis can still get a scent."

"I think I'll call Will early to tell him I need to speak to him. I won't mention searching his home. If he's our culprit, I'm sure he thinks he's fooled us so far. Honey, if you don't mind, I'll take Elvis with me in the morning."

Honey glanced at Elvis, then back to Hap. "I'm not certain how Elvis will respond after the way he acted at the hospital around Will."

Sam saw the concern on Honey's face. "Are you afraid he will react the way he did at the hospital?"

Honey replayed the scene of Elvis attacking Clive Barton in her mind. "I've never seen him attack anyone before. When he's protecting me, he's always just stood in front of me, intimidating people with his growl."

Sam tried to alleviate her fears. "Maybe he knows when there is an imminent threat, like he did today. He obviously knew the scent of Barton, from my shirt."

Honey nodded. "I'm sure you're right. He wouldn't attack anyone for no reason."

"If he seems aggressive in any way, I'll bring him home," Hap promised.

Honey trusted Hap to take care of Elvis. "Just drop him off at my office when you're finished. I have some errands to run and he likes to go to the pet store with me."

It was nearly eleven when Honey and Sam were finally alone. Sam reached for Honey's hand. "Come sit beside me."

Honey removed her shoes and climbed up beside him on the bed. "I might fall asleep."

"That's okay with me. I wouldn't mind if you slept with me all night, every night," Sam replied, his tone serious.

Honey frowned at him. "I don't think Woodrow, or your grandmother, would approve."

"I don't know about that, since I'm incapable of doing anything inappropriate right now. Besides, Elvis is watching. We must behave in front of our child."

Honey laughed. It was such a relief to hear him teasing again. The turquoise color had returned to his mischievous eyes. That told her he was definitely on the road to recovery. "How was your visit with Cam?"

"It was good. He's leaving tomorrow morning, and we said all the things we needed to say."

"I'm glad you're still friends. I guess he isn't going to get back together with Liz."

Sam shook his head. "It's over. She's tried to contact him, but he quit answering his phone." Taking her hand in his, Sam asked, "Did you mean what you whispered in my ear the other day?"

Honey looked up at him and smiled. "Are you certain you know what I said? You were pretty out of it."

"I heard you. You said you and Elvis couldn't live without me. Were you being nice, or did you mean it?"

"I meant it. I was scared, and I wanted you to know how much you mean to us."

"You've forgiven me for not telling you about Liz?"

"Of course."

He looked into her eyes. "I love you, Honey."

"I love you."

Sam leaned over, took her face in his hands, and kissed her softly, longingly.

Honey snuggled close to his side. "Am I hurting you?"

"No, you feel good."

Closing her eyes, Honey savored the feel of his warm body next to hers. She hadn't fully realized how much she loved him until she thought he might not survive. She would learn to live with his profession, because she didn't want to be without him.

Sam's thoughts seemed to be going in the same direction. "When I got shot…well, my thoughts were on you and Elvis. I wished I had told you that morning that I love you." He kissed her temple. "I'll never let another day pass without telling you. I want you to know how I feel every day."

"We should take lessons from Gramps. He says never to let the sun go down on anger. I know he told my grandmother how much he loved her as often he could, as she did him. They had a great love story."

"How would you feel if Woodrow wanted to marry my grandmother?"

"I would love it. They would have a good life together."

Sam told her about Woodrow's offer to sell him some property. "Would you want me to live so close to you?"

Honey didn't have to think about her response. She rose on one elbow and looked at him. "Seriously?"

Sam nodded. "I told him I would need to talk to you about it first."

"I would love it."

"What about Theo?"

"Theo and I will always be friends, but he knows I love you."

"Good answer."

CHAPTER THIRTY

EARLY THE NEXT MORNING, HAP and Elvis were ringing the doorbell at McNeal's home. Will answered the door, and while he was not thrilled to have Hap search his home, he consented.

Once Elvis started working, Will followed them from room to room, voicing his displeasure. "I can't believe you think I had something to do with Younger's murder. I'm going to be the next governor, and believe me, this will not bode well for you."

Hap stopped and faced him. He pushed his hat back and stared hard at him. "It's my job to do a thorough investigation of a murder. You had motive and opportunity. You should be eager to be cleared as a suspect."

Will threw his hands in the air. "I had no reason to kill him. I was going to win."

Hap's eyes widened at that ridiculous statement. "No?" Hap held up one finger and said, "Number one, he was your opponent." Another finger joined the first one. "You're sleeping with his wife." He lifted a third finger. "You and Younger argued constantly, and according to several witnesses, those arguments were quite heated." He glared at him. "Should I continue?" He wasn't going to mention Elvis's reaction to him at the hospital. Now that he thought about it, Elvis didn't react to him at all this morning.

"Have you searched the home of Terry Meiners? He was always arguing with Younger. Younger hated him. Meiners probably got tired of listening to him, and saw his opportunity at the party to get rid of the thorn in his side."

"We are investigating everyone," Hap responded and turned to look for Elvis.

"I'd say Meiners is the most likely suspect."

"I'll take your opinion for what it's worth." Hap turned his back and left McNeal standing there fuming alone. He found Elvis headed to the second floor, so he followed him up the stairs.

Elvis didn't find Younger's phone, and Hap drove him to Honey's office. Later that day, Honey took Elvis to the pet store where he could pick out his treats. Her last stop was the grocery to pick up a few items for the dinner she promised Sam.

"How are you feeling?" Terry asked when he walked into Sam's bedroom.

Sam pointed to a chair beside his bed. "Good. They are taking good care of me."

They chatted about Sam's recovery, and finally Terry asked about the investigation.

Sam saw no reason he couldn't discuss where they were with the case. Sam was confident Terry wasn't involved, and he thought he'd finally convinced Hap. "We are still looking for Younger's cell phone. Hap went to the McNeals' home today with Elvis." Sam went on to tell him how Elvis reacted to Susan and Will McNeal at the hospital.

"I can't imagine Will being involved. He doesn't seem like the type who would commit murder," Terry replied.

"I admit I didn't think Will was involved, but Elvis is never wrong. Not only that, but Will had motive and opportunity. You and Woodrow both said he was an excellent golfer. It makes sense to me that it took a good golfer to only take one swing and kill the guy. Even by the light of the moon, one shot had to be rather difficult."

"Did Elvis find anything at Will's home?" Terry asked.

Sam shrugged. "Hap hasn't called me yet. He had a busy day, so I'm sure he will call when he has a chance."

"Did you say Will was at the hospital with his wife?" Terry asked.

"Yes, why?"

"Just a thought, but do you think it's possible Elvis was reacting to Will's wife?"

Sam stared at him for a few seconds, his mind envisioning Susan McNeal as a murderer. He'd found her to be a rather skittish little woman. "She seems…I don't know…too timid. I wouldn't see her as much of a threat."

Terry chuckled. "I agree, she may be small and timid, but she has a better swing than her husband. She could have easily killed a man with one swing. She's probably one of the best female golfers at the club."

Sam gave him a steady look. "You're serious?"

"Yep. I'm telling you that woman has one heck of a swing."

Sam reached for his cell phone on the nightstand. He hit Hap's number.

As soon as Hap answered he told Sam he came up empty at Will's home.

"That's why I'm calling. Was Mrs. McNeal at home?"

"No, why?"

"How did Elvis react to Will?"

"He didn't have any reaction at all. I realized that as soon as we started searching."

"Terry is with me, and he says Mrs. McNeal is a better golfer than her husband. It's possible Elvis was responding to her, not Will."

"I'll go by their home right now and see if she is home. I'll call you back."

At the grocery, Elvis jumped from Honey's Jeep as soon as she attached his leash and opened the door.

Honey leapt from the Jeep and managed to step on his leash before he took off. "Elvis, you have to wait in the car." Picking up the leash, she said, "Come on, jump back in."

Elvis didn't budge, he stood rigid and stared. Honey turned to see what had caught his attention.

"Hi, Honey." Susan McNeal stopped a few feet away, her eyes focused on the intimidating canine growling. "That's the second time that dog has growled at me. Are you sure he's friendly?"

"Um, he's been under a lot of stress lately," Honey replied.

Elvis maneuvered his body in front of Honey, and she tightly gripped his leash.

Susan pointed to the car next to Honey's. "That's my car. Keep him away from me."

"Of course." She tried to pull Elvis closer to her, but Elvis lurched forward. He did stop growling as he pulled Honey toward Susan. Susan kept backing up, but Elvis managed to stick his nose on her purse. When he promptly sat down, Honey realized he was alerting her to his find. Susan tried to move away from them, but Elvis began growling again, so loudly that he was heard above the sounds of shopping carts rolling over the pavement, causing people to stop and stare.

"Elvis, stop." Honey patted him on the head and said softly, "Good job." Elvis allowed her to take him to the door of the Jeep. When she finally managed to open the door with one hand, Elvis was determined he was not going to jump inside. She knew he would listen to her command when she used her serious tone. It never failed to let him know that she meant business. "Elvis, come." Reluctantly, he slowly turned away from Susan and jumped into the Jeep. Once inside, he pressed his nose to the window, his big dark eyes remaining fixed on Susan. Honey quickly climbed behind the wheel and closed her door. She pushed her window down a few inches to hear what Susan was shouting.

"You shouldn't take that dog around people, he's dangerous." Susan hurried to the other side of her car and started loading her groceries in her back seat.

"Sorry," Honey mumbled, but she wasn't really sorry at all. As far as she was concerned, Elvis just solved another murder.

Sam had ended his call with Hap when his phone rang. Glancing at the screen, he said, "Excuse me, Terry, but Honey's calling."

"Sam, its Susan McNeal!" Honey shouted. "Elvis and I are at the grocery, she parked right next to me. Elvis jumped out before I could grab his leash and—"

"Honey, slow down." Sam looked at Terry and whispered, "Call Hap back."

As Terry hit Hap's number on his cell phone, Sam asked Honey, "Are you still at the grocery, Honey?"

"That's what I'm trying to tell you. Elvis saw Susan McNeal coming from the grocery and he jumped out of the Jeep. I grabbed his leash and held him back, but he was growling just like he did the last time he was near a murderer. He also alerted me to Susan's purse."

"Her purse?" Sam repeated.

"Yes, I bet Younger's phone is in her purse. You know he never forgets a scent."

"Hang on a sec, Honey." Sam could hear Hap on the other phone with Terry. "Terry, tell Hap to go to the grocery store. Susan McNeal is there and Honey thinks Elvis is alerting her to Susan's purse." Once Terry related the information to Hap, Sam said, "Honey, Hap is on the way. Has she left the parking lot?"

"No, she's putting her groceries in her car."

"Back your car out and park behind her. Turn it off and act like you're having car trouble. Hap will be there in a few minutes," Sam instructed.

Terry repeated the conversation to Hap. He looked at Sam and chuckled. "Hap said you are one devious son-of-a-gun."

Honey locked her doors and made sure her window was only open a few inches to prevent Elvis from taking matters into his own paws and jumping out of the Jeep. She pulled behind Susan's Mercedes and turned off her ignition as Susan slid behind the wheel and started her car.

Susan opened her window, stuck her head out and yelled, "Would you move your vehicle out of the way!"

"I'm sorry, it's stalled. I'm trying. Just give me a minute." Honey went through the motions, pretending as though she was trying to start her Jeep. She threw her hands in the air, and said, "I'm sorry, I think my battery is dead."

Jumping from her car, Susan marched toward Honey's Jeep. She came to a skidding halt when Elvis nudged Honey out of the way and pressed his snout to window and barked.

Honey thought he was so agitated that he might break the window. "Elvis, get back!"

Thankfully, Hap pulled up and parked behind Honey's Jeep,

effectively blocking both vehicles. He approached Honey's Jeep and asked, "Car problems, Honey?"

"Umm, yes." Honey's eyes slid to Susan. "I'm afraid I'm blocking Mrs. McNeal's car."

Hap nodded in Susan's direction. Susan had backed several feet away from Honey's Jeep.

"Can you help her get that car out of the way?" Susan asked Hap.

"I'll sure try." Hap look at Honey and winked. "Can you pop your hood?" As he walked to the front of Honey's Jeep, he said to Susan, "I was at your home early this morning, Mrs. McNeal, but you had already left."

"Yes, I had an early appointment. Now, can you help her get that car out of the way so I can get home?" Susan asked impatiently.

Hap opened the Jeep's hood and wiggled a few wires leading to the battery as he continued his conversation with Susan. "I'm sure Will told you he gave his permission to search your home and cars. I need to search your car while you're here."

"For what reason?" Susan demanded.

"We haven't found Younger's cell phone."

Susan sneered at him. "That's ridiculous to think I would have Younger's cell phone. Now, move that car, I need to go."

Hap turned to face her. "You're refusing to allow me to search your car?"

"Yes, I am." Susan opened her car door and slid behind the wheel.

Hap walked back to Honey's Jeep and whispered, "I need to talk to Sam, so I'll follow you home."

"Did you hear Elvis growling the entire time you spoke with her? Can't you look in her purse?"

"Not without a search warrant."

As soon as Hap, Honey, and Elvis joined Terry and Sam in the bedroom, Hap extended his hand to Terry. "Terry, I hope we're still friends."

Terry took his hand and laughed. "You don't think I'm going to let a little thing like being considered a murder suspect upset me, do you? I'm thankful you didn't arrest me."

"Sam wouldn't let me arrest you," Hap countered jokingly.

"You're going to owe him big for solving our murder," Sam chimed in.

Taking a seat near Sam's bed, Hap asked Terry why he thought Mrs. McNeal committed the murder.

"When Sam told me about Elvis's reaction to the McNeals at the hospital, and his theory that it had to be a pretty good golfer to kill Younger with one stroke, I thought it must be her. Susan has a great swing and strikes the ball with a lot of force. She's a better golfer than her husband. To be honest, I couldn't imagine Will killing anyone, and since all of the polls had him catching Younger, I thought that motive was eliminated."

Hap and Sam exchanged a look. "He had a few other motives that we can't discuss," Sam said.

"But you could see Susan murdering someone?" Hap asked.

"I don't know her well, so I couldn't really say," Terry answered. "Did you arrest her?"

"No, she refused to let us search her car. I need more evidence than Elvis's nose to arrest her."

"We could call Will and explain the situation. He might help us," Sam suggested.

"I was thinking the same thing, particularly considering his situation," Hap agreed. Neither Sam nor Hap wanted to advertise the relationship between Paige Younger and Will McNeal, so they were cautious in their conversation.

Honey looked at Terry and winked. She knew Terry would never gossip to anyone unless he knew the entire story. "They're talking about Will's feelings for Paige Younger."

"I figured as much," Terry replied. "I saw how they looked at each other at the party. I'm sure other people noticed something was going on there."

Honey threw her hands in the air. "That's what I told Sam, but he didn't believe me."

"I believed you, Honey," Sam told her.

"Am I the only one who didn't notice them the night of the party?" Hap asked.

"Apparently," Terry replied.

"We're overlooking one significant piece of evidence," Sam told them.

Everyone turned to look at him. "What?" Hap asked.

"No blood was found on her costume," Sam replied.

"Maybe she took her dress off," Terry suggested.

"You think she stripped down to commit murder?" Hap asked.

Everyone laughed but Sam. He thought Terry might be right. "Great way not to get caught with blood on your clothing. We know of at least four people who had removed their clothes that night. What's one more? But of course, that means it was premeditated."

Hap's phone rang, and seeing it was the station, he answered.

"Hap, we just received a 911 call, and it seems someone is wanting us to hear a conversation. I think you need to hear this. We're forwarding it you," Officer Reed said.

"Okay."

"I saw my husband's car and I'd like to know what he's doing here," a woman shouted.

Hap recognized the voice, so he hit speaker on his phone so Sam could hear the conversation.

A man's voice responded, "I came to see how she's doing."

"Really? Is that all you're doing?"

Hap whispered, "That's Susan McNeal."

"Susan, it's late," another woman said.

"That's Paige Younger's voice," Sam mouthed.

"I'm sure you don't mind if I join you," Susan McNeal replied.

"I was just leaving," the man said.

"It's a little late for that, don't you think, Will?" Susan said. "You two think you've been so smart sneaking around. Jeff knew what was going on, and he showed me the proof. He had video of you two."

"I'm sorry, Susan, but I love Paige. I'm sorry you had to find out from Jeff, but I'm glad I no longer have to pretend."

"So you think you're going to get rid of me as soon as you become governor. After all I've done to help you get to where you are? If not for my family and our money, you'd still be in that little Podunk town where you came from."

"Susan…" Will didn't continue because Susan interrupted, shouting, "Shut up!"

Will tried again, "Susan, I'm sorry…"

"I said to shut up! You're not going to get rid of me that easily!"

Hap jumped to his feet, and placed his palm over his phone. "Sam, call the station and tell Officer Reed to meet me at Younger's home. This doesn't sound good."

CHAPTER THIRTY-ONE

H AP AND OFFICER REED ARRIVED at the Younger home at the same time. They heard a woman yelling before they reached the front door. Hap knocked loudly, and within seconds Paige Younger opened the door. Hap read the relief on her face as soon as she saw him.

"Mrs. Younger, everything okay here?" Hap asked softly.

Her eyes widened and she shook her head from side to side. "Would you like to come inside?"

"Yes, I would." Hap and Officer Reed walked inside, and told Paige to remain in the foyer. Paige pointed to the sitting room off the foyer. As they approached, Hap saw Susan standing a few feet from her husband. He motioned for Officer Reed to stand by the doorway.

When he walked into the room, he nodded at Will, then glanced at Susan. "Would someone like to tell me what is going on here?"

"I thought it was time to confront my husband and his lover," Susan blurted out.

Will spoke up. "Susan, this is something we need to discuss in private."

Susan sneered at him. "Why? I'm certain he already knows about your tawdry little affair. I'm sure everyone in town knows by now, since you two haven't exactly been discreet." She glanced at Hap. "You do know, don't you?"

"I'd like to know when Jeff Younger showed you that video," Hap responded.

"What difference does that make? Apparently, Jeff knew about them for months. I think that's one of the reasons he was drinking so much."

"Did he show you the video on his laptop, or his phone?" Hap asked.

She was so enraged that she didn't consider her response. "He sent me the video on my phone. It was disgusting. At first, I thought he was blackmailing me. But that wasn't it at all; he said all he wanted was for me to keep my husband home at nights." She turned her frigid eyes on her husband. "I thought you were out every night trying to charm the voters. You've done nothing but use me for my money. I should have known better. My family tried to tell me not to marry someone like you. They said you needed my money and our family name for your ambitions. They were right all along."

Will lowered his eyes, his guilt weighing on him as he heard the truth in her words. "Susan, I'm sorry, but I'm in love with Paige. I can't change that now and we can't go back."

Looking at Susan's expression, Hap thought he could almost taste her rage. He wanted to make her angrier, hoping she'd made a mistake. "Susan, give me Jeff's phone."

"What are you talking about?"

Hap noticed how she tightened her grip on her purse. "The phone in your purse. It's Jeff's."

"Why would I have his phone?"

Will's eyes darted from Hap to his wife. "How did you get Jeff's phone? Is that why you left early this morning? Is that why you couldn't wait for Hap to arrive? You were afraid he would find Jeff's phone?"

"I said I don't have Jeff's phone!"

Will looked into her eyes and knew she was lying. He held out his hand. "You're lying. Give me your purse."

"It's a little late for you to act like a husband and give orders."

Hap moved between them. "We've been tracking Jeff's phone. I followed the signal here."

"That's impossible, it's dea..." As soon as the words left her mouth, she realized she had incriminated herself.

Hap knew he had her. He held out his hand. "Give me the phone."

Susan turned abruptly. "I'm leaving. If you want to search me or my property, you'd best get a search warrant." She glared back at Will, and added, "My *husband* doesn't have the right to give permission for me."

"Officer Reed is outside this door, and he is going to arrest you on murder charges," Hap told her before she took two steps.

She whirled back around to face him. "Murder? Why would I kill Jeff?"

"Either he was blackmailing you, or threatening to go to the press. I really don't care why you did it, I know you killed him, and I can prove it," Hap bluffed.

"That's ridiculous. You took my costume, and I'm sure you didn't find blood on it."

"You removed your costume before you killed him," Hap replied.

Susan laughed. "Do you know how ridiculous you sound? Who in the world would think of removing clothing to murder someone?"

"Someone who knew she was going to commit a murder." Remembering what Terry suggested earlier, Hap saw another opening to needle her some more. He hoped she didn't have a gun in her handbag, or a golf club. "You weren't the only one who took their clothes off that night. Maybe you even saw Younger on that bench with his mistress. Or, maybe you saw your husband with Mrs. Younger having a sexual encounter in that alcove. They were out there a long time, long enough for an audience to get an eyeful." That did it, he thought, flames were shooting from her eyes.

Susan took a step toward her husband, her face filled with such venom that he actually took a step back. "I'm sure everyone saw you that night. Saw how you looked at each other while you were dancing." She turned to Hap and said, "Yes, I saw them that night. Jeff told me he heard them plan their little rendezvous in the garden." Glaring at her husband, she said, "I think Jeff wanted me to kill you. He wanted to be governor. He said he would erase the photographs on his phone once you were out of the race. But I wasn't going to let you ruin everything we had worked for. I've spent years by your side, and you don't think I was going to let you disgrace me. You were going to win and I was finally going to be the governor's wife."

The shocked disbelief registered on Will's face. He couldn't wrap his brain around the fact that his wife had murdered his competitor, a man who had once been a friend. "You killed Jeff?"

Hap could hardly believe she was confessing in front of everyone. "Susan, I need to tell you your rights." Once he finished his rote recitation, he told her he was taking her to the station.

They walked to the front door with Will following close behind. "Susan, I'll call our attorney for you."

"I don't need your help. My family will make certain I don't go to jail." She saw Paige standing by the front door. "Don't think you've won, Paige. I intend to tell my story to anyone who will listen, and I know every newspaper in Kentucky will be interested. Everyone will know what a cheap woman you are. You'll never be the governor's wife."

"Come back to Woodrow's," Sam said to Hap when he called an hour later to tell them what had happened with Susan McNeal. "Everyone is still here, and we'll wait on you to order pizza. Honey didn't get to buy her groceries."

Hap arrived thirty minutes later and joined the group in Sam's bedroom. They stuffed themselves on pizza as Hap filled them in on Susan's confession.

"Terry, you were right," Hap said between bites.

"Words I love to hear," Terry teased. "But what was I right about this time?"

"Susan removed her costume to kill Jeff."

"Why did you even think of that?" Sam asked Terry.

"When you told me there wasn't blood on the costumes of the most likely suspects, I thought it was a possibility. Either that, or someone not invited to the party just came by to kill Jeff. That didn't seem likely."

"Maybe you should change professions," Hap teased.

Terry laughed. "No, thanks. I have an aversion to getting shot."

Honey handed Hap a beer. "Terry needs to stay on the radio. Everyone misses hearing his voice when he has a day off, especially Georgia. Plus, I don't want to worry about one more person getting shot."

Sam looked at her and he saw the concern in her eyes. He wondered how she would handle his profession if they were married. "No one is guaranteed tomorrow."

Honey met his gaze and gave him a tentative smile. "I know."

Sam glanced back at Terry. "If not for you, I'm not sure I would have thought of Susan McNeal as our murderer. I could still be working on that case."

Terry laughed. "I doubt that. Everyone tells me you are a great detective."

"I'm a pretty good detective, but I'm afraid where Mrs. McNeal was concerned, I hadn't even considered her. Normally, I can pick up vibes from people, but she had me fooled with her docile little woman act."

"I don't think it was an act," Honey responded. "I think she lost it that night."

Sam shook his head. "I might agree if she hadn't removed her dress. That tells me she knew exactly what she was going to do. It was a premeditated act."

"I agree with Sam. I'd feel sorry for her if she had acted out of a moment of rage. One could almost understand a moment of insanity since she'd just witnessed her husband with another woman, not to mention Younger was threatening to make the affair public. I think that would be tough for anyone to handle." Terry grinned at Sam. "If you ever need help in the future, you know where to reach me."

Sam chuckled. "I'll keep that in mind."

Hap finished telling them what Susan said in her confession. "At the party, she followed Will and Paige through the house. She said she thought they were headed to one of the bedrooms, but they walked into the kitchen. She waited in the hallway until they walked out the patio door. Elvis had apparently followed her into the kitchen, so she opened the pantry and gave him a bone. That's how he got locked in the pantry. She didn't want him following her outside."

"Did she break the glass on the pathway light?" Honey asked.

"She said she didn't. She first saw Jeff Younger with his girlfriend on the bench. But they didn't notice her. She then caught sight of her husband walking into that small private alcove in the garden. She admitted she watched them, and became so upset that she ran away. According to her, she remembered stepping on the broken glass from the light. Younger was alone on the bench at that time. He saw her approaching, and told her he was going to the press with the video if Jeff didn't pull out of the race. That's when she noticed the golf club leaning against the bench."

"I guess he didn't count on her wanting to be the governor's wife more than she cared about her husband having an affair," Sam mused.

"What did she do, tell him to hang on a minute while she undressed so she could kill him?" Terry asked.

Hap chuckled. "No, Younger actually propositioned her. He'd made advances before, which she says she always rebuffed. That night, she saw her chance to solve her problem. Of course, she said she didn't think Will was actually in love with Paige. She walked into the bushes to remove her dress, and when she returned to the bench with the golf club in hand, Younger was passed out."

"Hadn't his lover just left him?" Terry asked.

Hap nodded. "Yep. I asked her if she was planning on killing him when she undressed and she said that was her intention. She signed a confession before her attorney arrived. I imagine they'll use an insanity defense."

Honey stood and gathered everyone's plates. "That should be fair warning to all men who even consider having an affair."

"She didn't kill her husband," Terry reminded her.

"Well, they both ruined their lives. Will's affair will definitely get out in the press now," Honey replied.

Sam handed Honey his plate. "You told me early on that Will and Paige were truly in love."

"Yes, but they should have been honest with their spouses and divorced instead of ruining four lives."

"Does anyone know the protocol for one murdered gubernatorial candidate, and the other candidate forced to withdraw from the race because of a scandal?" Terry asked.

"It certainly is a mess," Hap acknowledged.

Woodrow and Virginia walked into Sam's bedroom, and Sam immediately noticed the sparkling diamond on his grandmother's left hand when she leaned over and kissed his cheek. He wanted them to make the announcement, so he didn't let them know he saw the ring.

After Hap repeated the details of Susan McNeal's arrest to them, Honey asked if they'd had dinner.

"Yes, we had a lovely dinner tonight," Woodrow answered, giving Virginia a warm smile.

Sam's gaze darted from Woodrow to Virginia. He couldn't wait any longer. "Anything you want to tell us?"

Woodrow reached over and linked hands with Virginia. "Would you like to tell them?"

"You can," Virginia answered.

"Well, one of you tell them," Sam suggested, laughing.

Honey looked at Sam. "What do you know?"

Woodrow grinned at Sam as he held Virginia's hand in the air so they could all see the engagement ring. "Sam knows that I asked Virginia to do me the honor of becoming my wife."

Sam extended his hand to Woodrow. "About time. Congratulations." He motioned his grandmother to his bedside so he could give her a kiss. "I know you will be very happy."

Honey jumped up and hugged her grandfather and Virginia. "This is wonderful news. I'm so happy for you both."

Hap and Terry offered their congratulations and best wishes.

"When is the big day?" Terry asked.

"At our age, we don't want a long engagement. We plan to wait until after Preston and Georgia's wedding. We are thinking after the first of the year. Of course, it will be a small affair," Virginia answered.

"We're thinking of having the wedding in the ballroom," Woodrow said.

Hap silently hoped that this event would go off without a murder on the property.

"Virginia has never been to Paris, so that's where we'll honeymoon," Woodrow said. "We plan to do some traveling through Europe for a month."

"Oh, that sounds so romantic," Honey exclaimed.

"Have you ever been to Paris, Honey?" Sam asked.

"No, but I've always wanted to go."

The discussion of the wedding ended, and Hap and Terry stood to leave, both offering their congratulations again. Woodrow walked the men to the door. As they walked down the hallway, Hap told Terry he could have his putter back now that the case was closed.

Terry shook his head. "Thanks, but I don't think I want it now."

Woodrow placed his arm over Terry's shoulder. "I owe you a new putter. If I hadn't asked you to show it to me that day, maybe this wouldn't have happened."

"I have a feeling she would have found something else to do the job," Terry replied.

Hap nodded. "You're right about that, Terry. A murderer will always find a way to do the dirty deed."

CHAPTER THIRTY-TWO

Honey removed the delicate tulle and lace veil from the box and passed it to Georgia's mother. After Mrs. Byrd secured the combs in Georgia's hair, they stood back and looked at her refection in the mirror.

To Honey's surprise, Georgia had dyed her hair a rich mahogany color, sans the blue streaks, and the result was stunning. Not only had she changed her hair, she further surprised Honey when she selected a Victorian-style wedding dress with a high neckline and long lace sleeves. "Georgia, you look so beautiful. That veil is perfect with your dress."

Georgia's mother beamed with pride at her daughter. "She does indeed."

Georgia smiled at her reflection. "Do you think Preston will recognize me without my combat boots?"

"I'm sure he will. Hopefully, he's not wearing his cowboy boots with his tux," Honey teased.

Mrs. Byrd leaned forward and placed her hands on her daughter's shoulders. "I already saw him and he looks very handsome. You are one lucky young woman to have found such a wonderful young man."

Georgia pulled the veil over her face. "Preston always looks handsome." She pointed to Honey. "It's in the genes."

"His best man is also a very a handsome man," Mrs. Byrd added.

Georgia's eyes widened at her mother's comment. "Mom, I'm going to tell Dad you have a crush on Detective Gorgeous."

Honey laughed at Mrs. Byrd's shocked expression. "Your mom would have to be blind not to notice Sam. I've never seen a black tux look so good." Honey knew how hard Sam had worked in rehab so he could return to work and attend the wedding without limping.

Hearing a soft knock, Honey hurried to the door. Thinking it might be Preston, she cracked the door open a few inches. "Seeing it was Terry, she pulled him inside the room and quickly closed the door. "I was afraid it was Preston knocking, and I wasn't going to let him see Georgia."

"He's still *waiting* at the altar with Sam." He glanced at Georgia, and after he told her she made a beautiful bride, he added, "Are we about ready to get this show on the road before the groom changes his mind and makes a run for it?"

Honey laughed, and reached for a single white rose boutonniere from the table. "No chance of that." She pinned the rose to Terry's lapel, and said, "You look great. That blue tie really compliments your eyes."

"Thank you." He opened the door and said, "Georgia, your dad is waiting outside the door. Ladies, get a move on before everyone falls asleep." He took a few steps, then turned back to Honey. "By the way, I never asked you if you found out who Marie Antoinette was at the ball."

Honey laughed. "I knew who she was. I was waiting for you to figure it out. Since you can't, I'll give you a hint. You might look closer to home."

Terry's eyes widened. "You're kidding."

Shaking her head from side to side, Honey smiled.

Honey stood at the double doors waiting for the bridesmaids to make their way down the aisle. The chapel had been beautifully decorated, but it wasn't the floral decorations that she found impressive. One wall of the chapel was glass from floor to ceiling, which afforded a view of the heavily wooded area just beyond. The pines were covered with a light dusting of freshly fallen snow, providing nature's beauty as the perfect setting for the occasion.

Before Honey took her first step, she glanced back at her future sister-in-law and smiled. As she made her way slowly down the aisle, she first spotted Elvis calmly sitting beside Woodrow, his eyes following every step she took. Georgia had insisted Elvis attend her wedding, and Honey knew he would be a perfect gentleman. Honey glanced at her brother, who had a big smile on his face. Honey returned his smile before sliding her gaze on the man standing next to Preston. Sam was, without a doubt, the most handsome man she'd ever seen. He was staring at her intently, as if he were trying to solve some great puzzle in his mind. Though he'd recovered from his injuries completely, she constantly worried about his safety, since they hadn't caught everyone involved in his ambush. Sam made certain he called, or stopped by her cottage, every night to alleviate her fears. Reaching the end of the aisle, Honey smiled at Terry before she took her position opposite the men.

As the music began, the guests stood and turned to watch Georgia walk down the aisle on the arm of her father. As soon as she came into view, the murmured oohs and aahs filled the room. Honey glanced at her brother and saw that he was smiling wide. Again, her gaze slid to Sam, but this time he winked at her and grinned.

Mr. Byrd kissed his daughter's cheek before he took his seat beside his wife in the front pew. Terry began the ceremony, his masterful, warm voice filling the chapel with words of love and promise. The vows were spoken and sealed with a kiss before Terry presented Mr. and Mrs. Preston Howell to the guests.

The reception was held in the ballroom at Woodrow's estate. After the reception line, the guests drank cocktails as Terry introduced the couple for their first dance. The musicians played "Can't Help Falling in Love," and Elvis's ears perked up at the familiar tune, but fortunately he didn't howl as was his habit when he heard Elvis's songs at home.

Everyone made their way to the huge tent where dinner was served, and Sam gave the first toast and speech, followed by Honey. Honey was thrilled when Sam danced nearly every dance with her. "Have I been forgiven for not dancing with you at the masquerade ball?"

"You have. But I didn't know you were such a good dancer."

Sam tightened his arm around her. "We haven't had much of an opportunity to dance."

"Are you tired?"

"Not on your life. I let Theo dance with you one time, and I'm not giving him another opportunity tonight. I may not be as good as Theo, but I'm keeping you in my arms tonight."

She did enjoy dancing with Theo, but it wasn't the same as dancing with Sam. "I noticed you were dancing with Bunny Spencer when I was dancing with Theo."

"She asked me. I was being polite."

It was well past midnight before Preston and Georgia cut the cake, and it was nearly three in the morning when the last guests departed. Woodrow drove Virginia home, and Honey, Sam, and Elvis walked Terry to the door.

"Terry, you made the evening so much fun. It was the perfect reception," Honey told him.

"Thank you, I had a great time," Terry replied.

After Terry drove away, Sam walked Honey and Elvis to the cottage. Sam slid his arm around her waist as they walked. "Terry did a wonderful job tonight."

"He's such a great guy and he has a wonderful sense of humor."

"Yeah. I can tell you really like him, plus I can understand why. He's a really good guy, and I've never met a more honest guy. Not a single person I interviewed had a negative thing to say about him."

They reached the cottage and Sam leaned down and kissed her. "Did I tell you how beautiful you look tonight?"

"Several times, but thank you. Of course, you know you were the most handsome man in the room."

"You think so?"

"Every woman thought so. I thought I was going to have to get out my Louisville Slugger to get them off of you."

Sam flashed her a big grin. "You have a Louisville Slugger?"

"Of course, and I'm pretty good with it."

Honey invited Sam to spend the remaining few hours before dawn.

"Do I have to sleep in the extra bedroom?" Sam asked with in a hopeful tone.

"You do, unless you want to sleep on one of the sofas."

He pulled her into his arms and whispered in her ear. "Only if you and Elvis share it with me."

Honey kissed his cheek. "Then let's get ready for bed."

Sam pulled back and looked at her. "You mean the bed bed?"

Honey laughed at his expression. "No, I mean the sofas."

Sam frowned. "If you're worried about my health, I assure you I'm fully recovered."

"As much as you danced tonight, I'm not worried about your health."

She turned to walk to her bedroom. "Your toothbrush is in the bathroom in the *extra* bedroom."

When Honey returned to the living room, Sam was sitting on the sofa with Elvis beside him. "Did you change your mind about staying?"

"No, Elvis and I want to talk to you." He patted the sofa next to him. Seeing she was wearing a tiny silky nightgown and robe, he hoped he could keep his mind on what he wanted to say.

The look on his face reminded her of how he looked earlier when she was walking down the aisle. She sat beside him, placed her hand on his thigh and looked into his eyes. "What is it? Is something wrong?"

Sam slid off the sofa onto one knee in front of her. "Honey, I love you." He stared at her bare thighs as he tried to remember his rehearsed speech. He was so distracted he couldn't form a thought, so he reached for her hands, linked his fingers through hers, and tried to refocus.

If she hadn't known know Sam so well, she would have thought he was nervous. But she'd never met a more confident, courageous man who had faced all manner of danger on a daily basis. He couldn't possibly be nervous. "Sam?" She didn't notice Elvis had leaped from the couch to sit beside Sam.

Taking a deep breath, Sam said, "I've asked for Elvis's approval, and I've already spoken to Woodrow and your father." He reached over and put his palm under Elvis's mouth. Elvis dropped a slobber-covered little velvet box in his hand.

Honey's eyes started to fill with tears.

Sam opened the box and pulled out a glittering round-cut diamond. His hand was steady when he held it to her. "Honey, would you do me the honor of marrying me?"

"Oh, Sam!" Honey threw her arms around his neck and hugged him to her. Within seconds, Elvis nudged his head between them.

Sam looped his arm around Elvis's neck. "Elvis, I think this means I'm going to be your dad."

I hope you enjoyed reading *Masquerade and Murder at the Bourbon Ball*. I love hearing from my readers, so please leave a review with your favorite retailer and tell me what you think!

SCARLETT DUNN BOOKS

<u>Historical Novels</u>

Promises Kept
Finding Promise
Last Promise
Christmas at Dove Creek
Whispering Pines
Return to Whispering Pines
Christmas in Whispering Pines
The Cowboy Who Saved Christmas (Christmas Road)
Chase the Wind (coming 2022)

<u>Mystery Novels</u>

Murder on the Bluegrass Bourbon Train
Masquerade and Murder at the Bourbon Ball

ABOUT THE AUTHOR

Scarlett Dunn is the acclaimed author of several historical romance novels, including the McBride Brothers trilogy and the Langtry Sisters series. She lives in Kentucky where she enjoys many outdoor activities as she plots her novels. Scarlett is presently working on another historical romance and a heavenly mystery—stay tuned.

Visit her website:
www.scarlettdunn.com

Llano Estacado 1862

A SENSE OF DOOM FLOODED LITTLE Flower's senses when she abruptly awoke from a deep sleep. She didn't know what woke her. On the fringes of her consciousness, she thought she heard someone scream. *I must have been dreaming.* She remained perfectly still as she tried to organize her thoughts, listening for—what? She didn't know. The crackling and hissing embers of the dying fire were the only sounds she heard. The air was cool and she shivered, not from the cold, but from the uneasy feeling she couldn't shake. She needed to add more wood to the fire, but she didn't want to leave the comforting warmth of the buffalo skins surrounding her.

Just as she closed her eyes, the reports of gunfire echoed through the air, followed by terror-filled screams. This time she knew she wasn't dreaming. *The village is under attack!* Panic replaced all rational thought. The deafening pounding of her heart made it impossible for her to hear anything else.

Though frozen in sheer terror, she told herself it was imperative for her survival to remember what she'd been instructed to do in the event of an attack. The most feared Comanche warrior, known by his enemies as

El Diablo de Ojos Verdes, had taught her how to protect herself, and her skills equaled most of the braves'. He'd told her that the enemy would show no mercy if they attacked their village and she would need to fight. His words echoed in her mind. *Stay calm and move fast! If you succumb to fear, the enemy has won.* But her friend wasn't beside her. She was alone and she was terrified.

With shaking hands, she tossed the buffalo hides aside and tried to stand, but her trembling legs folded beneath her like a newborn colt. On hands and knees she scrambled to the flap of the teepee and peeked out through a small slit. Odd, she thought, but the view in front of her teepee looked like a typical morning with the sun peeking over the skyline beyond the river. Shifting her position, she was able to see the interior of the camp. People were scrambling in all directions in their futile attempt to evade the men on horseback who were ruthlessly chasing them down. It was total pandemonium. The ground trembled as horses thundered through the village.

Turning back to the darkened expanse of the teepee, she scanned the space, searching for something she might use as a weapon. All she had was the knife she carried at her waist. There was no way she could defend herself against so many men. "Tell me what to do," she whispered to no one. She heard her friend's voice as clearly as if he were standing beside her. *If the enemy is great you should run. Live to fight another day.* Glancing at the buffalo hides, she considered sliding beneath them, but quickly dismissed that thought. Those men might set fire to the teepees. Her only chance was to run to the horses in the corral.

She hurried to the buffalo hides and grasped the one item she valued above all else: the beaded parfleche she'd made as a wedding gift for Running Deer, the brave she was to marry in two days. She held the pouch to her chest as if she could gather strength from the love she'd felt with every bead she'd sewn on the leather. Placing the strap over her shoulder, she pulled her knife and ran from the shelter of the teepee. She ran for her life.

Get that one, Curly," Vergil yelled above the commotion, waving his pistol in the direction of a young woman racing towards the trees.

Hearing Vergil's shout, Curly quickly reined his horse around to scan the area. With people darting about in every direction, along with the thick swirl of dust kicked up by the horses, Curly couldn't see anything that wasn't right next to him. He didn't know how Vergil could pick out one woman in the midst of the melee. With his head still thumping from a night of drinking too much whiskey, Curly was in no mood to give chase even if he saw the woman. He hadn't approved of this raid in the first place, knowing the fearsome Comanche who lived in this village could return at any moment. He figured Vergil was either plumb crazy, still half-drunk, or had a hankering to have his scalp lifted, to attack this particular village. At least Vergil had enough sense to wait until the warriors left for their hunt before they rode in with guns blazing.

They'd raided villages like this many times before, and they saw no reason to change what had always worked. Exactly as planned, they rode in at dawn, moving fast with pistols drawn and bullets flying with the intent of creating so much chaos that the people panicked and had no time to mount a defense. They quickly gunned down the young braves who were left behind to protect the people in camp. As adept as the young braves were with their bows and arrows, they were not prepared for ruthless men with pistols. Their arrows were no match for bullets. The old men who made a valiant attempt to battle were easily dispatched. Ear piercing shrieks filled the air as the young women tried to evade their attackers.

The women were the main reason these men raided the villages. They would sell the kidnapped women and children across the border. Comancheros would pay well for these captives, though not as handsomely as they did for the white women they preferred. It wasn't unusual for the Comancheros to ransom the women back to the villages where they'd been captured. Vergil usually traded with a Comanchero by the name of Velaso, but he didn't plan to tell him the women came from El Diablo's village. If Velasco found out, even that cold-blooded murderer would be too afraid to buy them.

The cloud of dust settled and Curly spotted the woman Vergil had indicated. Reluctantly, he whirled his mount around to give chase. Within seconds he was on the woman, bumping her body with his horse's flank, knocking her off stride. Reining his horse to a halt, Curly leaned over and grabbed the woman by the hair, preventing her from running again. Grasping her arm, he pulled her up on his horse and positioned her over his thighs. He pulled his pistol and placed the muzzle to her ear. The young woman was too terrified to move.

Out of the corner of his eye, Vergil spotted another young woman running toward the makeshift corral. Kicking his buckskin into a gallop, he raced to intercept her before she reached the horses.

Little Flower heard the horse bearing down on her as she ran. Reaching the corral, she ducked under the rope and zigzagged between horses. Vergil jumped off his horse and chased her through the small enclosure. When he closed the distance between them, he reached out to grab her shoulder, but his fingers closed over the strap of her pouch. Pulling away from his grip, Little Flower crawled beneath a horse and ran to the other side of the corral. She scrambled beneath the rope and dashed toward the river. Vergil was forced to maneuver around the horses, and by the time he exited the corral he was panting heavily, but his longer strides aided in his pursuit. When he was a few feet behind Little Flower, he hurled his big body through the air and caught her by the ankles, slamming her to the ground. The breath was momentarily knocked out of Vergil, and Little Flower turned on her side before he had time to react. She lurched forward with her knife and aimed it at his chest. Vergil reacted quickly, and with his overpowering strength, he easily subdued her, pinning her arm above her head. Little Flower used the palm of her other hand to drive his nose to his brain. Pain exploded in his skull. Through watery eyes, he drew back his meaty fist and smashed it hard to her chin. Little Flower's head lolled to one side.

Seeing she was out cold, Vergil straddled her hips. Pulling both of her arms above her head, he held them tightly with one hand. He picked up her knife and tucked the blade beneath her top and sliced the buckskin.

Little Flower's eyes fluttered opened, and when she felt the blade against her skin, she understood the man's intent. She summoned her courage and dug her heels into the ground, trying with every ounce of strength she possessed to buck him off.

Vergil moved the tip of the knife to her throat. "You better hold still or I'll mark you."

Not heeding his threat, she continued to resist, and the sharpened tip of the blade punctured the delicate skin at her throat. Vergil held the knife for her to see her blood dripping from the blade. Little Flower stilled. Her eyes widened as mind-numbing terror took hold.

Vergil figured he'd scared the fight out of her. He sliced the strap of the pouch she carried on her shoulder and tossed it aside. He then thrust the blade into the earth beside her hip.

Little Flower tried to twist her body from side to side, but her efforts were in vain. She couldn't budge him. She knew if he didn't kill her afterward, she would be sold as a slave. Death was her only answer.

Vergil laughed. "I like a woman who fights." Juice from the tobacco stuffed in his cheek trickled down his chin and dropped onto her bared skin. Tired of her struggling against him, Vergil drew back his fist and hit her on the side of her head. With that devastating blow, Little Flower stopped moving. Vergil wasted no time positioning himself on her thighs as he shoved her skirt up.

At that moment, Curly reined in beside Vergil and shook his head in disgust. "Come on, Vergil, we've got six women. We need to get out of here before those braves come back. If they find us here, we'll be wearing arrows for shirts." Now that Curly had sobered up, he couldn't get out of this village fast enough. He kept looking over his shoulder as if he half expected the demons from hell to ride up behind him.

Vergil looked at Curly. "This will only take a minute. She's a fighter and Velasco…"

Before Vergil finished his sentence, Little Flower pulled his knife sheathed on his belt. Curly whipped his pistol from his holster and pointed it directly at her head.

Little Flower's fearful gaze darted from Vergil's cruel dark eyes to the muzzle of Curly's deadly weapon. She glanced at Nadua, her friend across Curly's lap. She could tell by her vacant expression that she had given up hope. Her mind flashed to Running Deer. Just last night she'd placed all the little trinkets she'd collected for him inside the beaded parfleche. The few precious items would be meaningless to these vicious animals, but they meant everything to her. Running Deer would never see the little treasures: three white feathers, two arrowheads, a few pieces of sparkling quartz and a few small gold nuggets she'd found along the riverbank. Her most prized possession, a carved turquoise pendant, was also inside the pouch. The necklace was a gift from her friend, and she was going to wear it on her wedding day. She'd fallen asleep last night thinking of her marriage to Running Deer.

She quickly debated her fate. Knowing the intentions of these men, she couldn't abide the thought of disappointing Running Deer by being dishonored in such a way. A single tear trailed slowly down her temple. Running Deer would never see her wedding garment that had taken her months to make. Realizing the helplessness of her situation, her body went limp in defeat.

Vergil snatched the blade from her hand. He glanced up at Curly and smiled. "I think she finally understands."

Curly was losing patience with Vergil's stupidity. He holstered his revolver and growled, "Make it quick."

When Vergil made another comment to Curly, Little Flower felt his weight lift slightly and she thought she might have one last chance to escape. She brought her knees up hard, ramming Vergil in his groin. He yelped and fell to one side away from her body. Little Flower took that moment to scramble to her feet and started running as fast as she could toward the water without looking back. The river was only a few yards away and she was a good swimmer. She knew that would be her only chance to get away from these vicious men.

Curly pulled his pistol again and took aim.